C.J. looked him over. She smiled, feminine and mysterious as she engaged in just a touch of fantasy.

"What're you thinking?"

"Uh," C.J. said. "Just a few errant thoughts." She looked in her shopping basket. "It was nice chatting with you. I'd better run." She turned to go, but Wes captured her arm. White heat licked through her at the contact. C.J. sucked in her breath and looked at him.

"Pardon me," he said.

Before C.J. could ask why, his mouth closed over hers. She felt him take the small grocery cart from her hands and then his hands framed her face.

Desire rushed forward and reason scampered away. C.J., bold in her own yearning, stepped into his embrace. She opened her mouth and Wes accepted the gift. His lips, hard yet soft, teased her, filled her, claimed her. . . .

"Have dinner with me."

"Excuse me?" C.J. questioned.

Wes lifted a hand, one gentle finger traced her lips. "After that wonderful dessert I thought we should follow it up with dinner."

C.J. laughed. "That's the best pickup line I've heard in a while."

"What time would you like me to pick you up?" he asked.

"Seven-thirty." She gave him her address then left him standing in the aisle alone.

Wes shook his head as he watched her retreat. Mercy. The Good Lord knew what he was doing when he put that package together.

It wasn't until later Wes realized he didn't even know her name—and that she just might be off limits to him.

Pinnacle Books by Felicia Mason

FOR THE LOVE OF YOU

BODY AND SOUL

Felicia Mason

Seduction

PINNACLE BOOKS
KENSINGTON PUBLISHING CORP.

PINNACLE BOOKS are published by

Kensington Publishing Corp.
850 Third Avenue
New York, NY 10022

First Printing: August, 1996

Printed in the United States of America
10 9 8 7 6 5 4 3 2 1

For Monica Harris
an editor with vision; an editor who believed
Thank you, Monica

Acknowledgments

Many, many thanks to the U.S. Marshals Service in Arlington, Va., and to David M. Branham, U.S. Marshals Service public affairs specialist, for assisting with this project; and to Michelle Fronheiser whose prodding "just give it fifteen minutes" helped get me to the end.

Special thanks also to Chris Steuart, Tracy Palmer Parris, Michael T. Jackson, MaryAnne Gleason, Mike Gleason, and Adrien Creecy for moral support and answering myriad questions.

In Memory of William L. Mason Jr.

Prologue

C.J. Mayview stopped her car on the emergency pull off section of the bridge. She cut the engine, got out of the car, and stared back at the city. Twilight time. That half day, half night part of the day fell on the city with its purplish-blue hues.

C.J. soaked in the sight of the city before her. She loved the hushed pregnancy of twilight—the period as day ended and the quiet expectancy of night cast its shadows over the horizon. The night held secrets. Twilight, with the answers to those secrets, cast its warm glow through the sky: secret longings and secret dreams. The night held passion and crime. The cover of darkness that would come after twilight hid so much. C.J. watched twilight fold into night, long shadows chasing the hushed expectancy away.

Breathing in the scent, the fresh, free, freedom smell of saltwater and breeze, C.J. listened above the rush of traffic, listened to the water lapping against the bridge pilings. She listened and longed for the freedom of the waves.

Soon. Soon she would be free.

C.J. loved the water, and she loved the sight of the city coming to life in lights. Gazing out at the horizon she knew that any minute now a cop might come and ask if she was having car trouble, then chase her away. But right now, now it was just the twilight and the water.

She glanced at the car that held all the possessions she'd carry into her new life. It wasn't much, but that's the way she wanted it. The vehicle, a sturdy but unpretentious four-wheel drive, would get her where she wanted to go. It was a far cry from the preppy little BMWs she'd been driving for the last fifteen years of her life. She'd traded the latest Beamer in for the basic transportation that now held all the worldly possessions she'd deemed suitable for this new life. She had traded the old car in just as she was trading in that old lifestyle.

She again turned to contemplate the skyline. Night had fallen. Twilight, like the years of her life, had slipped away into something else; something dark, foreboding. As the night held its secrets, C.J. held her own. She was paying private retribution in the only way she knew how: by walking away from it all—from family, from friends, from a career she'd painstakingly built, from the addictions that threatened to consume her.

A solitary tear, one she couldn't even claim was of regret, fell as she said a quiet "Farewell" to all that remained familiar, all she knew and loved. Bending low to the ground, she felt around for a small reminder. Her fingers closed over a stone. The loose piece of granite she picked up wasn't smooth. That was appropriate, she thought. Nothing that she had done or become had been smooth, not in a lot of years. Maybe in the beginning she had been smooth, easy, laid back. But not now.

The stone, like C.J., was rugged, rough around the edges, as if it had had to toughen itself up to withstand the ravages of the elements. C.J. identified with the stone. She felt ravaged and ragged. A smooth edge peeked through but in no way dominated the texture of the rock. She liked that. The smoothness in the middle of the coarseness meant hope still existed. Over time, with steady care and constant polishing, the stone could be made smooth.

C.J. liked the analogy. With the stone in hand, she made her way back to the car. She strapped the seat belt around her and wiped away the single wet track on her face. She put the vehicle into drive and headed toward tomorrow.

One

Wes Donovan needed a cigarette. He reached for the pack tucked in his shirt pocket. Then, with a mixture of disgust and irritation, he remembered he'd given up the smokes. Wes squinted through the dark lenses of his wraparound sunglasses. He stared at the brick masonry of the federal building and frowned. God, he hated coming here.

He looked around to see if he could bum a smoke from anyone. But all the suits walking around him looked as if the stench of tobacco would never be something they inhaled, let alone enjoyed.

The tie at Wes's neck choked him. He hated ties. The one he wore today was nothing more than a facade, just like the black pinstripe suit he'd had to have dry cleaned and pressed before he could put it on and come down here for this meeting. Wes didn't have anything against suits—as long as the jacket and pants could be thrown in a washing machine. The contraption he'd bundled himself into today had been worn just twice. Wes shied away from thoughts of those two funerals.

Wes knew that to anyone paying attention he looked like all the other pinstripe suits scurrying about. Except, that is, for the shades and the custom-made cowboy boots. Wes patted the place where his smokes should have been, just to convince himself he really didn't have any. Then, with a sigh of resignation, he took a deep breath and hurried into the big building.

"Donovan? That really you?"

Wes turned and smiled. He recognized the voice. "Scotty, what's up man?"

The two old friends clasped hands then headed to the elevator.

"It's been a long time," Scotty said.

"Not long enough since I've been here," Wes answered as they got in the elevator.

"It's your attitude. You need to get it adjusted."

"Um hmm," Wes said, stepping aside to make room for a woman with a paper cup of coffee in her hands. Lips too small, chest too flat. Nice legs though, Wes thought.

"What you in for?" Scotty asked.

"Meeting."

"That would explain the suit," Scotty said dryly. "Almost didn't recognize you."

Wes smirked as the elevator lurched.

The woman with the coffee got off on three. Scotty stepped forward to depart on four.

"Gimme a call some time. Let's get together for a beer."

Noncommittal, Wes nodded as the elevator doors slid shut again. He wondered what time it was. He didn't wear watches. Despite the suits' preoccupation with time, Wes didn't think time was something to manage. It was to be spent, enjoyed, or in Wesley's case, a thing that was simply marked from one moment to the next, day in, day out, month after month. He wondered how many months it would take, how much time would have to pass, before he was able to forget . . . and forgive.

The doors swooshed open at the sixth floor. Wes stepped out and turned left. He reached in his jacket pocket for the magnetic ID badge that would allow him entrance. At a deceptively plain-looking door, Wes stuck the ID card in a slim gray hole, waited for the little green light to appear then punched in a short access code on the small keypad next to the slot.

The door popped open and Wes was inside.

He didn't recognize the woman who expectantly looked up at him from her receptionist's desk. Nice mouth, too much mascara and eye goop.

"May I help you, sir?"

Wes held out his identification badge. "Donovan. I'm in for a nine-thirty with Casey and Holloway."

The woman consulted some paperwork in front of her then smiled up at Wes. Nice smile, he thought.

"Right that way, Mr. Donovan," she said, pointing to her right. "They're expecting you."

A small, two-finger salute and an easy smile were his answers back to her. Wes headed toward Holloway's office, aware that the receptionist's gaze followed his progress.

"This job does have its assets."

Wes heard her mumbled comment and smiled to himself.

He found the door he was looking for and entered without knocking.

"Donovan, it must be that cold day in hell you mentioned the last time I saw you."

Wes smiled at Ann Marie Sinclair and fingered the lapel of his black suit. "That's the weather report I heard this morning."

He took a seat in the chair next to her desk and picked up a silver paperweight. "You're still the only reason coming down here is palatable."

Ann Marie shook her head and smiled. "Still a charmer." She stilled the hand that tumbled the paperweight. "Hey, Wes."

Slowly his eyes met hers. She waited until she had his full attention.

"Are you taking care of yourself?" she asked quietly.

Wes swallowed and looked away.

"Wes?"

He met her gaze this time. The gentleness in Ann Marie always soothed him. She knew more about him than a lot of people. And she understood far more than he found comfortable. "It still hurts," he said.

Ann Marie squeezed his hand. "I know, Wes. I know."

"Coming here doesn't help."

Ann Marie nodded then glanced at the telephone console on her desk. "Holloway's off the phone now."

"And Casey?"

"Not here yet," she said.

Wes rolled his eyes. "Probably off in a closet somewhere . . ."

"Watch your mouth, Donovan. You don't need to pick any fights today."

Wes looked at Ann Marie and smiled. "Forewarned," he said.

He stood up.

"Wes, anytime you need anything, you know I'm here for you."

Wes smiled at Ann Marie. He owed her a lot. They'd started working at the bureau the same day twelve years ago, Wes as a Deputy U.S. Marshal, Ann Marie as an office temp. She'd parlayed that temp assignment into a full-time position and had worked her way up the secretarial ranks. Few people knew how much power she actually wielded. Wes had always known.

Until just now, he'd had no idea why he'd been summoned to headquarters. The subtle warning she'd given him about the day was all he needed to prepare himself for this meeting. Wes steeled his back and rapped twice on Holloway's office door. Any trace of sensitive nineties guy, the type of man he could be only around Ann Marie and just a few others, disappeared completely as he took the first step into the office.

C.J. Mayview had come to the end of her endurance.

She'd survived far longer than she ever thought she would be able to manage. She congratulated herself on thirty whole days cold turkey. Thirty days of freedom. Thirty long, cold endless days and nights of nothing.

Her hands trembled as she flipped pages in the thin telephone book. She sighed a huge sigh of relief when she found the listing she wanted. She punched the numbers out on her telephone keypad and impatiently waited for the connection.

"Hi," she said as soon as a voice came on the line. "I need you to come out here as soon as possible. I don't care how much it costs. I just need you this afternoon. *Now* would be even better."

C.J. rolled her eyes at the response. "You don't understand. This is an emergency. I'm really, really desperate. And I'm not too proud to beg. I'll pay cash."

She listened again, then glanced at the wall clock. She was absolutely, positively going to die if she had to wait another four hours. She was so jumpy that even her fingers itched.

"Okay. Look. Where can I go right now and get what I need?"

C.J. scrambled over a well-worn plaid sofa to grab an ink pen off one of the cushions. She wrote the address on the palm of her hand. "Is that near the fire station?" She nodded. "Okay. Okay. I know where that is. Fine. I still need you to come out here, though. If I'm not here just walk in and leave everything I need. And make sure I get the royal treatment here. I'm hurting bad."

She listened again to the voice on the other line,

then answered. "That's right. Now my name is Jan Langley. That's L-A-N-G-L-E-Y. I'll leave the cash in an envelope on the sofa."

She completed the transaction and replaced the telephone receiver. Then she grabbed her wallet, pulled several bills out of it and stuffed them in an envelope. She tossed the envelope on the sofa

C.J. Mayview was a junkie. Trying to give up her habit, at least this one, had been a noble gesture but she couldn't take it another day.

If the cable company didn't get her hooked up to CNN today she was going to die. She'd been thirty whole days without the hypnotizing bass of James Earl Jones declaring, "This is CNN." Thirty days without round-the-clock instant news.

C.J. was a die-hard news junkie. For a month she'd been without cable, without even a newspaper or newsmagazine. No *Wall Street Journal,* no *Washington Post,* no local news, no nothing. The rest of the world could have fallen off the edge of the earth and she'd have been clueless.

She glanced at the address she'd scribbled in her hand. She draped the long, thin strap of her wallet over her body and dashed out the front door. She didn't bother to lock the door. Serenity Falls, North Carolina, had a zero crime rate. At her picket fence that needed a coat of paint, she glanced at her hand again. The cable guy said the hardware store next to the fire station had a TV department. She could go stand in front of the display models and get the fix of national and world news she so desperately needed. Maybe they'd even let her use the remote control.

The feel of the room was off. Tension vibrated through every part of Wes as he watched Casey. The man would not meet his eyes. Not a good sign, Wes thought. Sweat trickled down the middle of his broad back but none of the discomfort he felt showed as he stoically stood facing Holloway's desk. With his feet braced and his arms folded across his chest, Wes knew his stance intimidated most men. Casey, while of the male gender, couldn't signify as a man. Weasel, turncoat, jellyfish, wuss, mama's boy, all came to mind; but not man. Holloway on the other hand was a different story.

Wes didn't like him but he could respect him. Holloway had made a career out of his bureau work. Shrewd, cunning, and ruthless were apt adjectives. Wes didn't doubt for a moment that every breath Holloway took was a calculated move to advance him a step on the chess board. Wes could respect him, but he always, always watched his back around Holloway.

"Why don't you both have a seat," Holloway offered. Casey darted to a chair closest to Holloway. Wes snorted and rolled his eyes then took a seat in the straightback chair in front of Holloway's desk. He briefly wondered if he was about to get canned. After twelve years with the bureau, he'd be sorry to leave if that were the case. The only two bad things about the job were the times when he had to come in here and the wimp Casey. But he'd honed the skills necessary for the survival and sanity of every one of Casey's employees: how to work around and through the obstacle called Donald Casey. Long ago, Wes had stopped believing in a God, but he knew someone up there had been looking out for him. He could have been unlucky enough to be one of Casey's direct reports. It was bad enough being in his jurisdiction.

Wes did a quick mental inventory to see if there had been anything in the recent past to warrant this confab. He drew a blank. Not a good sign. He briefly wished that Ann Marie had given him some other clue.

Casey cleared his throat. Wes and Holloway both glanced at him.

"I know you're wondering why I called you in here today, Donovan," Holloway said.

"It had crossed my mind."

Holloway leveled a sharp glance at Wes. "Don't be wise, all right."

"That's right," Casey piped up from the safety of Holloway's desk. "One of these days Donovan, your mouth is gonna write a check that your behind can't cash."

"Any day, Casey. You name the time and the place," Wes said quietly.

Casey paled beneath his splotchy tan.

"That's enough," Holloway said.

Holloway walked around the perimeter of his desk and sat in the large tobacco-colored leather chair. "I called you two in here today because there's a case I want to assign you. Donovan, it'll require that you relocate. Casey, it'll mean you pick up any loose ends left from Donovan's case load."

Both men jumped up at the same time. Sputtering his indignation, Casey objected to the notion.

"I'm not some flunky you have whose sole purpose is to pick up the leftovers and dregs from the likes of him."

"I have about three highly sensitive cases I'm working. To bail now would mean losing months of work. And competent research," Wes added, looking in Casey's direction.

"Are you implying that my background work is incompetent?" Casey huffed.

"If the shoe fits," Wes replied.

Holloway ignored the byplay between the Deputy Marshals. Each, in his own way, was the best at what he did. It was a shame their personalities and work styles clashed so violently. They would be a formidable pair working as a team. That would happen the same day polar bears took flight.

"So wrap up what you can do on your caseload in the next week, Donovan. Leave the rest for Casey. On Monday you're on the road to Serenity Falls, North Carolina."

"North Carolina? No thanks. I decline," Wes said.

Holloway looked from one man to the other. "It's not an option," Holloway answered. The glacial stare backed up the statement.

"And if I make an issue of it?" Wes asked.

Holloway picked up a folder from a short stack on the right side of his desk. He tossed the not thin file to Wes.

"That's not an option either," Holloway said.

Wes reached for the folder and saw his own name neatly typed across the flap: DONOVAN, WESLEY K. He didn't need to open the file to know what it contained: Details of every run-in he'd ever had with Casey and probably an eyewitness accounting and report of the brawl before Marc's funeral. Three Deputy U.S. Marshals had to be rushed to the hospital by the time Wes was subdued by five deputies.

Wes took a deep breath and tossed the folder, unopened, back on Holloway's desk. So, this was to be his punishment. A two-week suspension hadn't been enough.

"What's in Serenity Falls, North Carolina?" he asked.

Holloway's smile was cold, just like his soul. He knew he'd won. "Have a seat, gentlemen."

Two

Serenity Falls had been home for a month. Now that she had cable and once again felt connected to the outside world, C.J. didn't think the town too shabby. She still resisted the local newspaper and even the big national dailies that could be found at Manheim Brothers Drug Store and Grill.

C.J. liked the intimacy of the small town. She was even getting used to saying "Hello" and chatting a few moments with strangers on the street. Leaving the house unlocked was still taking some getting used to. The day the cable installation guy came by was really the first time she'd done it. No way would she have even contemplated leaving her doors open in Baltimore. The condo she'd sold before moving to Serenity Falls was in an exclusive, upscale building with twenty-four-hour security. C.J. would no more have thought to leave a door unlatched than she would thought to stick her hand in the open flames of her brick fireplace back home.

She glanced around the small living room of the two-bedroom bungalow. It wouldn't be right to call this place shabby.

"You have character," she told the tiny living room. Only a couple of knickknacks, a vase here, an ottoman there, had made the trip with C.J. from Baltimore and that old life.

She'd spent much of the last month trying to figure out how to reupholster chairs. C.J. cocked her head and took a critical look at the two chairs that flanked a knicked coffee table. She'd painstakingly chosen the floral chintz fabric. One of the chairs looked better than the other but it didn't matter.

C.J. grinned, proud of her handiwork. No one in Baltimore, including herself, would ever believe that C.J. Mayview, Pulitzer-Prize-winning investigative journalist, Type A career woman, would be caught dead in small-town North Carolina. The nearest real department store was in Charlotte, a ways away. Most people here had never heard of espresso and thought cappuccino was the last name of some actor in Hollywood. Folks who wanted homemade bread kneaded it with their hands and let it rise on a kitchen counter. Bread machines and fancy coffee makers were for city folk.

C.J. couldn't wipe the grin from her face. Her biggest worry was not whether a crackhead would rob her in an alley or if a politician was lying to her. C.J.'s biggest dilemma rested in one monumental decision: whether to sand and refinish the coffee table next or to tackle the challenge of reupholstering the sofa.

She looked from the table to the sofa and chose neither.

"I'm going on to another project today. I'll get back to you guys soon."

With that she headed to the kitchen. From beneath the sink she pulled a pair of floral-print gardening gloves. She tugged them on and grabbed a small boom box from the counter. She kicked open the screen on the back door of her little two-bedroom bungalow. She'd fallen in love with the house on first sight, paid cash for it, and devoted part of her days into transforming a hard rock piece of soil in the backyard into a lush English garden—or at least her approximation of one. So far, she'd broken three nails and one shovel handle in the process, but, C.J. didn't mind. As a matter of fact, she thrived on the hard work of gardening and the honest day's labor of learning to repair furniture. It made it easier for her to appreciate what she had. And more importantly, it made it easier for her to forget what she'd left behind.

Wes Donovan rolled into town in a beat-up pickup. Sometimes he thought he was getting too old for these games and masquerades. The truck needed new shocks. Wes needed a shave, a cigarette, and the feel of his '67 Mustang under him. He briefly thought of what else would feel good under him. But he knew he'd be getting that about as soon as he'd get his own sports car back— not until this bogus job was done, which might be three weeks after never.

Wes jounced about in the cab of the truck. His gear, including his bike, was in the flatbed. At least he got to take the Harley this time. Small comfort. It would probably rain every day he was stuck in North Carolina.

The oil light came on in the dash. Wes swore out loud. This heap of rust had been Casey's doing. Wes figured that in another life Donald Casey must have been a real prick. He probably hadn't gotten it right then and was sent to this time for the sole purpose of tormenting Wes.

Wes glanced down at the map open on the seat next to him. This would be Main Street. Aptly named, Wes figured as he took in a hardware store, a grocery, a bank with a green ATM machine sign. At least the twentieth century had arrived here in Mayberry RFD.

He had vowed to himself never to set foot in another

place like this. His hometown was small enough for Wesley Donovan. Except for Mama Lo and her family, home was a place he'd just as soon forget ever existed. And now he found himself trapped in another tiny town. If this assignment could be likened to being shipped off to Siberia, Holloway couldn't have chosen a better punishment.

Making a right at a stop light, Wes turned onto Chauncey Street. He pulled into a service station just as steam started seeping from under the hood of the truck.

Wes hopped out of the cab and went around to the hood.

"Careful with that," a voice called out. "Looks like yur over heated."

"Yeah," Wes concurred as he raised the hood. The voice joined him at the truck. "Hey," Wes said, sticking a hand out. "You got a mechanic on duty?"

The man wiped one oily hand on his blue jean overalls before shaking Wes's outstretched one. "That'd be me. Name's Ray Bob."

"Hey man. I'm Wes. Can you take a look at my truck and get it fixed?"

"Gotta let it cool down first. Maybe a coupla hours."

Wes nodded. It figured as much. It would probably cost an arm and leg to get this clunker fixed. For the benefit of Ray Bob, Wes frowned. "Don't think it's gonna cost too much, do you?"

"Cain't say till I take a look at 'er."

Wes shielded his eyes from the sun. The profile on Serenity Falls, North Carolina, said blue collar. Real blue collar. "Got any jobs around here?" he asked Ray Bob.

"Hear tell the factory takin' on for second shift. They got a few midnight spots open, but those go real fast. You looking for work?"

"Low on cash. Gotta do something," Wes answered.

"Miss Clara Ann run a rooming house 'bout three blocks over. Lot of the single guys from the plant stay there."

"What's the name of it? I'll look it up."

"Ain't got a name. Just ask anybody for Miss Clara Ann's place. They point you in the right direction."

Wes tried to hide his sudden irritation. Any minute now he expected to see Andy and Aunt Bea walk up. Scotty had been right. Maybe what he needed more than a suspension, more than a vacation, more than this bogus assignment, was an attitude adjustment. And his hands around Casey's neck.

"Help me push this over there," Ray Bob said indicating a spot near the service station's double repair bay. "It'll be outta the way and you can come back for it in a coupla days."

Wes got the Harley and strapped his two bags to the back. In minutes he was headed out of the service station and back toward town.

The first thing C.J. registered was that the man in black looked like he had been made for the motorcycle he was riding down the street. He had on a black T-shirt, black jeans, black boots and looked like he was out for blood. C.J. was immediately attracted to him.

She paused to stare after the man. She liked bad boys. And this one knew how to handle the bike. For a brief moment, before the sun's glare forced her to turn away, C.J. got a glimpse of dark hair and rich copper skin. Her own skin tingled with the thought of what it would be like to be pressed against the hard body of that dark warrior as they rode through the streets and back hills of Serenity Falls.

C.J. shook her head. "Umph. It's been a long time since you had some of that."

As the motorcycle figure continued down the street and out of view, C.J. resumed her walk. The guy in black represented yet another thing she had spent the last month trying to purge from her system. Just because it felt good was no reason to jump in bed with a man. In her past, the one she'd closed the book on when she pulled out of Baltimore, C.J. had hopped in bed for reasons not even as noble as that one. That was the old C.J. The next time she gave herself, it would be for love—or the closest thing to love she was capable of feeling.

She put the thought and the vision of the dark warrior on the motorcycle out of her mind. Today she was in search of herbs to start a small herb garden in a raised area near the back porch. The owner of one of the town's three lawn and garden stores had told her to come back when she was ready to plant. C.J. was now ready.

Wesley drove around for a while then found the rooming house. Serenity Falls was bigger than he'd first thought. The town had a Wal-Mart, a three-screen cinema, and what billed itself as an all-night skating rink/bowling alley. Wes couldn't remember the last time he'd been bowling.

He kicked the bike's stand down and swung a long leg over the seat. Taking the stairs to Miss Clara Ann's two at a time, he admired the pots of geraniums on the steps. Miss Clara Ann obviously liked flowers.

Wes rang the doorbell.

"Come on in. It's open," a voice from somewhere inside called out.

Wes gave the door a dubious look. These people left their doors unlocked? He really had landed himself in the middle of Mayberry.

Wes took the last step up and into a Florida room. "Hi there, young man. How're you doing today? My you are a big one. If you're looking for a room, you're in luck. I got one with a bed big enough and long enough for the likes of you. Are you hungry, baby?"

Wes glanced down at the diminutive lady in front of him. He liked her on the spot. The top of her head, covered with a green scarf tied back, came just about to his navel. The dish cloth in her hand and the apron around her waist told him she'd probably been in the kitchen cooking or cleaning. She had to be seventy if she were a day.

"Are you Miss Clara Ann?"

She looked up at him and laughed. "Well, who else would I be? This is my house. I'm Clara Ann. What's your name, baby?"

"I'm Wesley, ma'am. Ray Bob over at the Texaco said you might have a room to rent. I'd just need it until I find myself an apartment."

"Shoot child, stay as long as you like. The room is seventy-five a week. That includes linens, a wake up call, and a bottomless cup of coffee. If you want meals it'll be another twenty-five."

"Don't you want to check my references or anything first?"

Clara Ann laughed out loud. "Whatever for? If you're in Serenity Falls and Ray Bob sent you this way, you don't need no other reference."

Wes shook his head then grinned. Small-town life sure had a different feel to it.

"Come on this way, Wesley. I'll give you the key to your room. You're from the city aren't ya? I can always tell. City folks the ones who want to know about references and damage deposits. The way I figure it, if you damage something, you pay. Folks who ain't decent enough to do that, well, the Lord'll make sure they get theirs."

Miss Clara Ann opened room number five and

waved Wes in. "This is the big room. It has its own bathroom. I usually charge extra for that."

"How much?" Wes asked.

"Oh, don't worry about it. Right now there are only four other people staying here. One's a regular. I have eight rooms that I let out though."

Miss Clara Ann walked into the room and opened the three windows. "See, it's got a TV with the cable. The bathroom's that way. I leave fresh linen every other day. The door has a deadbolt lock. No cooking, no loud music, no parties, no drugs. What you do in your room is your own business, meaning I don't mind if you have company. Just don't disturb the other guests. There's a little parking lot in back. Long time ago that used to be my vegetable garden. Use the spot that's the same number as your room."

"What time are the meals?" Wes asked.

"Breakfast is from six to eight. Don't serve lunch. Dinner is six to eight. If you are working over at the plant and on midnight or four to twelve, I leave a plate."

Wes smiled. "I'll take it."

He slipped a hand in his back pocket and pulled out a well-worn leather wallet. He peeled out two hundred twenty-five dollars and handed the money to Miss Clara Ann.

"What's the extra twenty-five for?"

"The bathroom."

Miss Clara Ann took the money then tapped Wes on the forearm with it. "You and me gonna get along just fine."

After she left, Wes searched the room. It was unlikely that anything had been planted there. He'd chosen the place on the spot. But in his line of work, Wes learned early that you could never be too careful.

When he was sure both the room and adjoining bath were clean, he left the room, locking the door behind him. He'd grab his gear, park the bike, then get a feel for the town on foot before making his way over to the plant to fill out an employment application.

C.J., with her head stuck in the directions she'd been given on starting her herb garden, walked smack dab into the wall of a mountain. It took her a full minute to register that there weren't any mountains in Serenity Falls. She looked up into the face of the solid force in front of her. C.J. caught her breath and at the same time marveled that she'd finally figured out what it meant to get weak in the knees over a man.

"Dark warrior."

"I beg your pardon? Are you all right, miss?"

"Sorry about that. I wasn't paying attention." Only then, after speaking a few words, did she realize that he was supporting her arms. C.J. got her balance but didn't move out of his sheltering embrace. He smelled the way a man was supposed to smell, of time and sweat and hunger. And just beneath the surface, teasing her senses, C.J. picked up a faint scent of an earthy cologne or after shave. Just from the smell of him she wanted to crawl in his arms and hold on tight.

In another time he would have been a king or a warrior. She knew that just like she knew that this man would belong to her. C.J. didn't question her instinct or the fact that people didn't belong to each other. This man with his chiseled features and hard mouth, needed tenderness the way a flower needed rain.

C.J., fairly tall for a woman, didn't necessarily feel dwarfed in his presence. Her five-foot-eight frame was sheltered in his arms. The solid wall she'd walked into turned out to be a broad chest covered in thin black cotton. Without thinking, C.J. raised a hand and touched. Beneath the T-shirt, she could feel the strength of him flex.

She felt more than heard him draw in a breath.

She had eyes the color of dark chocolate, eyes in which he could see the dawn of civilization; from the pyramids of ancient Egypt to the longing dreams and desires of the special creature called woman. Wes looked into her eyes and felt something in him shift, reconfigure, and settle. Eyes, he'd always read, were the window to a person's soul. This woman's soul was old and proud and passionate.

At her full lips, she wore just a hint of color. The shade enhanced her cinnamon and sugar complexion. Wes held his breath. If that mouth, that gorgeous, gorgeous mouth parted any more, Wes wasn't going to be able to stand it.

Wes had definitely had his share of women but he couldn't remember the last time he'd been so attracted to a woman so fast. He wanted her now and hard and fast. Standing up right here in the street would do. But Wes also knew he couldn't have her. Not now, probably not ever. She'd called him Dark Warrior. She was the one he'd been sent here to protect.

With more will than he thought he possessed, Wes stepped away from her.

"You're the most beautiful man I've ever met."

What was almost a small smile curved his mouth. "Isn't that supposed to be my line?"

C.J. smiled. Before he could stop himself, Wes lifted a hand to caress those perfect lips. This woman's mouth was made for kissing. He wanted to see her lips swollen with the pressure of his own. His thumb, in a whisper of a caress, brushed the side of her mouth. When her lips parted, Wes lowered his head.

Closing his eyes, he sighed. Wes took one deep breath and moved away from her. This woman, no matter how kissable, was off limits to him. There were lines. And this was one he didn't believe in crossing. By law he couldn't cross it. Wes had never mixed business with pleasure and wasn't about to start now in the middle of Main Street in Serenity Falls, North Carolina.

C.J. watched the fleeting expressions cross his face before he dropped a concealing mask over himself. She wanted to know the man under the mask, not the one who now stood before her looking like an unforgiving rock of a mountain. C.J. was intrigued, as she always was by challenges. She liked chameleons because they adapted to their surroundings. C.J. got a feeling that the man standing before her had many of the characteristics of a chameleon.

"What changed your mind?" she asked, sure that he would know exactly what she meant. She didn't regret or apologize for the come on. What would be the point? They were both adults. Even consenting ones. She ignored the little voice in the back of her head reminding her that this constituted one of the things she was supposed to be purging from her system.

Wes took a step back and studied her. One of those string purses women liked so much was draped across her body. The strap divided her breasts. Wes took a deep breath and tried not to focus his attention there. "You called me Dark Warrior. Why?"

Her brows furrowed and she cocked her head. A tiny smile splayed at her mouth. Then with a deliberate sensuality that made Wes ache, she checked him out from the top of his head to his boot-enclosed feet. Her gaze lingered and assessed in some of the places along his body. Wes felt as if he'd been plugged into an electrical outlet. She hadn't touched him but his body felt like she'd run a thousand ostrich feathers over his naked skin.

She licked her lips then smiled coyly at him.

"No reason," she said. Then, with a look that belied her words, "Sorry I ran into you." She paused just long enough to make sure she had his undivided attention. She did.

"I wasn't watching where I was going. See you around."

With that she pulled a Houdini on him. By the time Wes found his way out of the sensual fog that enveloped him, she was nowhere in sight. He scanned the street and shop fronts. No one about even remotely resembled the woman. It was almost as if she'd never been standing in front of him. Wes could hardly be classified as a man given to delusion or illusion. And besides, more than anything else, more than the magic in her eyes, the challenge in her voice, or the sweet honey of her mouth, the very solid erection in his jeans let Wes know the woman had been real.

Now all he had to do was find her again. And make her his.

Three

Careful not to get stuck by the coil spring that had poked its way to the surface of the old plaid couch in her living room, C.J. sat on the edge of the sofa. Her herb garden forgotten, at least for now, she tried to assess her feelings. In addition to the physical work she'd been doing at the house in the last month, she'd been spending quite a bit of time getting in touch with her inner self, a being that had been suppressed for so long that sometimes the hard truths she'd unearthed had been painful lessons in self-identity.

One of the lessons she'd learned about the real C.J. was that "C.J. the reporter" did things so methodically and meticulously that "C.J. the woman" frequently—usually—took third place on the priority list.

C.J. closed her eyes and practiced the deep breathing exercise her older brother had taught her. With each exhale she drew closer to her true self as well as the feelings and emotions coursing through her being. Adrenaline was there. So was desire. No. Desire was too tame a word for what she felt toward the dark warrior. She felt primal and passionate. Primal passion.

She inhaled then exhaled, cleaning out and sorting through her feelings. There also existed an element of fear and danger. Not fear for her physical safety.

No. Not that. The threat posed constituted an emotional one. It would be all or nothing with that man.

"Breathe, C.J. Don't forget to breathe."

Inhale, exhale. Desire, passion, fear . . . and peace? Peace? That was an odd addition but just thinking the word soothed her. It fit.

Deep inhale, slow exhale. C.J. slowly opened her eyes. She'd courted danger on the sidewalk today in Serenity Falls. The experience hadn't really diminished any of the progress she'd made so far on this mission to recovery. If she put the man with his solid good looks out of her mind and focused her attention in the right place, everything would be just fine.

"So why does the right place seem to be the backseat of a Harley?"

She didn't have an answer to that, but she did have a solution. Work. She went to her bedroom, changed out of the slacks and blouse she'd worn into town and slipped on a pair of jeans and a lightweight Fisk University sweatshirt. She grabbed all of her supplies, including the gloves that would protect her hands, and headed to the backyard.

Back in his room at Miss Clara Ann's boarding house, Wesley placed a call on a small flip telephone he pulled from his bag.

"Dark Warrior has landed at the desert rendezvous. Recon in progress."

He didn't wait for a reply. Wes flipped the phone off and tucked it back in a black leather backpack. From another satchel he pulled the few clothes he'd traveled with: clean shirts, briefs, socks, moccasins and loafers, two additional pairs of jeans, one blue, the other black like the ones he wore, and an easy wear suit that would need just a little pressing to be ready to roll. He placed a small toiletries kit on the vanity in the bathroom and eyed himself in the mirror.

He ran one large hand over his chin. "You're not losing your touch. This is probably what scared her away, old pal."

Wes pulled off the black T-shirt and reached for a white hand towel draped over a rack on the door. He tossed the towel over his shoulder and turned the faucet on. A quick shave would help him feel more human. Wes grinned at his reflection. Actually, nothing could make him feel more human than the honest male response he'd had to the woman on the street. He liked the fact that she didn't overdo it on the makeup. She wore enough to enhance her God-given assets, high cheekbones, a full mouth, and expressive eyes.

He lathered up his face with shaving cream then began the smooth strokes down his face that would clear away the shadow of the beard. He did, after all, want to make a good impression when he showed up to fill out an application for work at the plant.

Wes wondered what kind of impression he'd made on the woman. He didn't even know her name. After the stop at the factory, he would begin an earnest search for her. But Wes smiled as he cleared away more of the shaving cream from his face.

If she was who he thought she was, she'd be in search of him soon and would likely find him faster than he'd be able to locate her.

The smile became a grin. "Sometimes, you know, Wesley, this job is a whole lot of fun."

Later that day Wes arrived back at Miss Clara Ann's with the satisfaction that he'd secured a job at the recycling plant. He had been somewhat surprised to discover that the company had a human resources department. He'd fully expected to make application at a trailer stuck off to the side of the entrance. He'd anticipated a broken-down step, the stale smell of old coffee and cigarette smoke, and a general order of disarray. What he'd found instead was a coolly efficient and well-run HR office.

"You're going to have to cease with the preconceived notions about small towns, Wesley," he chided himself as he kicked the Harley's stand down in his parking space. "It makes you slack in your thinking."

If the recycling plant had been what he'd expected— like the coal mining companies he grew up with—workers were either hired or rejected on the spot in a rusted-out white trailer. As it stood now, he'd have to wait three days for the HR types to run a drug test, handwriting analysis, driving record, and criminal background check.

He had no doubt that everything would come back clear. It just meant he had some extra time and a weekend to kill. He could get a lot done under the guise of waiting for a job call back.

Wes smiled as he made his way around extensive flower beds to the front door of Miss Clara Ann's. He wondered what *she* did there. And he wondered what her name was. With her exotic eyes and arched brows, the woman he'd met on the street today could be an Eve or maybe a Zora. She'd have a strong feminine name. Of that he was sure. He wondered if she had one of the Afrocentric names that had been popular in the late sixties and early seventies. Maybe she was a Nia or an Ashanti.

He guessed her to be in her mid- to late twenties, five foot eight, one twenty five to one thirty, size 10, B cup that was doing its best to spill into C.

Wes grinned and took the steps two at a time.

"Share the humor," a light feminine voice said.

Wes turned. His mind had been so focused on the

woman he'd met on the street that he'd almost run down a woman at the door who held an armful of books.

She tried to extend her hand but thought better of it. "Hi. My name's Margaret. Are you a resident here, too?"

"Yes. Let me get the door for you." Wes pulled open the door and picked up a bag near her feet. "Is this yours as well?"

Margaret looked over her shoulder. "Oh, yes. But don't pick it up. It's quite heavy."

Wes smiled and hefted the bag in his hand for her to see.

"Ooohh, so strong," she cooed.

The woman made her way to the front parlor. Wes rolled his eyes and followed her through the Florida room. Then he raised an eyebrow and reassessed. Her back side might be a bit broad for his tastes, but she sure knew how to work that walk and make a man take notice.

He followed her to the front parlor where Miss Clara Ann sat in a wooden rocker with a cup of tea.

"Oh. There you are, Margaret. I was sitting here figuring you wouldn't make it in tonight. Come here girl and let me take a look at ya."

Wes placed Margaret's bag at the foot of the stairs then found his arms filled with books.

"Would you hold these for a second? Thanks," Margaret called back to him, already on her way across the room to greet Miss Clara Ann. Wes raised both brows at the woman's familiarity with him. Did she think he was the hired help? There was nothing worse in Wes's book than bourgeois black folk. He'd had enough to deal with trying to cope with his mother's airs. Just the thought of Eileen, the woman who gave birth to him but could never be called a mother, made him frown.

He stared after Margaret who was now kissing Miss Clara Ann on each cheek.

Wes unceremoniously dumped the books on the closest step then leaned back on the banister with one booted foot resting on a step behind him.

"Oh, good, I sees you done met Wesley. He joined us just today. Come on in baby and get a proper introduction. This here is my niece, Margaret. She come to stay here in Serenity Falls for a little spell."

When he hesitated, Miss Clara Ann prodded him. "Come on now, baby."

He didn't particularly want to be rude, at least not to Miss Clara Ann. Wes pushed himself away from the stairwell and sauntered across the room.

He stuck out a hand in greeting to Margaret even as his brows drew together. There was something vaguely familiar about this woman. "Nice to meet you."

"It's all my pleasure," she assured him.

"Margaret here hasn't managed to snag herself a husband yet," Miss Clara Ann said. "And she's almost thirty years old."

"Aunt Clara!"

"So I told her to come on down here. We got lots of eligible bachelors. What about you Wesley, you hitched up?"

Wes swallowed a smile at the blatant matchmaking but ignored the curious hopeful expression on Margaret's face. "No, ma'am. Can't say that I am. I like being footloose and fancy free."

Miss Clara Ann grunted. "Hmmph, that's what you say now. You just ain't found the right woman. The right one'll change that thinking in a flash."

"Aunt Clara, which room is mine?"

"Don't be trying to change the subject on me, girl. Ya'll two young folks, both of you single, standing here looking like you don't know which way is up. I tell you.

You would think that after almost seventy-five years on this earth that I could find a little peace. But I can see that ain't to be yet. My work is still cut out for me."

"Aunt Clara, please."

Wes grinned. Miss Clara Ann had gumption. She'd obviously been a beauty in her day. Her hair was more white than gray, and her mahogany skin, while it had a few lines, still shone with youthful vigor. She'd probably spent her whole life meddling in other people's business. And he'd bet the Harley that she would have been a pistol in her prime.

Wes glanced at Margaret and actually felt sorry for the woman. With Miss Clara Ann as an aunt, Margaret would probably find herself marching down the aisle to a husband whether she wanted one or not. Wes knew one thing for sure, though: He wasn't the man for her.

With her pert nose and bow mouth, Margaret was attractive in her own right. Wes, however, had always been attracted to the sensual Earth Mothers over some of the more traditional standards of beauty. The face of the woman on the street came to him and Wesley smiled.

"You're embarrassing him and me," Margaret said, waving a hand in Wes's direction.

Miss Clara Ann sucked her teeth and pushed back to get the rocker going. "I think I'll put you right next door to young Wesley. Take room four, Margaret."

"Aunt Clara, that's really not necessary. I'll go up to the third floor."

"Cain't do that. I got an artist living up there. He's in residence. Says he gets his inspiration out on the widow's walk. I think he's been talking to the pigeons too much. Ain't seen a nary painting from him and he's been here four months. Pays on time though and don't cause no trouble, so he can talk to the pigeons all he wants."

Wes realized something, something that should have hit him when he first met Miss Clara Ann. Here was a woman who probably knew every person in town and all their relatives back to the day the ship arrived from the motherland. Maybe instead of courting Margaret as Miss Clara Ann seemed so intent on him doing, he'd court Miss Clara Ann herself.

He smiled. "If you two ladies would excuse me, I have a little work to do." With that, Wes bent low, kissed Miss Clara Ann on the cheek then headed out the parlor and up to his rented room.

From a pink plastic water pot with a sunflower emblazoned on its side, C.J. gently watered the peppermint sprigs she'd just planted. She patted the rich soil then sat back on her haunches to admire her work.

"It looks good, Jan."

C.J. looked up, responding more to a voice than to the name. She was still trying to get used to the fact that she'd told people her name was Jan. When she'd closed on the house deal and signed her name on the paperwork she'd almost written her full formal name, Cassandra Ja'Niece Mayview. Jan was totally foreign but it was the first thing that came to mind when someone had asked her name. Remembering her fake last name was a little easier. Langley had been her mother's maiden name. C.J. didn't really care who Jan Langley was. Her purpose for being in Serenity Falls was to discover who C.J. Mayview was.

Her new friend Amber Baldwin stood near the cracked bird fountain in C.J.'s backyard. The toddler on her hip gurgled and swatted at a butterfly.

"Hi, Amber," C.J. said, dusting her hands on her jeans. She tugged the gardening gloves off and got up to meet Amber.

"Hope you don't mind I came on back here. I didn't get an answer at the front door."

"Not a problem. It's good to see you and the baby."

C.J. wasn't real sure how to deal with little people, particularly ones this small. Children mystified her, always had. C.J. had never had a single maternal instinct in her. Maybe that's what her problem was. She reached a hand out and offered the baby a finger. The child tugged the finger to his mouth.

"Frank Jr. stop that," Amber scolded as she gently batted at the boy's hands.

C.J. took the opportunity to recapture her hand and finger, then surreptitiously wiped her finger on her jeans.

"Do you mind if we stopped over? I thought we'd take a short walk and get some air and when I looked up, we were on your street."

"I was just about to take a breather for a minute."

C.J. sat on the bottom step. Amber put the toddler down and watched as he stumbled across the grass to chase another butterfly.

Amber settled on a step where she could keep watch over the baby. "Do you mind if he runs around?"

"Amber, what I mind is you always asking 'Do you mind?' No, I don't mind. It's grass. Kids are supposed to play in it. Just say what's on your mind. You don't have to preface everything you say or do by getting someone else's permission. You're your own woman."

Amber looked away and then back at C.J. But when she spoke, she couldn't meet C.J.'s eyes.

"That's what I like so much about you, Jan. You're independent and free thinking. Me, well, all I've got is Frankie and Frank Jr." She glanced at her son who was busy inspecting the trunk of one of the two apple trees in the far corner of the backyard. "I was brought up to believe a woman's place was in her house, minding her man and her babies."

C.J. rolled her eyes. "Hmmph."

Amber smiled shyly. "See, that's what I mean. I don't know what you did before you came to Serenity Falls, but me, well, the only time I've ever seen any of that women's empowerment stuff is on TV and everybody knows those people aren't real."

As she'd done in every previous conversation with Amber and anyone else who'd asked, C.J. ignored the questions about her past. With Amber, it was simpler. The woman never asked a direct question. That alone nearly drove C.J. crazy. The woman's self-esteem was nonexistent. Amber was an attractive woman but you'd never know it by the way she carried herself.

The woman's thick dark hair was combed straight back and secured with a headband. She never wore any makeup, not even a hint of color on her mouth. C.J. was willing to grant that some of it had to do with having an eighteen-month-old on her hands. But still . . .

"Amber, a lot of women are out there with successful careers and family lives. Some of them are burned out now because for so long they've been burning the candle at both ends. But at least they can say they made the effort." That was about as close as C.J. would get to explaining her previous life.

The young woman shook her head. "Maybe there was a time when I thought I could be one of those women but now . . ." Amber shrugged. "Remember that old commercial about women bringing home the bacon and frying it up in a pan? Frankie and I saw that on one of those funniest video shows a little while back. He said that's what's wrong with America now: Too many women are out there trying to be men."

That did it. C.J. had never met Frankie Baldwin but she was sure she didn't like the man. He'd crushed all the potential out of Amber just like his son was about to crush a petunia C.J. had planted. C.J. frowned at the toddler. Then she inhaled and exhaled. Relax. It was just a flower. Definitely not the end of the world. She gave herself points for being calm—another of the lessons she'd been spending time on in the last month. If Frank Jr. crushed a flower, she could plant another. If Frank Sr. further crushed the spirit of his wife, that might not be as easy to replace.

C.J. looked at Amber and smiled.

"What? What're you up to, Jan?" Amber asked. "That smile looks devilish to me."

"Oh, nothing. I was just thinking about all the projects I have to do around the house." C.J. slapped both hands on her jeans-clad thighs. "How about we break for cookies and lemonade?"

"Sounds good to me."

C.J. held the screen door while Amber collected the baby from a half-planted flower bed at the foot of the back porch steps. She followed Amber and Frank Jr. into the house.

C.J. had added another item to her list of projects: Amber Baldwin.

The first thing C.J. noticed later that afternoon as she approached the grocery store was a black Harley-Davidson motorcycle in the lot. She wondered if it belonged to him. It looked like the one she'd seen earlier in the day. But before she had the chance to conjure an image of the dark warrior and match him with a motorcycle, a commotion near the entrance of the store got her attention.

Several people crowded around a person on the sidewalk. C.J.'s reporter instincts kicked in as she approached the throng. She scanned the crowd getting a feel for place, time, and people, storing information as if she were taking a snapshot. A man in dark pants and an electric blue jacket with white racing stripes peeped around metal grocery carts lined up near the front of the store. He looked up, saw C.J. watching

him, and ducked into the store. A little boy about
seven or eight tugged on his mother's sleeve pointing
to the video store next to the supermarket. The
mother ignored him, and like the rest of the crowd,
hovered near to see what the fuss was all about.

"Give the man some air," someone said. "How can
he breathe with all you folks in his face."

"Someone call 9-1-1," a woman called out.

"Hey, mister, is he gonna be okay?"

C.J. edged forward and around a heavyset woman
who was trying to get a better view.

"What happened?" C.J. asked.

"Mr. Parker was standing there and then he just collapsed," the woman said. She turned to get a look at
who she was talking to. "Oh, hi there, Miz Langley.
Remember me, Bettina, from the bakery? You asked
me about biscotti."

C.J. smiled and nodded. She'd remembered to remember that her name was Jan Langley. "Hi, yes. I'm
going to stop by for more of those brownies of yours."
She'd settled for a brownie with her coffee because
biscotti, like bread machines and cappuccino, were foreign in this small town.

"Come on over. I always have brownies," the baker
said before turning her attention back to the scene.

The shrill wail of an ambulance's siren parted the
crowd. People moved aside as the emergency medical
technicians leaped from the ambulance to tend to the
fallen man.

When the crowd parted, C.J. got a good look at the
victim and at the person on the ground administering
CPR.

The dark warrior was saving a man's life.

Four

C.J. stepped aside to let the ambulance attendants wheel a gurney next to the fallen man but her fascinated gaze remained glued on the dark warrior who breathed the breath of life. She watched him breathe and push and count, one, two, three.

One of the emergency technicians got across from the man and picked up the rhythm of the cardiopulmonary resuscitation procedure.

"Breathe, dammit. Breathe," she heard the dark warrior command as he continued the maneuver. A few moments later, the man sputtered and coughed and the crowd sighed in relief.

In minutes, the attendants had the man secured on the gurney and headed into the ambulance. C.J. offered up a quick prayer as she watched the vehicle race down the street. When she turned back her heart beat faster than usual.

Used to the adrenaline rushes that came with the excitement of chasing a good news story, C.J. knew that the moment, watching a man's life being saved, could cause that adrenaline. Ever honest with herself though, she knew what she was feeling had little to do with the moment. It was the man.

He sat on the curb wiping his face with the tail of his T-shirt as people patted him on the back.

"Nice job there, mister," a man said. "Your quick thinking probably saved old Jesse Parker."

"I'm sure glad you knew how to do that," a woman with a yellow scarf tied over hair rollers told him. "I've seen it on those rescue programs on TV, but now I'm gonna take a class to learn how to do what you did. You never know when you might need to do it. I sure hope Mr. Parker is gonna be okay."

"Hey, mister? That was really cool. Are you okay? You need some water or something?" a teen asked.

As other people jostled forward to congratulate the man on his heroic deed, C.J. saw a photographer snap a picture then drop the camera back on his chest. The photographer scribbled something in a notebook and asked a question. C.J. pegged the young man as somewhere in his mid- to late-twenties, probably the local reporter working double-time as staff photographer.

A woman in an apron emblazoned with the store logo pressed something in her hand and nodded toward the man. C.J. looked down. Bottled water.

"Would you give that to the man, please," the woman asked.

C.J. looked from the plastic bottle in her hand to the dark warrior who was rising from the curb. A dark trail of perspiration dampened the blue T-shirt. C.J. wanted to trace that trail and lick up the moisture of his skin. He tugged the shirt down and tucked it into his pants. Her eyes followed the movement then dipped lower to assess. He was a man's man and C.J. liked every inch of what she was seeing. When she'd gotten to be so shallow she wasn't really sure. The outside wrapping didn't ensure that the inside was any good. But, Lord, the outside sure made her want to explore the rest. Besides, she figured, a biker who does CPR can't be all bad.

"Sir, hello. My name is Kenny Sheldon. I'm a reporter for the *Serenity Falls Gazette*. People are telling me you're a hero. What happened here?"

Wesley looked at the reporter and sighed. All he'd wanted was to get a quart of milk and some chips and stare at the packages of cigarettes. He hadn't bargained on this. And had this guy taken his photograph?

"Nothing really. I did what anyone would do."

The reporter chuckled. "Modest I see. What's your name?"

Wes eyed the camera. "I'd really rather not be in the paper if you don't mind."

"Oh, this. I just got a good scene shot of all the people talking to you."

Wesley sighed then looked to his left in the direction the ambulance had taken. His gaze connected with a serenely beautiful woman who stared back at him. It was her! She was standing right in front of him.

"Hi. Here's some water for you," C.J. said. "A store employee brought it out for you."

Wes accepted the bottle, twisted the cap, and took a deep swallow. His eyes never left hers. She was exquisite, just as beautiful as she'd seemed earlier in the day.

"Thank you."

"Anytime," she said.

"I'm Wes Donovan," he said, extending his hand to her.

The reporter jotted the information down.

"Nice to meet you. That was a great thing you did here. You probably saved that man's life."

"If it meant the opportunity to meet you, then that's

two good things that will have come out of this. You pulled a disappearing act on me earlier."

She shrugged and smiled. Wes was lost. "Listen," he said. "I was just on my way into the store to grab a couple of things. How can I thank you?" he said, holding up the bottle of water.

"I told you, it was from the store."

"Then how can I get to know you better?"

"Why?"

"Why?" he asked back. "Well, lots of reasons." Smooth skin, pretty brown eyes. A mouth that begged to be kissed. Full breasts. And hips and thighs that promised a dance of delight.

She folded one arm over the other and rested her chin in her hand. "Well, I'm waiting," she said.

Wes loved a challenge. "For what?"

"One of those reasons."

Wes laughed out loud. "You have a beautiful smile."

She gave him a look that said You-could-have-come-up-with-something-better-than-that.

"Thank you," she said, acknowledging the compliment. "I'm here to pick up a couple of items. Yogurt and cottage cheese."

Wes couldn't keep the grimace from his face.

"Not your taste, huh?" she asked. "The grocery has lots of selections. There are other things you can eat."

Wes knew better than to mention where that comment took his thinking.

"Mr. Donovan, may I have a few minutes? I promise I won't take up much of your time."

Wes had forgotten about the reporter. "No, thanks. I decline Sheldon. These folks out here can tell you what happened."

With that, Wes took her elbow and guided her into the grocery store.

C.J. picked up a small basket. Wes did the same.

"Why didn't you talk to that reporter? He seemed like a nice enough guy."

"I like to keep a low profile."

C.J. wondered why but let the obvious follow-up question go. Her reporting days were over. She'd joined the ranks of regular citizens. They headed in the direction of the dairy products aisle. C.J. picked over the yogurt, checking expiration dates and frowning at the flavors offered.

"You know, that stuff'll kill you. Too healthy," Wes said.

C.J. selected several containers of strawberry, blueberry, and raspberry yogurt and put them in her basket. "Have you ever even eaten yogurt?"

Wes shook his head and regarded her. "Nope. Just like chitlins, don't like the smell of it. I'll stick to frozen yogurt. At least it looks like the ice cream it's pretending to be."

C.J. laughed. "Yogurt is not like chitlins."

"How would you know? You've probably never eaten a chitlin in your life."

He was right but she wasn't about to admit it. "What do you know?" She pulled a container of strawberry yogurt from the dairy shelf. "Here, try this," she said, putting it in his basket. "It's blended yogurt so it'll taste and look more like the frozen yogurt you're used to."

She moved a few steps down and picked up a container of cottage cheese. "Why'd you say that?"

Wes followed her. He placed his basket on top of the sour cream containers. "Say what?"

"That I'd probably never eaten chitlins."

"You were standing there grumbling because the store doesn't carry apricot yogurt. A woman who eats apricot yogurt just doesn't strike me a chitlins and cornbread type."

C.J. was insulted but she couldn't quite put her finger on the reason why. "And you are?"

"If they're cleaned and cooked right. Mama Lo makes the best. But it took her a long, long time to get me to taste 'em."

C.J. smiled, forgiving. "Then you should give yogurt a chance like you gave the chitlins. Who's Mama Lo?"

"She's my . . ." Wes paused for a moment. "She's my mother," he finished.

C.J. looked him over. She'd bet his parents were striking people. To produce a son who rivaled the Greek gods, they'd have to have some good genes. His bronzed skin was rich. She wondered if he'd gotten his height from his father, from Mama Lo, or from some other ancestor. He'd shaved since the morning. C.J. couldn't decide which she liked better, clean shaven or the touch of whiskers. Whisker burns came to mind and she smiled, feminine and mysterious as she engaged in just a touch of fantasy about this man and certain parts of her own body. He would lick slow and easy, like savoring in ever tightening swirls, a delicious ice cream cone.

"What're you thinking?"

"Uh, just a few errant thoughts."

C.J. looked in her basket. "It was nice chatting with you. I'd better run." She turned to go, but he captured her arm. White heat licked through her at the contact. C.J. sucked in her breath and looked at him.

"Pardon me," he said.

Before C.J. could ask why, his mouth closed over hers. She felt him take the small grocery cart from her hands and then his hands framed her face.

Desire rushed forward and reason scampered away. C.J., bold in her own yearning, stepped into his embrace. She opened her mouth and Wes accepted the gift. His lips, hard yet soft, teased her, filled her, claimed her.

A hot ache consumed her, and C.J. realized she'd never before been this hungry. Nor had she ever been as conscious of her own femininity as she was in Wes's arms. She felt small, delicate.

As Wes roused her passion, his own grew stronger. He pulled her closer to the erection that was filling his jeans. She swiveled her hips and Wes groaned. His mouth moved from hers, to her neck where he rained tiny kisses along her earlobes.

A polite clearing of the throat brought them back to the surface. C.J. blushed and stepped back. She fought for breath but failed when she realized his gaze was riveted on her breasts, her hard nipples telling him exactly what her body wanted.

"Mouth to mouth resuscitation is your forte I see," an amused male voice said. The man stuck out his hand to Wes. "Hi, I'm Rusty York, the store manager. I was in the back when the heroics were going on. My people told me what you did. Thank you."

"No problem," Wes said.

C.J. retrieved her basket from the sour cream display where Wes had put it. "I'll see you around." With that, she took off at a fast pace down the aisle.

"Hey, wait a minute," Wes called after C.J. "Be right back," he told the store manager.

With a few long strides he caught up with her. "Why are you running away from me?"

"I don't know you," she pointed out. "You could be a killer or a rapist for all I know."

Wes cocked his head. "I'm not and you don't believe any of those things. I'm a good guy. Ask my mom."

C.J. couldn't stop the smile. "I'm sure your Mama Lo would vouch for you."

"Have dinner with me."

"Excuse me?"

Wes lifted a hand, one gentle finger traced her lips. "After that wonderful dessert I thought we should follow it up with dinner."

C.J. laughed. The sound of her voice rushed through Wes like wildfire. He stifled a groan.

"That's the best pickup line I've heard in a while."

"What time would you like me to pick you up?" he asked.

"Seven-thirty." She gave him her address then left him standing in the aisle alone.

Wes shook his head as he watched her retreat. Mercy. The Lord knew what he was doing when he put that package together. Wes turned to head back to the store manager and the milk he needed to buy. He added condoms to the list of items to pick up.

It wasn't until later he realized he didn't even know her name—and that she just might be off limits to him.

Five

Amber Baldwin was frightened.

"Frankie, don't talk like that. You scare me when you talk like that."

Amber went to Frank Jr.'s playpen and lifted the toddler in her arms. She held the baby, shielding it from his father's ranting.

"Look at you," Frankie smirked. "You're gonna turn him into a pansy boy the way you smother the kid. Let 'im be. God, I tell you, Amber Faye, you are worse than your mama. No wonder that low-life brother of yours is a . . ."

"Frankie, you said you weren't gonna talk about that anymore." Amber hugged the baby closer to her. It pained her when he spoke ill of her family, a family he would no longer allow her to see or communicate with.

Frank glanced over his shoulder then quickly peeked out their open living room curtains. "Yeah, well, I'm not. I was just using that as an example."

He walked over to the telephone on the crate-style end table. Amber watched as he twisted open the two ends and looked under the speaking and listening apparatus. She was used to the obsessive ritual her husband had. He believed that "they" were listening in and trying to catch him. Who "they" were, she'd never been able to get out of Frank. But the one thing she'd learned and learned well, was fear. Fear and living on the run.

They'd lived in Serenity Falls the longest. Eight months. Long enough to put down a few roots, make a few friends. But Frank always cautioned her against friends. "Friends turn on you," he always said. Amber thought about Jan Langley. Jan wouldn't turn on her. She was too nice. Frank didn't know about Jan, and Amber intended to keep it that way. If she got too friendly with anyone, Frank would just pick them up to move again.

When they met in Las Vegas two years ago, Amber had been a cocktail waitress at a casino on the strip. Frank Baldwin was a regular with a wad of cash and a serious line of credit. Three months after meeting him, they were married in one of the classier wedding chapels. Frank treated her like a queen for the first few months. They lived on champagne and pâté and he lavished her and her family with expensive gifts. Then he said they would winter on the Florida coast.

Amber had never been to Florida and was excited about the trip. But when they arrived, they didn't stay at a fancy hotel or even a nice house. Frank drove up to a dilapidated trailer in a trailer park and said they would stay there for a while. When she'd questioned him about it, he said he wanted to "see how the other half lived."

That trailer had been the worst but not the last one they lived in. They'd been observing the other half for some time now, from roach-infested trailers to run-down apartments in not-so-good neighborhoods. Amber was more than ready to return to the lifestyle they'd known in Vegas.

Amber shifted Frank Jr. to her hip and followed Frankie into the kitchen of their apartment. "Frankie, what kind of trouble are you in? Let's talk about this together. Maybe together we can come up with a solution."

Frank turned from his inspection of the telephone

on the kitchen counter. "I told you, princess. I'm not in any kind of trouble."

"Then why do you always check the phones? They're the same everyday. Nobody comes in here."

Frank replaced the receiver and walked up to her. He pulled her chin in his hand and planted a quick kiss on her lips. "Hang tough with me, Amber Faye. One more month and we'll be home free."

"Da," the baby said.

"Hey, little man," Frank answered, lifting the baby from Amber's arms. "What say you and me watch a ball game while Momma fixes us up some supper?"

The baby grinned. Frank patted Amber on the behind as he left the kitchen. "Hurry it up, too, babe. I'm hungry."

Amber went to the sink to rinse off the chicken she was going to fry for dinner. She ran cold water on the poultry then turned to stare at the telephone so recently checked out by Frankie. One more month and they'd be home free.

At Miss Clara Ann's house, Margaret reviewed her strategy. First she'd lure her prey, then she'd reel him in with teasing promises and whispered entreaties. She knew she could count on Aunt Clara Ann to both wittingly and unwittingly assist her in her plan.

Margaret smiled into the bureau mirror in her room. She spritzed herself with a light, flirtatious cologne and freshened up her lipstick. She loved these games, loved the thrill of the hunt. And this time, her prize would be a big one.

Kenny Sheldon typed the last paragraph of his story, then sat back and smiled. He'd done a good job. And he hadn't had a lot to work with. The eyewitness accounts were good. He just wished that the hero of the day, Wes Donovan, had been more willing to talk.

Kenny picked up the telephone and called the nurse's station at County General.

"Hi there," he said when he got someone. "This is Kenny Sheldon over at the *Gazette.* I was just calling to check on Mr. Parker's condition one more time before I turn my story in." Kenny listened for a moment then, "Sure, I'll hold."

While waiting for the nurse's report, Kenny picked up the black and white print of the scene at the grocery store. He nodded, pleased with his work. He'd captured the moment: a weary rescuer sitting on the curb with his head down being comforted by townsfolk.

"That Donovan sure is a big one," he observed, not for the first time. For a moment earlier that day, Kenny had been almost certain the modest hero who had to be about six four, two twenty, was about to land him one in the face. Thank goodness that woman was there.

Kenny had seen her around town once or twice. She was pretty and for the most part seemed to stick to herself. If he himself had felt more comfortable around beautiful women, he may have asked her out on a date.

"It's not too late, Clark Kent," he said, then smiled to himself. "Oh, yes. I'm still here," he said into the receiver. "Guarded but stable. Got it. Thanks a bunch. You have a good evening."

Kenny replaced the receiver, pushed his horn-rimmed glasses up then updated his story, made a print out of it, and shipped it to his editor. The *Gazette* had finally joined the twentieth century with four computers. Kenny had one, the newspaper's features reporter had one, the editor had one, and the layout guy in the backroom used a Mac to do the page design.

Kenny Sheldon was biding his time. He'd been on

staff at the *Serenity Falls Gazette* for a year and a half. He'd started as a correspondent writing up the county high school sports stories. Now he was a full-time sports and news reporter. He figured he'd stay one more year then make his break to the big time. What he needed was a big story that the editor could put out on the wires with the byline Kenneth J. Sheldon. But nothing big ever happened in Serenity Falls, North Carolina. Even though the town could boast more than twenty-five thousand residents, it remained small town U.S.A.

Kenny sighed. Maybe he'd give the *Gazette* only another six months instead of a year.

C.J. opened her front door to a smiling Yancey Yardley. If ever there were a made up name, Yancey had it. But time and again, he swore on his "dear, departed mother's soul, bless her heart," that that was the name he'd been given at birth.

"Yancey, what brings you here, tonight?"

"Just passing through, so to speak," he said.

C.J. laughed. Yancey lived on the other side of town, in the opposite direction of the established little street C.J. lived on. "Um hmm," she said.

If Yancey was waiting for an invite in, he'd be disappointed tonight. He obviously was coming straight from work; he still wore the telltale blue shirt with the plant seal at the breast. The matching pants completed the uniform. Yancey, with his blue eyes, short afro, deep tan, and engaging smile, reminded her of singer Tom Jones in his prime. Normally she liked shooting the breeze with the truck driver. Yancey offered a perspective on the town that C.J. had been unable to get anywhere else.

But tonight she was keyed up and anxious about her date with Wes Donovan. C.J. had never been one to let grass grow under her feet when it came to a man she'd like to get to know better. She still hadn't decided what to wear. But before she could do that, she had to get rid of Yancey, no easy feat if he was in one of his usual talkative moods.

"Come on, now, Jan . . ."

C.J.'s smile faltered a bit at the name.

"You know I take this route home every night."

"Whatever you say, Yancey," she answered. "What's up though? I'm kind of in a hurry."

Yancey shifted his feet and stepped aside. He hefted up four cardboard boxes. "The rose bushes you special ordered came in. I was over at the lawn and garden shop picking up some crab grass killer. Mrs. Charleston was telling me about your pretty roses. I mentioned I was headed over this way and voila! Personal delivery."

"That was sweet of you. Why don't you bring them this way."

C.J. opened the door wider and followed Yancey.

"Where do you want them?"

"Kitchen counter will do. I want to read the directions first."

Yancey did as he was bid.

"Thanks so much," she told him.

Yancey eyed the cookie jar on the counter. He'd somehow gotten the notion that C.J. cooked. C.J.'s idea of cooking was nuking restaurant leftovers. "No cookies, Yancey. But I do have some brownies from Bettina's Bakery. Picked them up fresh this afternoon."

C.J. offered him the waxed bag.

"Don't mind if I do. Hey, did I ever tell you about the time—"

C.J. cut him off at the pass. "Yancey, I'm really running late. We can talk maybe tomorrow."

"Oh, yeah. You did say you were in a hurry. Where you headed?"

There were some things C.J. detested about small

town life. This was one of them: why everybody assumed they should know everything about you.

"Out."

Yancey looked hurt. C.J. felt bad. She'd never been really good at subtleties. She left those things for people like her brother, Robinson, who both enjoyed and was good at the art of the nuance.

"Yancey, I'm sorry. I didn't mean to be rude. Thank you for bringing the rose bushes over. Have another brownie. Forgive me?"

Yancey grinned. His blue eyes sparkled. "No harm, no foul, Jan. I'd better be going." He stuck his hand in the waxed bag and pulled out another brownie. "Bettina makes the best," he said.

C.J. followed him to the front door. Yancey pushed the screen door open and stepped out on the porch. "Hey, did you hear about old man Jesse Parker? Had a heart attack or something right outside the grocery today. They said some guy on a motorcycle stopped and gave him CPR."

C.J. nodded. "Yeah, I was down there today."

"I sure hope Mr. Parker's gonna be okay. He's a nice old man. Well, you have a good night. Let me know when those pretty roses of yours bloom. I'd like to see them."

"I will. You have a good evening, too."

Finally he was gone. C.J. sighed. All of this good will and small talk was draining. People in the city just sort of ignored you. C.J. was discovering that perhaps that wasn't so bad after all.

She went to the kitchen to look at the clock on the stove. She had less than half an hour to get dressed for her dinner date with Wes Donovan.

C.J. looked at the rose bush boxes marked FRAGILE—LIVING. They could wait. Getting dressed couldn't.

Since she wasn't sure where they were going, she

opted for an outfit that could pass for dressy or casual: a silky loose burnt orange shift with a black miniskirt. C.J. thought her legs were her best feature, not that anyone in her former life would know that. She'd never been a power suit type, preferring loose, casual clothing, usually slacks, designed for comfort rather than style.

She plucked from a jumbled pile of jewelry a cowrie shell necklace. She wrapped the necklace over her right wrist several times to form a five-layered bracelet. She found a pair of funky earrings designed from cowrie shells and put them in her ears.

Adeptly applying makeup so it looked like she wasn't wearing any, C.J. finished dressing just as the doorbell rang. She opted against a purse or bag. She slipped her driver's license, some "just-in-case" cash, and house key in a slim skirt pocket and went to the door.

Wes Donovan looked good enough to eat. The bad boy image personified, he wore a black shirt, black slacks, and black boots. If he didn't carry it so well she may have made a comment about being a Johnny Cash wanna-be. The black clothing is where the Johnny Cash resemblance stopped though. If she were to hazard a guess, she'd figure that in addition to the African influence, Wes Donovan had more than a little Native American and Mediterranean blood flowing in him. His dark skin was flawless, his facial features hard, like she suspected all the rest of him would be. His thick brows hooded eyes that seemed to undress her as she stood in the doorway.

"Hi. You look great," he said.

"You're not so shabby either."

"Hungry?" he asked.

C.J. looked him over. Wes took a step forward.

"Um hmm," she just about purred.

He chuckled, the sound a rumbling like thunder in

the distance. "How about some more dessert before we go to dinner?"

He pulled her into his arms. His lips were hard and searching, hot and searing. But before C.J. could get her arms up and around his broad back, Wes stepped away.

"Let's go before I get some other ideas," he said.

Oddly disappointed, yet at the same time pleasantly surprised, C.J. locked her front door, a habit she couldn't quite break. When she turned to follow him she met the wall of his chest. He braced her so she didn't stumble.

"I don't even know your name," he pointed out.

C.J. had a choice. She could tell him the truth or she could lie the same way she'd been doing with everyone she met in Serenity Falls. For some reason, the simple lie didn't seem so simple and she couldn't quite roll it off her tongue as she'd learned to do in the last month. She looked into the face of this man and knew that to lie to him would be like lying to herself. Funny thing, though, she'd been lying to herself about so many things for so long that that no longer seemed like a sin; it was just more of the masquerade she'd perfected to a science.

In the end, caution won out. She'd come too far to blow it all now and just for a piece of a hard body.

"Jan Langley," she mumbled.

Wes looked at her oddly before heading down the walkway and to the gate. "You know, it's a funny thing about names. I would have bet money that you had a strong, Earth Mother name."

Affronted, C.J. fired back, "What's wrong with Jan?" It was, after all, her middle name . . . sort of.

Wes opened the gate and let her walk through it before him. "You could use a paint job on this," he absently observed. Then, answering her question, "Nothing. It just doesn't seem to fit. You're dark and mysterious. I guess I was expecting something like Eve or Zora."

C.J. smiled. "I love her stuff."

Wes lifted a brow. "Zora Neale Hurston? Yeah, I like the short stories better than some of the longer work. But the autobiography *Dust Tracks on a Road* is probably my favorite."

C.J. was surprised . . . and well, surprised: a bad boy biker who was familiar with the writing of a black feminist author who lived before her time. She half expected him to next tell her that he had a Ph.D. in anthropology and was fluent in Mandarin Chinese. She didn't bother to ask though. With her interviewing skills, honed over the years as a beat reporter, she knew she'd know everything she wanted to know about Wes Donovan by the end of the evening.

The Harley-Davidson was propped up at her curb.

Wes looked from the bike to C.J. in the short skirt and black pumps. "Hmm."

"Not a problem," she said stepping up to the bike.

"You want to drive your car?" he asked.

"Nope. I'll hang on to you real tight. I've always wanted to ride on the back of a Harley."

Wes grinned as he handed her his helmet. He hopped on the bike then turned to see that C.J. got settled. "I like tight," he said.

"I'll just bet you do."

With that, Wes took off.

Six

He felt a twinge of guilt. She was obviously someone with something to hide. Weren't they all? Every person in the government's Witness Protection Program had something to hide. He wondered what secrets Jan Langley held and who she'd been before being relocated to Serenity Falls.

Then again, Wes figured, maybe she was what she looked like, a woman living alone in a small town. But Wes had been a Deputy U.S. Marshal too long to believe that. He'd ruled out the possibility that she was his own contact. He was here to assess the alleged breach of security on a relocated witness. That didn't mean that there was just one protected and relocated witness in the town. For all he knew, Jan could be one of many. She acted like a woman with a lot of secrets.

The secrecy and need-to-know status of many of the Marshals Service's cases made it impossible for him to know the details of every file. And in this case, Holloway had been unnecessarily vague on just who Wes was to be meeting. Since the recycling plant was the largest employer in the area, it stood to reason that his guy worked there.

As for Jan Langley, he'd drop a few well-placed clues throughout the evening. She'd open up before the night was over and he'd know what he wanted to know. In the meantime, it was hard, pun intended, he thought to himself, to concentrate on guilt when her soft hands were wrapped around him and surreptitiously inching lower. If she kept that up, he was going to have to find a hotel in the town and take care of business. But then again, if her hands didn't do him in it would be those smooth thighs flush against him.

The bike was covering some ground. Behind him, Jan let fly a whoop and a holler.

Up front, Wes grinned. He turned back to take a quick look at her then put his attention back on the road. "Having fun?"

She pressed closer to him and held on tighter as he made a sharp left turn. "Awesome."

A few minutes later, they pulled into the parking lot of McCall's Restaurant. C.J. had heard good things about the food and had passed by the place several times but had never had a meal there. Wes cut the engine on the bike. C.J. got off then tugged at her skirt.

Wes didn't miss the motion or the fact that she'd done that with more grace than many women would have mustered. He settled the bike then joined Jan, following her with his hand at her waist. Maybe a beer would cool him off a bit.

At Miss Clara Ann's, Margaret made an entrance into the dining room. The low-cut blouse was provocative but not too daring. A man at the table with Aunt Clara stood up when she walked in.

"Good evening," he said.

"Hello. Hi Aunt Clara."

The man pulled a chair out at the table and helped her take her seat.

"Thank you."

Miss Clara Ann shook her head. "You're too late. He left 'bout half an hour ago," she said with no additional explanation. "Garrison, I'd like you to meet my niece, Margaret. Margaret, this is Garrison, the artist I was telling you about who's staying up on the third floor."

Margaret smiled and managed to hide her disappointment. She'd heard him come in his room and had timed her arrival in the dining room so he'd be about midway through his meal when she arrived. Instead, here was some artist who was just starting on a salad.

"Are you visiting?" he asked.

Margaret managed not to roll her eyes. Of course she was visiting. This guy had probably been breathing too many paint fumes. "Yes, I'll be here a few weeks," she said sweetly then helped herself to a small portion of salad from the large bowl on the table.

As usual, Aunt Clara had prepared a big spread. Ham and okra with mashed sweet potatoes, corn on the cob, and spoon bread. She'd have to make sure to go jogging in the morning, maybe tonight, too.

Maybe she'd catch Wesley at breakfast. With that thought, Margaret cheered up and asked the artist about his latest work.

Wes led C.J. to a table. McCall's was obviously having an identity crisis. It seemed the place couldn't decide if it wanted to be a country western theme joint, a sports bar, or a family restaurant. Wes hoped the menu wasn't too schizoid. He would have preferred cooking himself. But living in a rooming house didn't give him that luxury. He'd found this place while on his way to the job interview earlier in the day.

"This is nice," C.J. said as she settled in their booth. "I've never been here."

Wes held his comment and ordered a beer when the waitress placed menus before them.

"What can I get you to drink, ma'am?"

"Do you have herbal tea?"

"I'm sorry, no. We have iced tea. Would you like a glass of that?"

"Sure."

"Be right back to take your orders."

The waitress walked away. C.J. and Wes studied their menus for a minute.

"Steak and potatoes for me," Wes said.

A traditionalist, C.J. thought. A meat and potatoes kind of man appealed to her on lots of levels.

She pondered the choices a while longer. "I'm trying to decide between the grilled chicken and the Santa Fe salmon."

When the waitress returned with beer and iced tea, Wes looked at C.J. After a quick question to their server, she settled on the salmon. Wes then ordered his steak, medium rare.

"I'll get some bread and house salads to you just as soon as I place your order," the waitress said as she collected their menus.

Wes downed a considerable portion of the beer. C.J. watched him drink and licked her lips imagining the cool refreshing taste of the imported brew. She added sugar to her tea, squeezed a lemon over the ice and stirred it, then sipped at the beverage.

Wes leaned back so his head rested on the high cushion padding of the booth. "So, tell me, why did you call me Dark Warrior?"

"When did I call you that?"

"Earlier today. On the street when you bumped into me."

C.J. smiled. "Oh. I didn't realize I'd said that out loud." She studied him for a moment. "Because you're dark, almost swarthy, like a pirate or a desert sheik. And when I walked into you today, sorry about that, you stood before me scowling and glaring like an ancient warrior king."

Wes smiled. "So, you're a fiction writer?"

C.J. watched him take another swallow of beer, she really would have preferred the brew over the tea. One step at a time, she told herself, one day at a time. She lifted the glass of iced tea to her mouth, pretended it was an icy cold one then answered his question with a question. "Why do you say that?"

"The imagery of your description."

She smiled. "That's not imagery. It's the truth through my eyes."

"And they are beautiful," he said.

"Flattery will, of course, get you . . ." she paused long enough to make him wait, "anything you want," she added softly.

Wes leaned forward. "Well, in that case, let me tell you about those legs you had wrapped around me. And your mouth . . ."

C.J. sat back, smiled and wagged a finger at him. "Unh uh. It has to be sincere flattery."

There was a faint glimmer of humor in his eyes, and then they darkened even more. C.J. felt as if she were standing on the edge of a two-thousand-year-old volcano that was about to blow its top for the first time. She smoldered under his intense gaze and knew like she knew her name that she'd be with this man. It no longer was a matter of *if*, if she could even claim she'd ever really doubted it, but a matter of *when* and where.

Without a word, he continued to stare at her. C.J., unable to tear her eyes away from him, met him unflinching, gaze for gaze.

"I want you," he said smoothly, with no expression on his face or inflection in his voice. He stated it as simple fact. C.J.'s breathing deepened and her eyes dilated.

She was spared an answer when the waitress arrived with a small loaf of fresh-baked bread and two generous green salads.

"Here you go, folks," she said. "Be careful with the bread, it's straight from the hearth. The butter spreads are honey maple, strawberry kiwi, and boysenberry. If you'd like some regular I can get some for you." She placed the bread on the table then put a salad in front of each of them. "Fresh ground pepper?"

"No thanks. I'm hot enough as it is," C.J. mumbled.

Wes smiled and shook his head no.

"Another beer for you, sir?"

"Yes, please. Jan, would you like a glass of wine?"

What C.J. really wanted was a double scotch on the rocks and a cold shower. "I'll take more tea, please. Thank you."

"Sounds good. Your meals will be up in a few minutes. I'll come back by to refill your drinks and bring you some more bread if you'd like it."

When the waitress left, Wes turned up the heat again. "Do I make you nervous?"

Her mouth quirked with humor. "That's not exactly the word I'd use."

"Then what word would you use?"

"Needy. Achy."

Wes smiled in masculine understanding. "Good," he said simply. Then he turned his attention to the salad before him.

C.J. watched him eat and wondered when he'd gotten the upper hand of the conversation. It was time he squirmed a bit.

"Do you come on quite so strong with every woman you meet?"

"No. It hasn't been necessary. I've never felt this way before."

"How do you feel?" she asked.

Wes paused, salad fork speared with a black olive, he looked at her. His gaze dipped to her breasts then meandered back to her face. "Needy. Achy."

C.J. downed the last of the iced tea in record haste.

By the time the waitress brought their entrees the conversation had shifted to more neutral ground.

"How did you come to be in Serenity Falls?" she asked.

"Mostly just passing through," he said. "It seemed like a nice enough place to pause for a while."

"Where are you from?"

"West Virginia. And you?"

"Originally from Maryland. But I've been around, here and there most of my life." She hoped the answer was vague enough for him to avoid a more specific follow-up question.

"I've been to Baltimore several times," he said. "I love the Inner Harbor and the aquarium. Have you ever been there?"

He was dancing awfully close to home, too close for comfort. C.J. nodded vaguely and then lobbed another question statement his way, one she hoped would steer him away from the subject of Maryland and her hometown Baltimore.

"So, tell me about yourself. You handled that CPR today like a pro."

Wes smiled. "I try to keep current. You never know when you'll need to know something. Or when you might be a contestant on 'Jeopardy.' "

"What other things do you know?" she asked with a teasing smile.

"A few foreign languages, mostly enough to get by, enough tae kwon do to have earned a black belt, how to rebuild the engine on a '67 Mustang, and which fork to use at a formal banquet."

"I'm suitably impressed."

"You should be," he grinned.

"Any of it true?" she asked.

Wes let loose with laughter that was deep, warm, and rich. C.J. fell in love with the sound.

He answered her in smooth French.

C.J. blinked. Her French skills were rusty. Practicing the language was not something she got a chance to do often while she reported stories from low-income areas of Baltimore.

It took her a moment but she managed to translate most of his statement. He'd said: "Only that which you choose to believe."

After another moment of thought, she answered back in French: "I'll grant you the benefit of the doubt for now and believe it all."

Wes smiled and held his glass up to her in salute.

"To the here and now," he said in English.

C.J. clinked her iced tea glass with his.

They ate in silence for a few minutes. The waitress replaced their bread round then slipped away.

"Your turn to impress me," he said.

The comment was simple and it was fair; they were getting to know each other. But C.J., for the second time that night, found herself debating about telling him the truth or telling him the vague tale she'd used to fend off the more curious of Serenity Falls's inhabitants.

Lying came moderately easy for C.J. But it felt wrong, as if she would be cheating not only herself but Wes if she told him less than the truth. Rare was the occasion when she even thought twice about bending or stretching the truth when it came to getting information she needed. She really hated the getting to know you part of relationships. It generally proved tedious beyond measure. And now, she not only had to contend with that part but the minefield of half-truths she'd so recently created. It was far easier to just acknowledge mutual lust, grab a couple of condoms and bid someone a fond but forever farewell in the morning.

"What do you want to know?" she finally asked him.

"What do you do for fun?"

C.J. could have wept in relief. If that was the toughest question she had to tap dance around, the rest of the night would be a breeze.

"I garden. I've spent the last few weekends trying to turn part of my backyard into an English garden. I'm also experimenting with an herb garden. My newest recreational activity is reupholstering and refinishing furniture—or at least trying to."

Wes's brow furrowed, he peered closer at C.J. She swallowed her last bite of salmon and laughed.

"What?" she said smiling. "Not exactly what you were expecting?"

"To be honest, no," he said. "I sort of figured you for an outdoors type but outdoor sports."

"That's just like a man to think something like that. I play a pretty mean game of tennis," she admitted. But she left out her better than average golf and lacrosse games. Telling him about the country club sports she'd grown up with would give too much away. She also didn't count the two grueling hours she put in in aerobics every morning. Well, every morning before moving to North Carolina. She'd ceased that obsessive activity as soon as she arrived and now contented herself with half an hour of step aerobics in her living room every morning.

"So, you have a green thumb?"

C.J. held her right thumb up and turned it one way

and then the other. "Looks brown to me," she said, smiling. "Actually, no. That's why I decided to try my hand," she said, tipping her hand to him at the small pun, "at gardening."

Back in Baltimore, she'd had a service come in to take care of the few plants she did maintain. If left up to C.J., the ficus trees and houseplants scattered about would have died of neglect and dehydration. One of the reasons she'd decided to do the outdoor garden when she arrived in Serenity Falls was because if and when she tired of the notion of playing Miss Green Thumb, the natural rain and sunshine would take better care of the plants than C.J. ever would.

"What do you do, as in for a living?"

This one was easy, she thought. "Whatever I want to. I'm recuperating."

She waited for the inevitable next question. Most people assumed recuperating meant you'd been in an accident or had had an illness. C.J. let the good people of Serenity Falls believe what they wanted to. So half of the folks in town that she'd met thought she'd been sick and the other half thought she'd been in a car accident.

Wes smiled. "We all need to recuperate sometimes."

C.J. sat back, cocked her head to the side and regarded him. "You surprise me, Wes Donovan."

Wes took the last bite of the baked potato on his plate. He chewed and swallowed. "How so?"

"Oh, you just do," she said. "Do you come from a large family?"

Wes shook his head. "Immediate family, no. Extended family, yes. What about you?"

C.J. smiled. Obviously, the man was adept at not answering questions, even simple yes/no ones. She wondered how he got to be that way. "One older brother."

They sat back when the waitress arrived to clear their

dinner plates. "Can I interest you folks in dessert? We have some really good ones."

"Dessert's my favorite," C.J. said with a wink at Wes.

"Mine, too," he said.

"Well, then, I'll be right back with the menu and dessert tray. Would you like coffee?"

"Yes, please," Wes said. C.J. asked for hot tea.

A few minutes later, Wes was putting serious dents in a generous helping of apple pie à la mode while C.J. worked on strawberry cream pie.

"You said you were just passing through Serenity Falls," she said. "What do *you* do for a living?"

"Well, right now I'm hoping to get on at the plant and earn back the money I'm spending to get my truck fixed. Usually though I work on call as a trouble-shooter for a government contractor. I show up where they send me, assess the situations, fix them if I can, call in for assistance if I can't. It's pretty good work."

"What have been some of the situations?"

C.J. could have sworn he looked surprised at the question. If he seemed to take a while thinking about the answer, she let it go as trying to come up with a suitable example to impress her.

"My juris . . . My work takes me lots of places. There was this guy in Silicon Valley who'd lost a whole lot of money for his company. I came in as a management consultant so to speak and got him squared away."

C.J. noted and stored the fact that he seemed about to say "My jurisdiction," and "management consultant" as she well knew from doing several stories about criminals, covered a wide spectrum. For all she knew this guy could be a cop or a bank robber. But seeing that he spoke several languages, or said he did, and claimed to be a black belt in martial arts, if he were indeed a criminal she decided he'd be a jewel thief.

But he said he was a government contractor. Maybe he was an arms smuggler.

She smiled at her fancy. "It's been too long," she said.

"Too long what?"

"I was just thinking out loud. Too long since I've been in the company of an interesting man." She'd always been quick thinking on her feet. The real answer though was too long since she ever took what people said at face value, simply as the truth as they perceived it. Maybe it was time to stop looking for the next great story, the next conspiracy theory. It was past time to just relax, enjoy life, and take people at their word.

They finished up their dessert. Wes patted his shirt pocket. Then sighed.

C.J. smiled in understanding humor. She'd seen that gesture enough in the newsroom to interpret it. "How long has it been?"

A full brow lifted in question.

"Since you gave up smoking?"

"Not long enough."

C.J. leaned forward, rested both elbows on the table and her chin in the cradle of her hands. "So, what do we do now?"

"Sex sounds good to me," he said.

Seven

"Let's do it," she said.

If Wes was surprised by her answer it didn't show. He signaled for their waitress, settled the bill, and within five minutes had C.J. on the back of the motorcycle. He handed her his helmet then bent low for a kiss. Hot and hungry, it promised heaven. Wes settled himself on the bike, and with C.J.'s arms wrapped about his waist they headed to her house.

Without a word spoken between them, C.J. led him through the dark bungalow and to her bedroom. Wes felt along the wall for a light switch but C.J. stilled him. She pressed her soft woman's body against him. Wes closed his arms around her and inhaled her scent.

Clasping her face in his large hands, he lowered his head and their mouths met. His covered hers hungrily, with the same gusto and enthusiasm with which he'd devoured the steak during their meal.

C.J. ran her hands up the hard wall of his chest then around to his back. She smoothed her palms along him until she grasped his buttocks. When she squeezed he whirled her around and braced her against the wall. C.J. wrapped her arms around his neck as his tongue left her mouth and staked a claim on her neck.

She gave herself up to the hot licks of fire that ran

up and down her spine in concert with the movement of his mouth at her neck and nape.

C.J. moaned. Or was it him?

She pushed at his broad shoulders until he stepped away, a question in his eyes.

C.J. backed him up to her bed. When the back of his legs hit the mattress she reached up and pressed on his shoulders until he sat.

Wesley smiled.

She stepped away from him and lit several candles scattered about the room; well aware that his gaze followed her every movement. She returned to the bed a few minutes later. Leaning forward to brush his lips against hers, she kissed him slow and easy as if time and the moment existed solely for them to share the nectar of the gods.

When Wes lifted his arms to pull her closer to him, she took three steps back and shook her head.

Wes smiled and rested his arms behind him on the firm but soft mattress.

Slowly, with a deliberate taunting that made him sit up and lick his lips, C.J. came out of every piece of clothing. Her hips undulated as blouse, skirt, and bra pooled at her feet. A gentle kick, sent the clothing out of the way.

She stood before him in high-heeled black pumps and hose. The triangle of her white panties peeked through the hose. She parted her legs. Wes stood up.

With a taunting smile she wagged a finger at him. He got the message and sat back on the edge of the bed. The tension in the room was palpable. Swinging her hips with each slow step, C.J. came to him. She held her full breasts, one in each palm and offered the erect tips to him. When Wes opened his mouth to capture the treat, C.J. chuckled and shook her head. Starting with the button at his collar band, she undid each of the small black buttons on his shirt. When his skin was bare, she ran her hands over his chest, kissed each of his small male nipples, then pushed him backward on the bed. She climbed astride him and in no time found herself flat on her back with Wes's head buried in her breasts.

She allowed him that because to deny him would be to deny her own pleasure.

Except there was one thing wrong.

She watched as Wes suckled and nipped. He gave one more delicious swirl at her breasts and then sat up long enough to pull out of the rest of his shirt, kick off his boots and get out of his pants. He left his white boxer shorts on but there was no denying he filled them up—completely and then some. The soft candlelight cast him in flickering shadows that enhanced C.J.'s feeling that she was about to be loved by a god come to life.

But there was one thing wrong.

"May I break the silence?" he asked quietly.

C.J. nodded.

"I need to go."

"Go?"

"All the beer."

She smiled. "Oh. Then go. Over there," she said, pointing toward the door that led to her bathroom.

Wes seared her with a kiss. C.J. felt scorched all the way to her toenails.

"Hold that thought," he said huskily.

Wes swung across her and off the bed.

C.J. took the time his absence afforded to kick off her shoes and hose. When Wes returned a few minutes later, she was sitting up in bed, her back against the wooden headboard, her chest bare but a sheet pulled to her waist.

Wes sat on the edge of the bed facing her. He

reached one hand out to fondle the ripe fruit of her breasts.

C.J. giggled.

"What?" he said, smiling.

Her giggle became a quiet reflective laugh. "We're not really going to do this are we?" she asked.

Wes pulled his hand away. He shook his head. "I don't think so." Then, with a slight frown, "Why not?"

C.J. scooted down on the mattress until they sat face to face. She kissed him lightly on the lips. "I'll make us some tea."

Wes nodded. He stood and assisted C.J. from the bed.

Unmindful of her nakedness, she walked to her closet, pulled out a long burgundy and pink robe and wrapped it about her body.

"We can sit out back," she said.

A few minutes later they sat on the steps of C.J.'s back porch quietly contemplating the stars visible in the night sky.

"I blew the candles out," he said. Then, after a short pause, "What was that all about?"

C.J. sipped from her mug then turned her head to look at him. "I don't know. Mutual lust."

"But definitely the wrong way to start a relationship?" he asked.

"Are we starting a relationship?"

"I don't know. You tell me."

"I don't know you. You don't know me."

Wes placed his mug on the step next to him then reached one bronzed hand into the folds of her robe. C.J.'s breast puckered in anticipation. He rubbed her until the relaxed nipple was again a hard pebble and warm heat flowed through her.

With his free hand he removed the mug from her hands and set it aside. Guiding her small hand to his lap he curled her fingers around the hard length of his erection.

Wes took a deep breath when her hand began a slow rhythm. "We have this in common," he said, as his own hand gently squeezed her breast. "And this is gonna be good. But if we want something more, it can't be based on sex alone."

"I agree," she said.

"So, where do we go from here?"

"Maybe you should leave," she suggested.

"I'd rather cut off an ear."

C.J. smiled. "Then let's say we stop tormenting each other and take things as they progress." She removed her hand from him but was unable to halt the sigh of disappointment when his strong hand ceased its gentle kneading. She watched as he quietly adjusted the fold of her robe.

C.J. picked up his mug and handed it to him. She lifted her own and sipped from the warm tea. They sat quietly and watched the stillness of the night. A steady chirping of crickets and the occasional croak of a frog filled the air, a natural symphony that more than anything else, served as a quiet reminder to C.J. that the world didn't have to be a hectic, ugly place.

She wrapped her hands around her mug and stared into the darkness. "I moved to Serenity Falls to get away from this sort of destructive behavior. I figured I wouldn't get myself in trouble or be overly tempted in a serene North Carolina town so I relocated here. I'd thought I was doing okay," she said. Then quietly added, "Until I bumped into you."

Wes evaluated her words and sighed inwardly. Relocated. That was one of the specialties of his line of work. He had no business getting involved with this woman. He could probably get fired for what had happened so far. But still he wanted her. He wanted her like he'd wanted no other woman, ever.

In the quiet of the night, Wes figured that was a bonus punishment that Holloway hadn't figured on, one that would do more to break his spirit, even more than Marc's death had done. Jan Langley was beautiful and off limits. And still he wanted her.

He tried to guess what she had done or been in her past life. What she knew or had seen that had gotten her a new identity fully paid for by the U.S. government. Wes glanced at her. In profile, she looked like an African queen: proud, arrogant, confident. Her features, perfectly shaped, fit her face, the smooth brown skin beckoned his touch. An arched brow tapered off. Wes wanted to run one finger along the small waves in her hair.

Wesley's gaze next examined her ear and the place on her neck he wanted to again bury his head. She smelled of woman and of exotic nights. Wes smiled. She had two holes in her left ear visible above the big earrings she wore.

"What did you do before?" Even as he asked the question Wes knew it was inappropriate. If she were indeed a good witness, no matter what she told him, it would be a lie. She'd protect her old identity.

She turned to him and smiled, no longer a serene smile. "Let's not talk about that. Tell me about growing up in West Virginia."

Wes accepted her answer for what it was: the best truth she could offer him. He'd get the information he wanted to know another way. There was always another way. He sipped from his cup, frowned when he realized she really had made tea, then lowered the cup and silently watched the night.

"West Virginia was a long time ago," he said after awhile. "I haven't been home, what you'd probably call home, in more years than I care to remember. It doesn't necessarily bring back fond memories."

"What about Mama Lo?"

For a moment, Wesley looked surprised. Then he remembered he'd mentioned Mama Lo's cooking to Jan earlier in the day. He nodded and smiled. "Yeah. It would be nice to see Mama Lo."

He hadn't seen her since the funeral. She'd looked older then, old and tired. Wes hoped that healing had started for her by now. He couldn't say the same for himself but he wished healing and comfort for the woman who was like a mother to him.

"I've been thinking," he said.

"About what?" she asked.

"The sex thing."

"We are two consenting adults," she pointed out.

"I have condoms."

C.J. put her mug to the side and moved to the step in front on him. She settled between his legs and leaned back. She smiled when his legs opened wider and he draped his arms about her neck and shoulders. She turned her head back and they kissed, this time letting the need in them flower slowly.

Safe within the shelter of his embrace C.J. faced the night again and contemplated the moonlight between the trees in her backyard. The soft night and the gentle stroking of his hand along her neck soothed C.J. in a place where for too long she'd felt turmoil. This man's hungry kisses and gentle embraces fed a place in her that she didn't realize was lacking. She wanted him. She knew she'd have him. But she wondered if having him would make him just like all the others, a mountain once conquered, no longer a mystery or thing to be desired.

She sensed within him a power restrained, a harnessed energy waiting for the right moment. Given her

own track record, C.J. knew that giving in with Wes
Donovan would mean one of two things: destroying
him like she did every man she'd ever had a sexual
relationship with or so deeply losing herself that she'd
be forever lost in a mire of dependency just like her
new friend Amber. C.J. could see no balance, no middle ground anywhere between the two extremes. She'd
bought hook, line, and sinker the spirit of the 1980s
overachievers: work and play hard. She'd extended
that notion to every aspect of her life and was now
faced with a question that had never needed answering—what comes after you work hard and play hard?

"Why did we stop earlier?" Wes quietly asked.

She smiled to herself at the question. Then she felt
him shift behind her. His head nuzzled her neck and
his hands began a slow exploration. C.J. sank deeper
into his embrace.

"I was just thinking about that," she said.

"And did you come up with an answer?"

"No. Not really," she said. She captured one of his
hands and kissed the palm. "This is going to happen.
But I don't think it should be tonight."

She surprised herself with that answer. Did that
mean she was maturing? It had to be, she figured, because she'd never denied herself pleasure before, and
the one thing she wanted most in the world right now
was for Wes Donovan to keep doing all the things he
was doing with his hands, with his mouth, with the
erection she felt pressed into her back.

But even as she prided herself on her newfound re-
straint, a part of her was pissed off that it had to come
now, with this man. Waiting, patiently waiting, was not
one of her strong points unless it had to do with fer-
reting out a story. And what she was feeling now had
not even a smidgen to do with newsgathering.

C.J. leaned forward out of his embrace and then

stood up and faced him. Wes silently watched her. She pushed him back until his back lay on the wooden planks of her porch. C.J. crawled along his long body, pausing here and there to explore an interesting tidbit.

She heard Wes suck in his breath. "I thought you just said 'Not tonight.' "

"I'm not a tease," she said. "I've run hot and cold tonight. And that's not fair to you."

Her hand traced the now full erection in his jeans.

"Let me ease your pain," she said, as her hand slowly unfastened the top and worked at the zipper.

A shuddering sigh was Wesley's answer.

Back in his room at Miss Clara Ann's Wes thought about what had transpired this night. He had stopped her on the porch. At the time, he didn't know why. He wanted her with every fiber of his being. But he wanted her right, and right meant together and whole. Damned if he could figure out why it made any difference. It never had before. But he wanted the total woman, not the Jan who gave of herself while he lapped up all the sweetness and offered her little or nothing in return.

The lady had said no, then seemed to change her mind. He wondered at her choice of words. She'd distinctly said that she moved to Serenity Falls to cease "this sort of destructive behavior." Since the only behavior that had been going on was their foreplay, Wes concluded that maybe she'd been a high-level call girl. He did a mental inventory but came up blank in trying to remember if there had been a prostitution bust or case in the recent past that would warrant Witness Security and relocation. Maybe she was the girlfriend of a Mafia boss or a gang leader.

But that just didn't fit. "The woman speaks French for God's sake," he said.

Yeah, Wes, and think back to the most dazzling courtesans of old, he argued with himself. Lots of them were bi-, tri-, and quadlingual, just part of the package.

Wes pulled off his shirt and boots and padded into the bathroom. Grateful he'd gotten a room with a private bath, he turned the shower on. A strong steady stream of water poured forth. Wes stuck his hand in the spray to test the water temperature. He shook his head.

"That won't do." He adjusted the water.

He came out of the rest of his clothes, dropping the jeans and shorts over the commode. Wes gritted his teeth and stepped into the now icy stream. "This better work," he mumbled.

It didn't.

Eight

Old habits die hard. Without the benefit of an alarm clock, Wes woke up at four in the morning. He pulled on a pair of running shorts, socks, and athletic shoes then dug out of his bag an old gray sweatshirt with the sleeves ripped off. Less than ten minutes after waking he was out the front door of Miss Clara Ann's and running the dark, deserted streets of Serenity Falls.

In the room next door to Wes's, Margaret swore out loud. She guessed that he might be a runner. He had to do some sort of regular intense physical activity to maintain the physique he had. Glancing at the digital travel alarm she'd placed on the night stand next to the bed, Margaret calculated how long he might be out. She jogged almost two miles every day but got started at the more civilized hour of five-thirty; she guessed Wesley might do a three- or four-mile run.

Aunt Clara had given him a room with an adjoining bath so she couldn't contrive to "accidentally" walk in on him while he showered. Breakfast might be her next best opportunity after this one. Margaret smiled in the dark as she tossed off the percale sheet that covered her. She had plenty of time to set her bait and lure in her prey.

"And what a fine specimen he is," she said while pulling on a bright pink running suit.

Running cleared Wes's mind. He generally spent the first two miles monitoring his breathing and clearing his head of all thoughts except the process of running, of putting one foot in front of the other. The second two miles he took in his surroundings, and the last two he always spent organizing his day—except for this morning when his thoughts were so very narrowly focused. When he got to the organizing his day part he tried to come up with a legit reason to stop by Jan Langley's. He failed to create one but didn't sweat it; he'd see her today by one means or another.

He'd check on the truck then scope out his guy. Orders from Holloway had been not to spook the witness just make contact and assess the situation. The witness's field inspector, whose job it was to remain in total contact with the witness, had landed himself in a cast from ankle to hip and would be out of commission for at least ten weeks. Wes smirked as he ran by the closed up stores of downtown Serenity Falls. Everything about this assignment smelled bogus. What kind of marshal tripped over a trash can, fell down a flight of steps, and wound up totally out of commission? There probably wasn't even a protected witness in Serenity Falls.

Except for Jan Langley.

He'd run a make on her. With any luck, the sort of luck that would keep him employed, she'd be just what she said she was, a woman recuperating in a small town. He hadn't bothered to ask recuperating from what. Wes wasn't really interested in whatever lie she needed to tell to maintain her former identity.

Wes sensed before he heard the other presence. Imperceptively he slowed his pace a bit. He let the other person draw near. Tense but loose Wes was ready for action.

"Geez, oh man. They told me you got up real early. This is crazy," the runner said from a few feet behind.

Wes glanced at the person trying to keep pace with him. He slowed up a bit more. "Good morning."

The runner grunted and caught up. "It was until I had to sit up all night waiting to see if you'd be out. I think somebody has made me."

"Made you what?"

The runner snorted. "You Marshals are the most cloak-and-dagger James Bond people I've ever met. Look, are you here to protect me or what?"

"What's the problem?"

"I think somebody knows who I am or rather who I was. Look, can you slow up a bit. I'm in fair shape, or thought I was. You're going to give me heart failure."

Wes came to a quick halt that threw his partner off guard. The runner stopped a few feet ahead and then walked back to where Wes stood stretching and limbering. Wesley took a good, long look at his contact. He'd need to be able to recognize this person under any circumstance, any time of day or night.

The jogger looked left and right and then leaned forward. "You know that accident that Jackson had? Messed up his leg."

Wes didn't give any indication that he knew one way or another.

The jogger leaned closer still then imitated the stretching exercise Wes had done. "I don't think it was an accident," the runner whispered. "I think that was a message to me. You know, 'You can run but you can't hide.'"

Wes began to jog in place. His shadow did the same. "What else can you tell me?" he asked.

"That's about it for now."

"What do you mean 'For now'?"

The witness shrugged. "How do I know I can trust you?"

"Sometimes in life you have to trust people."

"Yeah, right. The last time I did that I almost ended up dead." The witness again looked to the left and then to the right checking for eavesdroppers. "I'm outta here. This is making me crazy out here in the middle of the night. For all I know a sniper with night vision glasses is scoped on us right now."

To anyone who may have been observing so early in the morning, Wesley's run had been random. But he'd spent most of the time surveilling the area. With no backup security detail, he couldn't be 100 percent sure, but he was 80 percent sure there were no snipers on any of Serenity Falls's roofs. Wes had to admit, however, that those odds sucked. That 20 percent could have just as soon been 100 percent for all the difference it made.

"I'll be in touch," he told the witness. Wes watched the jogger nod and then duck around an industrial-size recycling bin and disappear.

Wes continued his run, eventually making his way back to Miss Clara Ann's. Well, he thought, it looked like there actually was a witness in town after all. He had some work to do.

A little more than an hour later Wes scowled over a cup of black coffee and the morning edition of the *Serenity Falls Gazette*. He sat by himself at Miss Clara Ann's guest dining room table. In the next room over, he could hear the early morning news on television as Miss Clara Ann prepared breakfast. The smell of frying bacon, more than hunger, kept him in his seat. Every now and then he'd hear her short bark of laughter or a sassy comeback to some of the morning anchors' witty repartee.

He read the first few paragraphs of the rescue story. Kenneth J. Sheldon obviously fancied himself as a grand journalist in the Woodward and Bernstein tradition. But stories about Little League and the county bake-off weren't going to win the guy any Pulitzers. The lead story in the paper was the so-called "miraculous rescue," for God's sake. The only good thing Wes could say about the story on the *Gazette*'s front page was that his name was spelled correctly and the photo didn't show his face.

Wes wasn't so much worried about working undercover, he rarely did that these days, but he was real concerned about keeping a low profile. He'd purposely come into town looking and acting like a regular Joe. It felt odd to travel without the heavy firepower though he had enough heat to get him out of basic types of trouble. And the claptrap truck Casey had set him up with couldn't even claim to be a fully outfitted armored government vehicle in disguise. It was exactly what it looked like, metal and rust that had seen better days.

Seeing his picture on the front page of the paper didn't serve any of his purposes for being in Serenity Falls. With luck, the paper didn't circulate anywhere out of the small northwestern North Carolina county. The way the media operated, Wes knew how futile that hope could be.

The scent teased him first. He didn't turn around or in any way acknowledge it. He smelled it above the bacon and eggs and coffee. It wasn't heavy but it wasn't light, the essence heady and straightforward and all woman. The scent had to have been formulated for the sole purpose of capturing a man's attention. It worked.

Margaret slid into the seat next to him at the table. Wes bit back a smile. A tigress was on the loose, he'd have to be careful. Knowing it would come quickly, he waited for her first move.

"Good morning," she said. "I heard you prowling around early this morning. Have a rough night sleeping?"

She had not just a nice voice, she had a great voice. It curled around him, reminding Wes of smooth, rich honey. He'd have to be careful not to be a fly stuck in that honey.

"No. I'm just an early riser."

"Me, too. Dawn is my favorite part of the day. You learn a lot when you're up and about early."

Wes glanced at Margaret. Her short, bobbed haircut flattered her face. She looked familiar in the way some black women did, like she'd stepped from the pages of *Essence* magazine, strong, black, and in charge. Her features, including the pert nose and the bow mouth, were attractive. But Wes didn't find himself responding to her obvious appeal.

"Morning's my favorite part of the day, too," he said.

Miss Clara Ann backed into the room carrying a platter heaped high with bacon and eggs. She settled it on the table. "Be right back with some biscuits hot from the oven. Mornin' Margaret, didn't think you got up this early," she said before heading back into the kitchen.

Wes bit the smile that threatened. Margaret said nothing.

The three ate breakfast with general conversation about the weather and the morning news.

"Wesley here is a hero," Miss Clara Ann said. "Helped save old Jesse Parker. Don't know why you bothered though, Jesse's nothing but an old rogue, chasing after some young thing is what probably give him a heart attack in the first place."

"What'd you do?" Margaret asked.

Wes buttered another flaky biscuit. "Nothing really."

"Shoot. Where's that paper, boy?"

Wes smiled in good humor and handed the newspaper to Miss Clara Ann who proceeded to pass it on to Margaret.

"I like that photograph. It captures your weariness," Margaret observed. "The mayor should give you a citation for bravery," she said after reading the story.

That was the last thing he needed. But Wes didn't say that. "I'm just glad the man's going to be okay."

After downing another cup of coffee and what he deemed a suitable amount of time, Wes excused himself from the table with the excuse that he wanted to go explore the town.

Margaret dabbed her mouth with a paper napkin. "Mind if I join you? It's been a while since I was here. I'm sure things have changed."

Miss Clara Ann saved Wes from having to respond.

"Margaret, stay back would you? There's a coupla family matters we need to discuss."

Wes caught Margaret's look of exasperation before she masked it and smiled sweetly at her aunt.

"Of course, Aunt Clara."

Wes beat a hasty retreat but did overhear Miss Clara Ann scold Margaret.

"If you want to capture that man, you needs to listen to me girl cause I ain't seen no moves on your part that would make him interested. What'd you do this morning, fall in a bottle of perfume?"

Wes grinned all the way to his room.

From a pay phone about an hour later he put in a call to headquarters and got his old buddy Scotty to agree to run a check on Jan Langley. Citing his need to know as an "integral part of the current operation,"

Wes secured an albeit reluctant Scotty to do what he could.

His next stop was to the service station to check on his truck.

"Be good as new in about two hours," Ray Bob assured him. "She needs a couple of hoses, some other parts, and some transmission fluid."

"How much is it gonna run?" Wes asked.

Ray Bob scratched his head and looked at the sky. "Don't rightly know yet. I'll leave a message for you at Miss Clara Ann's place. That's where you're puttin' up, right?"

Wes nodded. This guy was going to try to take him on this. Wes decided to let the mechanic know he knew cars. "If it'll save on the labor I'll just buy the parts. If I rebuilt my Mustang's engine I can handle a couple of hoses. I have time this weekend."

Ray Bob eyed him, obviously skeptical, but Wes figured, not willing to lose any work. Ray Bob studied the oil and dirt under his fingernails for a moment.

"Yeah, well, it won't likely be that much."

Wes smiled. "Thanks. Appreciate it."

"I heard 'bout what you did for Jesse Parker. Figure that counts for something."

Wes nodded, not quite sure how the man who collapsed equated with work he needed done on his truck. But he wasn't of a mind to figure it out. He had an important destination.

"I'll swing by later today. What time you close up?"

"Don't really," Ray Bob answered. "I live upstairs," he said, pointing to an above garage apartment. "If I'm not out here, just knock on the door and we'll settle up."

"Good enough." Wes put the dark glasses on and swung a muscled leg over the seat of the motorcycle.

With a two-finger salute to Ray Bob, Wes pulled out of the station garage.

It took him less than fifteen minutes to make his way to Jan Langley's small house. He kicked the stand down on the bike and sat for a moment looking at her home. It was small, old and comfortable looking, one of the few houses on the street with a detached garage instead of a covered breezeway. A few bushes in the front could use a trim but the grass was cut. The gate definitely needed a coat of paint. He could grab a couple of gallons at the hardware store he'd seen and probably get the job done in a few hours.

Wes blinked. Where in the world did that come from? he asked while unfastening his helmet and getting off the bike. Being in this town less than forty-eight hours has you acting like a Mark Twain character.

The last time he'd done any painting he and Marcus had redone Mama Lo's dining room and kitchen. They'd gotten her instructions backward though and had painted the dining room walls yellow and the kitchen a pale blue. Wes smiled as he remembered Marc trying to sweet talk Mama Lo into leaving the walls the way they were.

"Blue gives the kitchen a soothing, restful feeling," Marc had pointed out.

"You won't be feeling too soothed or restful if you and Wesley don't do these walls the right way," she'd shot back.

It took them another eight hours after the paint dried to do the job right.

Wes was still smiling at the memory when C.J. opened the door.

He hadn't been a figment of her imagination. She'd been having a difficult time coming to grips with the fact that she and this man had been naked in bed together . . . and had done nothing. Not one blessed thing.

"Hi."

"I spent a little time trying to manufacture a reason to come and see you. Then I said what the hell. I'd just come."

"I'm glad you did," she said more candidly than she'd anticipated. "I didn't get much sleep last night."

Wes smiled. "Why is that?"

"I kept thinking about what we, what I, was missing out on."

Wes knew the feeling. But until he got the "all clear" from Scotty, Wes had to have a care about what he said with and did to this woman. Why did life have to be so complicated sometimes? He'd worked with liars and low-lifes so long that when he found a little ray of sunshine it seemed all the more bright and tempting to him. Jan was that sunshine. And right now, she was off limits. Sort of.

But off limits didn't mean they couldn't spend time together.

"Have you ever been fishing?" he asked.

"You mean like bait, hook, line, worms?"

"Those things generally define it."

She smiled, saucy and challenging. "Then no. I've never been fishing."

"Wanna go?"

"When?" she asked.

"How about now? I'm free."

C.J. cocked her head and stared up at him. "On one condition."

"Your wish is my command."

"Don't say that, dark warrior, we'd never leave the house if that were the case."

Her provocative words had an immediate masculine effect on him. The cold shower hadn't worked last night and Wes knew he couldn't count on any sort of relief by trying to psyche himself out now. What was it about this woman that was so hot? That made him so hot?

His voice was huskier than normal when he asked what her condition was.

"I need a couple of hours to finish up the project I'm working on."

"Granted. On one condition," he said.

A small smile tugged at her mouth. She folded her arms and leaned against the doorjamb. "What?"

"Let me kiss you."

The small smile slowly transformed into feminine awareness. The space around them crackled with sensual electricity. He had to feel it like she did. In one forward motion she was in his arms. She caught his breath, warm and moist against her face, a moment before his mouth closed over hers. The velvet warmth of his tongue aroused her further as they drank from each other. Her mouth burned with a fire she didn't want quenched, not now, not ever. Nothing and no one had ever made her feel this way: cherished and sexy and hot; achy and needy and wanting more. So much more.

As if sensing her need, Wes clasped her buttocks and lifted her up and closer to him, closer to the erection he didn't want to conceal. He claimed her with his mouth and knew an ecstasy he'd never imagined. God, he wanted to be inside this woman. Inside her so deep he forgot where he ended and she began.

C.J. ran her hands over his short cropped hair. Blood pounded in her veins and her heart swelled. This felt so right, so good.

A dog's barking drew them apart. C.J. opened her eyes and stared into Wesley's brown ones.

"Wow."

"Yeah, wow," he said. He slowly lowered her, the feel of her firm body cascading down his did nothing to lower his temperature.

C.J.'s breath came in short but deep gasps. She had to get oxygen to her brain. It couldn't be possible for one man to make her feel like this. She almost told him to bag the fishing date. She could think of far better things they could bait than fish.

"Give me two hours," she told him.

Wes leaned forward for another kiss, this one short and sweet. But if C.J. thought she'd gotten control of herself, she was mistaken. Wesley's hand caressed her from the bridge of her nose, slowly around her mouth and over the bottom of her full lips. That large, smooth hand curved around her chin and trailed down her neck in a maddeningly slow descent. When his palm closed over the fullness of her breast, it came as no surprise to C.J. that her nipple was hard and ripe, ready for him, aching for him. He squeezed the delicate flesh. C.J. moaned and turned into the embrace; closing her eyes giving herself to him in this small way.

"Open your eyes."

When she did, his mouth closed over hers, hot and hungry. Then he released her, all of her, by stepping back. "I'll pick you up at ten-thirty," he said.

C.J. nodded and leaned against the door. She watched his retreat down her walkway and out the wooden gate. C.J. swallowed. Wesley Donovan was an addiction she'd like to never give up.

Wes killed time by crisscrossing the town and outlying area. By the time he got back to Main Street people were out and about and the shops open. And Wes could get anywhere in a twenty-five mile radius practically with his eyes closed. He believed it important to know the lay of the land. That information could come in handy down the road.

He stopped in a convenience store and got a cup of coffee. Then, outside on the far edge of the store's parking lot, he pulled a flip telephone from a small pack on the bike.

Wes punched out a number on the cell phone and sipped at the coffee while waiting for the connection. Scotty, his old buddy from headquarters, picked up on the first ring. "Hey, man," Wes said. "Got anything for me?"

"Yeah and no, Donovan. I can tell you this. If she's one of ours she's deep, real deep. No paper anywhere."

"Keep looking." The request sounded more like a command.

"I can get into some deep shit about this, Donovan. You know the rules. Why do you need this woman made?"

"Part of the case," Wes lied. "I need to know what's going on down here. She may be part of it, might not be. Come on Scotty. I swear to God I won't bother you again if you can pull up some background on this woman."

"You're supposed to be down there working on an attitude adjustment. At least that's the word that's going around here," Scotty said. "It sure doesn't sound like you've made any progress. Still as insolent and demanding as ever."

Wes chuckled. "Part of my charm. Interesting spin on this assignment. Particularly since I was thinking the same thing. You start that rumor?"

He kept to himself the early morning encounter he'd had. If word was going around that he'd been sent to North Carolina to get his attitude adjusted, chances were that Holloway had kept a lid on what

Wes was really up to. More and more, it was looking like his assignment wasn't bogus after all.

"You wound me, Donovan. You really do," Scotty said. "I'll see what else I can find out about your woman. Don't hold your breath though on this one."

Wes rang off with Scotty. He'd been in this business so long that he was suspicious of everyone he met— and with good reason. Most of the people, men and women alike, who crossed his path generally had criminal records or ties longer than his arm. For a moment, just a brief one, Wes longed for the old days when he served warrants for the Marshals Service. Busting down doors and arresting the bad guys, even if you'd been on a stakeout for weeks or months, had a certain satisfaction to it, certainly more appeal than his current assignment.

He stashed the phone in his gear bag and finished the coffee. Crumpling the cup, he tossed it in a trash can. It was time to go check on his truck and pick up Jan Langley for their fishing date.

"There is no conflict of interest," he said aloud.

Maybe if he kept telling himself that he'd believe it.

Nine

When Wes arrived to pick her up, C.J. had a wicker basket waiting on the porch.

"Lunch?" he asked hopefully.

"Not exactly. Something to put lunch in. I found it in a closet in the house. I figured we'd pick up something to eat along the way."

He looked good enough to eat but C.J. kept that thought to herself. He'd traded the boots he'd worn the night before for a pair of scuffed moccasins. A long-sleeved plaid shirt worn open and on top of a white T-shirt tucked in well-worn jeans made him look rugged yet comfortable. C.J. in knee-length khaki shorts, a matching top, and loafers felt positively overdressed.

She locked her front door, tucked the key in a pocket, and picked up the basket.

"There's a bakery in town that has wonderful brownies. We can stop and get some for lunch."

"Are they chocolate?"

C.J. nodded and licked her lips. "Double chocolate. Some have white and dark chocolate with nuts and fudge icing. They're to die for."

Wes grimaced. "You can say that again. I'm allergic."

He held the gate open for her and she walked through before him.

"Really? That's too bad. Chocolate is wonderful. Sometimes better than sex."

"I doubt it," he mumbled, watching the sway of her hips as she walked.

C.J. laughed over her shoulder. "I heard that. Better Than Sex is an awesome cookie recipe. As a matter of fact, it's the only thing I know how to make besides tea."

"You don't cook?"

C.J. shook her head and eyed the truck. It had seen better days. "I thought we were going on the bike."

"You like the Harley, huh?"

She climbed into the cab of the truck and watched as he walked around to the other side and got in. "I liked the wind on my face and the hard body on my chest," she answered.

Wesley, about to turn the key in the truck's ignition, paused and looked at her. "We don't have to go. There are other ways we can . . ." he paused and let his gaze linger over her eyes, her mouth, her breasts, "get to know each other better."

C.J. smiled and faced forward. "Drive, Donovan, before I forget my resolve."

He continued to stare at her until she glanced at him and then, flushed and unaccountably shy, she looked away and out the passenger window. Wes cleared his throat, turned the ignition key, and pulled out.

"I figured we'd get outfitted at the Wal-Mart. They should have everything we need."

"Do I get a pair of those big rubber boots?" C.J. asked.

He had an idea about rubbers but they had nothing to do with boots or fishing. "Sure, if you want to. This isn't fly fishing though. We'll be on the bank of the river. I found a good spot for us this morning. It's shaded and it looked like the fish were jumping."

A few minutes later Wes pulled the truck into a parking spot at the local Wal-Mart. The lot, crowded with vehicles and folks pushing package-laden carts to their cars, had more people in it than C.J. had seen in her entire month in Serenity Falls.

"Are they having some sort of special sale today?" she asked.

Wes killed the engine. "There's always a sale at Wal-Mart."

"Must be a good one. The place is jammed. I've never been in one before."

Wes couldn't hide his incredulousness. "You've never been in a Wal-Mart?"

C.J. shook her head and pushed open her door. "Nope. I've seen their commercials though."

"Well, this should be interesting," Wes said, joining her.

Tires screeched.

Wes dashed into the road. Amid horn blowing and a woman's scream, he snatched a toddler up a moment before a station wagon hit the child.

Everything happened fast. Wes, with the child safe in his arms, dashed to the frantic woman. An infant in a carrier on the woman's shopping cart cried. The driver of the station wagon shook his head, then swearing about unattended kids, drove off.

"Oh, my God! Oh, my God! Are you okay, Jeremy?"

Wes handed the child to the mother.

"He's OK, ma'am. Just a little frightened about all the commotion."

The woman hugged the now crying toddler to her and then scolded. "Haven't I told you not to go wandering off. Stay here by me and you'll be safe."

Wes chucked the child under the chin. "You listen to your mom, champ. Okay?"

The child wiped his nose and nodded.

"Thank you," the mother said.

C.J. eyed Wes as he ruffled the kid's hair and said a few words to the frightened mother. Not very many people had reflexes that fast. She hadn't even seen the child in the street. Just who was Wes Donovan? So far he seemed to be a French-speaking Ninja-looking rescuer who favored cowboy boots and black. He seemed to have a knack for being where the action was. One thing she knew without any doubt, Wes Donovan was a man's man . . . and he belonged to her. For all she knew though, he could be married with a wife and kids.

His interaction with the small child in the parking lot sure looked fatherly. She'd have to find out. But she got distracted watching him walk back to her. He walked slow but with a moderated ease and purpose that reminded her not so much of a swagger but of a black panther slowly stalking its prey—modulated, easy, always ready to attack, to protect, to make slow, sweet love to her.

C.J.'s stomach tightened as heat engulfed her. She'd met this guy yesterday and had wanted him from the get-go.

He draped an arm about her shoulder. She slipped her own arm around his waist and hugged him. "You're awfully good at that," she said.

"What?"

Arm in arm, they walked to the store entrance. "Helping people out, responding quickly to emergencies. Take yesterday for example. You didn't have to stop to help that man."

Wes shrugged.

"Good morning. Welcome to Wal-Mart," called out a smiling greeter in a blue jacket.

"Hey," Wes said. "We're looking for fishing gear."

"Sporting goods department is right over there," the greeter said, pointing in a direction near the back of the store.

"Thanks."

C.J. accepted a shopping cart and Wes fell into step beside her. "This place is huge," she observed, looking around at the various departments.

As they wheeled by the intimate apparel department C.J. grinned when Wes slowed his pace and eyed the lacy teddies and camisoles. He looked from the silky lingerie to C.J. She stopped pushing the cart. "Yes?" she said, dragging the word out.

"Oh, nothing," he said, fingering the edge of a creamy vanilla camisole.

C.J. sucked in a breath. She felt as if his finger, slowly outlining the fabric on the hanger, were on her own flesh. Wes moved to another piece and then inspected some ultrafeminine bras in bold, bright colors. He selected one from a dainty hanger and turned to assess C.J.'s chest. Eyeing her full bosom he shook his head and picked another one with a considerably larger cup. He looked from her to the bra, her again then back to the bra and raised his eyebrows.

She folded her arms and bit back a grin. "I thought we were getting fishing rods."

"Yeah, we'll get some of those. I like being a careful shopper though. Don't want to miss any good deals."

He put the brassiere back in its spot then walked around a display of lace-edged, hi-cut teddies. Wes picked one off the display and returned to where C.J. stood at the shopping cart. He held the champagne-colored garment up to her.

"It compliments your skin," he said.

C.J. swallowed. "I wear a ten/twelve."

"That a fact?" He looked at the size tag in the teddy, then took the piece back to the rack. He picked out one in the right size and put it in the basket. "Funny, you didn't offer up your bra size."

C.J. cleared her throat and looked away. Wes chuckled.

"Thirty-four B but spilling out of it. Spilling out of it big time," he added.

She didn't give him the satisfaction of an answer. How could she when he was right on the money. She glanced down into the basket. "We, uh, need a teddy to go fishing?"

"Is that what you call that, a teddy?"

She nodded.

Wes grinned. "Yeah. It distracts the fish and makes 'em rise to the bait."

C.J.'s eyes roamed over him. Things were definitely rising. She refrained from comment though and fell in step as Wes, chuckling to himself, pushed the cart away from lingerie and toward sporting goods.

She breathed a sigh of relief when they made it to the fishing section without any other distracting stops.

"Okay. We need rods, reels, line, lures, and a tackle box."

"It all looks the same to me," C.J. said. She picked out two rods from the display and stuck them in the basket.

"There are differences," Wes said from where he crouched looking at lures on a low shelf. He selected what he wanted and tossed them in the basket. When he looked up, she was gone.

"Jan?"

"Over here. The next aisle," she called out.

Wes grinned. He liked the sound of her voice. Actually, he liked a lot of things about Jan Langley. Like how she stuck her tongue in the corner of her mouth and looked away when she was embarrassed. She'd done it twice today. He wondered if she was as aroused as he was. The episode at the lingerie department had cost him more than he cared to admit. He'd taken one look at the soft, sexy garments and imagined the soft, sexy woman wearing them.

Wes stood up and grabbed the first tackle box he saw. He dropped it in the cart then wheeled around to the next aisle.

Jan had a hunter green fishing hat on her head and was shrugging into a sleeveless net jacket.

She saw him and smiled. "Fishing guys on TV always have on these things. I need some of those feathers and what-not for the hat."

Wes smiled. Feathers and what-not. This woman called out and appealed to him on so many levels Wes couldn't even begin to comprehend the complexity of his feelings. He answered the call the best way he knew how. He bent his head and captured her mouth with his. His tongue explored the recesses of her mouth. The hat fell off her head. Wes took advantage of that and ran one large hand up over her nape. She was a heady sensation for him as she kissed back, just as hot and eager as he was.

Reluctantly Wes eased up. He nibbled at her lower lip, kissed her nose, her brow and then hugged her to him.

"You don't know what you do to me," he said.

"Yes, I do. It's the same thing you do to me."

"I want you."

She glanced around. "This isn't really a good place."

Wes looked left at a row of canoes and oars, then to the right at life vests and fishing jackets. "I guess you're right. We have everything we need. Let's head to checkout."

He picked up the hat and dropped it in the cart. The playfulness of their earlier encounter had disappeared, replaced by the restless humming of sexual need.

They wheeled the cart through the store. Wes paused at the linen department. "Did you put a blanket in that wicker basket?"

C.J. shook her head in the negative. Wes grabbed the first one he saw and tossed it in the basket. "For our lunch picnic," he said.

"Um hmm."

Wes looked at her, grinned, then shrugged. They made their way to a snack food section. "Grab what you like. I'm going to see if they have any Vienna sausage."

C.J. tried not to crinkle her nose. If this guy's idea of good eating was Vienna sausage, they were going to have some major compatibility problems. "Is that what you're eating for lunch?"

Wes laughed. "That's what the fish will eat for lunch. We'll use it as bait. We're gonna eat well. We can stop at the deli next to that bakery in town and pick up some sandwiches."

C.J. breathed a sigh of relief. While Wes searched the aisle for the canned meat, C.J. picked up potato chips, pickle slices, and M&M's. Their shopping cart was getting full. She shrugged out of the fishing jacket and added it to the other merchandise they'd selected.

"Got it," Wes called out. He returned bearing two of the small cans of meat.

"Wouldn't they prefer caviar or pâté?" C.J. asked.

"Caviar would be cruel and pâté's consistency isn't thick enough. Come on, city girl. Let's get this date started. The day's a wastin', as Mama Lo would say."

They headed to the checkout aisles. "You sure know your way around this store," C.J. observed. "I thought you'd just arrived in Serenity Falls."

"I do and I did. All Wal-Marts have basically the same layout no matter where you are in the country. This is my store. I get just about everything I need here."

C.J. looked around. The place did have a certain appeal. She thought about all the upscale malls and exclusive boutiques she normally shopped in. Once a year, C.J. and her mother flew to Paris to get undergarments. She had a feeling though that she was going to cherish the lacy teddy Wes picked for her more than any of her froufrou silks and satins.

Wes paid the bill with a credit card. C.J. watched him sign his name in bold but meticulous detail. She liked a detail man. Actually she liked everything about him. Including the way he handled himself in tough situations. Wes Donovan was the kind of person you'd want to watch your back. C.J. looked at Wesley's back as he accepted packages from the cashier and put them in the cart.

Without thinking she raised a hand and smoothed it over the broad expanse of his back. She flushed all over as she remembered exactly how his skin felt, how hot and hard and broad he was.

Wes turned, a tender smile playing at his mouth. "Ready?"

"More than you know," she mumbled.

They made a gas stop, picked up sandwiches, fruit, and bottled water at the deli then headed to the river.

"How'd you find this place?" C.J. asked as she followed Wes through a clearing and to a glade sheltered by tall trees.

"I was out running this morning and came up on the water. I checked down at the hardware store to see if the river is good for fishing. The man there directed me to several likely spots. And I picked up a couple of licenses."

"So this is a popular spot?"

Wes shrugged. "Don't know. I ignored all the ones he suggested and scoped this one out myself."

He put the fishing gear on the ground. C.J did the same with the picnic basket. She looked around and found a relatively flat spot with a big rock. A frog sat atop the rock sunning itself.

"Mind if we share?" she asked the frog.

"What was that?"

She looked over her shoulder at Wes and smiled. "Nothing. Talking to myself." C.J. spread the blanket about a foot from the base of the boulder.

She went back to where she'd left the hamper and put it on the edge of the blanket. When she turned to see what Wes was doing she found him staring at her.

"What?"

"I don't think we're going to get a lot of fishing done."

C.J. met his intense gaze. "I think you're right but let's give it the old college try."

"Whatever you say." Wes reached into one of the bags for the line and lures. "Come on over here and I'll show you how to get everything set up."

He kicked off the moccasins and sank to the ground in a fluid motion. C.J. watched him in a quiet awe. "Do you dance?"

Wes looked up. "I beg your pardon?"

C.J. sat on the ground next to him in what she knew was not as naturally graceful a movement as he'd achieved. She crossed her legs and rested her arms on her knees.

"Have you danced professionally? Like ballet."

Wes chuckled. "No. What would make you ask that?"

"You're very light on your feet, and quite graceful for a man."

Wes laughed out loud. "There's an insult in there somewhere isn't there?"

C.J. smiled and shook her head. Maybe it was his martial arts training. "Okay, professor. Show me what to do."

Wes spent the next half hour teaching C.J. about hooking, baiting, and casting. When she was ready, they stood.

"Oh, wait. I can't do it without my hat and jacket."

Grinning, Wes pulled the garments from one of the bags and handed them to her. C.J. ripped off the price tags and tucked them in one of the mesh pockets on the jacket. When the hat wouldn't quite fit on her head, she removed the two combs that held her hair up and put them in another of the jacket pockets. She pushed the hat into place, and then, like Wes, kicked off her shoes.

Standing with legs spread and the fishing rod held in her hands like a flag pole, she announced, "Okay. I'm ready now."

Wes shook his head and smiled.

They moved a little closer to the water's edge. Wes cast his line and watched as C.J. did the same. She kept waiting for it to land in the water with a quiet plop like Wes's did. She turned to question him.

A rumbling like thunder in the distance made her scowl, particularly when she recognized the rumbling as his laughter. "What?"

"You're supposed to aim for the water."

"Where's the line?" she asked.

Wes pointed to a bush to the back and left of C.J., her hook and line tangled in the brush.

"Oh."

"Hold on to this," he said, handing her his own rod.

C.J. put hers on the ground and accepted his. Wes went to the bush to inspect and recapture C.J.'s line.

He untangled the mess.

"Uh, Wes. There's something tugging on this."

He ran back to where she stood at the shore, feet braced and pulling on the rod.

"Reel it in," he instructed.

"What do you . . . Oh, this." C.J. reeled the line in taking steps backward as she did.

"Hold still. Just keep reeling."

A six-inch fish hung at the end of her line. Wes grabbed the line and swung it in. "Nice job."

"It's so little. It's gonna die."

Wes laughed. "That's the point, Jan."

C.J. frowned—at the fish, at Wes, and at the name. She watched him unhook the catch and drop it in a bucket he'd brought from the truck and filled with river water.

"Wes, it's not like we're hunters and gatherers. We don't need that fish to live. Can't we let it go?"

Wes smiled and gave in. "We'll let them all go when we're done. That make you feel better, city girl."

"Don't call me that."

Wes came up behind her and circled one large arm around her waist. He leaned forward and nibbled on her ear. "Okay."

C.J. forgot what she'd been mildly miffed about. She sank into his embrace, loving the feel of him at her back.

"Okay. Time for another casting lesson," he said.

He positioned her hands around the rod she held. "Stand like this," he instructed as his muscular thighs shifted hers to the right position. "Now, when you cast off, keep your wrist steady, lean back just a bit." He guided her body in the proper motion. "Let it flow from you, steady, easy."

The line plopped into the water about twenty feet out.

"I did it!"

Both of Wes's hands snaked around her waist. She felt so right in his arms. "Yes, you did." He lowered his head and licked her neck.

C.J. arched into him and moaned.

"Look," he said, his hot breath at her right ear. "We can pretend that there isn't fire between us or we can dive right in, burn ourselves to ashes and then see if anything, like the phoenix, rises from those ashes."

In answer C.J. dropped the fishing rod and stepped out of his embrace. She didn't say a word as she turned to face him. She shrugged out of the jacket then crossed her arms at the edges of her khaki shirt and pulled the cotton top over her head.

Wes's mouth went dry. She wore no bra. The ripe fruit was his for the taking.

Ten

She lifted her breasts to him in silent offering. With one step forward he stood before her then lowered his head. Capturing first one firm nipple in his mouth and then the other, Wes gently bit into her. C.J. cried out at the pleasure pain. Wes bent at the knees, suckling, nibbling, swirling his hot tongue over her until she swayed on her feet.

With one final lap at her breast he chucked out of his clothes then knelt before her.

"What, what are you doing?"

"Loving you," he murmured. His hands unfastened the belt at her waist. Unzipping the shorts she wore and skimming them over her thighs and legs came easy. The sight left for him made Wes glad he was already on his knees.

His hands revered her smooth brown skin. She stepped out of the shorts and kicked them aside. Wes buried his head in her navel, lapping and licking while murmuring words and sounds of extreme male delight.

C.J. thought she'd die of the pleasure. He moved too fast . . . and too slow. She crushed his head to her belly and cried out when his mouth rimmed the thin band of the string panties she wore. By the time he'd worked them down over her hips C.J. was ready for him like she'd never been ready for a man before.

She tugged at his shoulders, encouraging him to rise. But Wes grunted, pulled her hips closer to him and used one large hand to part her thighs. When he buried his head between her legs, C.J. almost doubled over his back. She cried out for mercy but he was relentless in the thorough examination of her core. She exploded in a million pieces and called his name over and over.

Before she thoroughly recovered, Wes reached into the pocket of his pants, found one of the condoms he had and put it on.

"Wes," she panted. "Wes?"

A slow finger meandering up her leg and then higher to her inner thigh was the answer she got. C.J. sighed and then gasped when she was lifted in his arms a moment later.

"Wrap your legs around my waist."

She did and was hefted higher. The blunt maleness of his erection pulsated hot and heavy at the place she wanted him most.

"Now, Wesley. Now!"

He thrust into her and they both cried out. C.J. threw her head forward and bit into his neck. The intensity of their desire and the rough play turned her on as much as the man who pounded himself into her like there was no tomorrow.

She felt her climax coming and tried to wait for him. She shivered and cried out his name. Wesley followed shortly after her.

He carried her to the blanket she'd spread out on the ground. Then, kissing her the whole time, he slowly let her languid body slide over his until she again stood on her feet. Wesley helped her to the blanket and they stretched out together.

She lay drowned in a floodtide of emotions, physically spent yet wanting him again . . . and again.

"I have never, ever . . ." her voice trailed off on a soft gasp when his palm circled a full breast. "Wow. You wow me, Wesley Donovan."

"I'm glad you think so because I delight in your body. You're strong and soft, tight and warm."

C.J. sat up and leaned on one elbow. Her other hand strayed to wander over his chest. Well-defined pecs captured her attention. She leaned over him and licked the small male nipples so alike, and yet so different from her own.

Wes shuddered and stilled her soft hand. "Rest."

"I'm not sleepy," she said. Her hand skimmed down his flat stomach and to his inner thigh. "And neither are you," she noted at a certain part of him.

"Where are the other condoms?" she asked.

"Pants pocket."

C.J. leaned over and kissed him on the mouth. "Be right back."

A while later they remembered the fishing. Wes sat up from his spot on the blanket. The rod she'd dropped was nowhere in sight. He grinned. With his luck, a twenty-five-pound catfish had probably swum off with the thing. Wes glanced down at a dozing Jan. A fish may have captured his fishing rod, but he'd gotten the better catch with his own.

He got up and went to the pile of clothes they'd shed at the shore. Pulling on his shorts and pants, he saw the rod submerged in shallow water. He grinned and retrieved it.

"Best fishing lesson you've ever given," he said. He dumped the bucket with Jan's small catch back into the river. Turning to look at the sleeping Jan, Wesley smiled. Then he came to a grim conclusion: If she was a protected witness he was screwed because he wanted her for his, for always. But he didn't want to think about that now.

After tidying up the fishing gear, Wes picked up his shirts and Jan's clothes and returned to her.

She watched him approach and wondered if what she felt meant she was falling in love. C.J. had had her share—and probably some other women's share—of relationships. But nothing and no one had ever left her wanting more. She knew how quickly she tired of new things and wondered if, now that she'd had the dark warrior, she'd be ready to move on to the next challenge, the next hard body.

But as she looked inside herself while watching him put his clothes on, the only answer she'd found was more. She wanted more of Wesley Donovan. Not just more sex, that had been hot and wild, just the way she liked it, but even with Wes the sex had been different. The why of the difference eluded her. And so she watched him.

"Hey, beautiful. You're awake."

"I've been awake since you left me. I wanted to watch that warrior king body of yours without you knowing I spied."

"You can spy on me anytime. But don't be alarmed if you see a marked physical reaction as a result."

C.J.'s smile contained a sensuous flame, one that needed little encouragement to grow into a larger conflagration.

He handed her her clothing. "If you don't put something on, I won't be responsible for my actions."

In response she leaned back on the blanket, opened her legs wide and lay spreadeagled before him. Wesley fell on her with a ravenous hunger that surprised neither of them.

About an hour later, after they'd both dressed they sat cross-legged on the blanket munching on the sandwiches and fruit they'd bought for lunch.

C.J. took a swig of the bottled water to wash her sandwich down then ripped open a package of M&M's.

"Have you always been allergic to chocolate?"

Wes reached for the half sandwich C.J. hadn't eaten. "As long as I can remember. Although in the beginning we didn't know it was chocolate that was causing me to break out. My mother just thought I'd been playing in the poison ivy."

"Didn't Mama Lo know the difference?"

Wes nodded. "Mama Lo did. My mother, Eileen, was too drunk to care or to investigate."

C.J. looked at him. She'd thought the Mama Lo he'd so lovingly referred to was his mother, or maybe his grandmother.

"You and your mother aren't close."

Wes looked up, surprised. "Eileen? Hell, no. The only thing she's ever been close to was her bottle of Thunderbird."

C.J. winced at the venom coming from him. She knew, well knew, what it was like to be close to a bottle. She'd counted almost fifty days of sobriety. She'd given up the bottles before leaving Baltimore. Every day was a struggle. Every day she took it one moment, one day at a time. She wondered if Eileen fought the same demons.

"It's an illness," she said. "Not everyone can control it."

"Eileen never wanted to control it. Why control something that brings you your greatest pleasure . . . and your worst nightmare."

"Is she still living?" C.J. asked.

Wes shrugged and bit into a pear. "Don't know. I haven't seen her in years. The last time I heard from her she wanted a thousand dollars. Said she was going to go clean and check herself into a detox center, start going to AA meetings. Stupid me, I sent the money."

"What happened?"

"She stockpiled liquor at her house and then crashed her car into a light pole coming home from a party. Unfortunately, only the light pole suffered."

C.J. hurt for Eileen, but mostly she hurt for Wes. Given her own loving relationship with her parents, she couldn't imagine not communicating with them. Genevieve and Robinson Mayview, for example, hadn't agreed with their daughter's decision to quit her job and leave Baltimore, but they understood her need to do so. What they didn't understand or know about was her alcoholism and the little white pills she used to keep her going.

C.J. had finally admitted she was powerless over the addictions. She'd busted every bottle in her house, flushed all the prescription pills down a toilet, and then sat in her dark living room crying. Afraid to ask for help, afraid she'd go out and buy a drink, she'd called the only person she knew she could trust to keep her secret. She called her older brother, Robinson.

It had been Rob's idea that she get away for a little while. "Take a vacation, go stay at the beach house in Rehobeth for a couple of weeks. You deserve a vacation. You haven't stopped running since you accepted that Pulitzer. Did I ever tell you how proud I am of you?"

She'd nodded and then cried in his arms. All the world thought she had it totally going on. What few people knew was how miserable she was. C.J. had taken Rob's advice; taken it to the extreme. She turned in a letter of resignation at the newspaper, sold her condo, sold her new BMW and all her furniture. She stuffed only the clothes and things she needed in a four-wheel drive Cherokee she bought used and headed southeast. She drove past Rehobeth. She drove past Virginia.

A detour on the road and a need to fill up the gas tank found her in Serenity Falls, North Carolina. She liked the name of the town. She liked its smallness. She stayed. She'd stayed and was slowly recuperating, finding the self she'd lost somewhere between her first job as a cop reporter and winning a Pulitzer Prize.

"Maybe she wonders about you," she told Wes as she made a mental note to call her own parents that night.

"Eileen doesn't wonder about anything except where her next drink is coming from. Look, why are we talking about this anyway?"

His gruffness hurt her but she understood the source of his anger just as she could understand some if not all the depth of his pain.

Suddenly no longer desiring the taste, C.J. put the chocolate candy away. She reached for an apple and bit into it.

Wes smiled a small smile. He leaned forward to catch the juice that ran down her chin. "I didn't mean to snap at you."

"I know."

"You want to fish some more?"

Her smile was radiant. "I'll never look at fishing in the same light again." She shook her head no. "If we try to do another fishing lesson, it'll be well past dark before we ever leave this spot."

Wes leaned forward to steal a kiss. "You're probably right. I want you again."

"I want you, too."

Wes took the fruit from her hand and cleared the remains of their lunch from the blanket by tossing it all in the wicker hamper. He then reached for her and slowly lowered her to the soft padding of the blanket on the ground.

This time when they made love, it was slow and tender, with a poignant sweetness that brought tears to C.J.'s eyes. She held him and loved him and gave to him all the gentleness that he'd never found in his mother's arms. She gave him hope and strength and something she'd never given before: 100 percent of herself.

Eleven

It was dusk when Wesley dropped her off at her house. At her door, he kissed her.

"Stay the night."

"I'd like to," he said. "But there are a couple of things I need to check on." Like what kind of job I can land after being fired for getting romantically involved with someone in the Witness Security Program. But with a clarity that rocked him, Wes realized he didn't care. Jan Langley was worth losing his job over. She was special.

"Tomorrow?" she asked.

Wes nodded. "Tomorrow. I'll call before I come over. What's your number?"

She gave it to him. He repeated it back to her and had it memorized.

Wesley pulled her into his arms and pressed her close to the part of him that still, amazingly, reacted to her closeness. He ran a hand down her back and cupped her firm rear. "Tomorrow can't get here fast enough."

With a reluctance they both felt, Wes let her go. He waited until she was safely inside and he heard the deadbolt click before leaving.

Halfway down the steps he thought of something.

Jan Langley had city locks on her doors, the kind of protection someone with something to worry about might have even in the midst of wholesome small-town America. Wes sighed. The sooner he found out who she was the easier he'd stop feeling so conflicted.

You didn't feel too much of a conflict down by the river, his conscience pointed out.

"Shut up."

Not that he was particularly hungry, but Wes figured he'd better grab something to eat if he wanted dinner. He'd probably missed Miss Clara Ann's cut off time for serving dinner. He climbed into the truck and pulled away from the curb.

The piece of junk Casey had supplied him with didn't have a cassette player in it. It barely had a radio. Good thing he wasn't a big music person. He liked to work out to classic rock but that was about it. Wes found one crackly AM station that played country music. He thought he recognized Patsy Cline's plaintive tone but it could have just as easily been the contemporary country artist k.d. lang who sometimes had a Patsy Cline sound.

The song reminded Wes of Eileen. He scowled and turned the radio off. His mother had always pretended she was white, using her light skin as a bargaining chip in the community. She never knew how people, black and white, laughed behind her back and called her a lush.

She'd sent her husband, Wesley's father, to an early grave with her false airs and nagging. People around town said Winton Donovan died of the black lung after working so many years below ground in the mines. But Wesley knew better. The coal dust may have contributed a bit, but his daddy had been nagged to death.

With Winton gone, yelling at Wes when he made friends with dark-skinned kids seemed to be one of Eileen's favorite pastimes. Sometimes, Wes admitted, he did it on purpose. Eileen had never forgiven herself for getting knocked up by a dark man. Her plan had been to marry white and eventually deny any black blood in her own veins. But too much to drink at a party one night put a halt to those plans. Winton Donovan had done the right thing and married Eileen. But through their entire marriage Eileen never let him or her son forget that they both had been bad mistakes.

Yelling at Wes was high up on Eileen's list of priorities, right after beating him for reasons as lame as daring to wake her up from a blackout to tell her he'd gotten an A on his geography test. But Wes had taken his last beating from Eileen more than twenty years ago. Once, just once, he'd struck back. Eileen tore into such a rage that he still bore a small scar in the place where the sharp edge of a kitchen utensil had sliced into his arm.

If she was sober enough to see, he knew Eileen would be appalled at how her son turned out. He was black and proud of it, glad that his father's darker genes were dominant in his skin, and secure in the knowledge that he didn't judge people on the hue of their skin. Wes was good at what he did and, for the most part, liked and respected among his colleagues. He'd dated women of all races, but none seriously. In his line of work, he wasn't willing to put a woman through the changes and the violence that were a necessary part of his job.

Jan Langley would be different. If she was indeed a protected witness she'd understand those things.

Wes pounded the steering wheel in frustration. He hoped Scotty had an answer for him.

He picked up dinner at a drive-through chicken place and made his way to Miss Clara Ann's.

A couple of residents were watching television in the parlor. Wes stopped in and met Garrison the artist and a quiet man who looked up from his book only long enough to grunt a brusque "Hello."

Miss Clara Ann sat in her rocker with an afghan thrown over her knees.

The tigress was nowhere to be found so Wesley decided to linger for a while. Maybe Miss Clara Ann could tell him something about Jan Langley. He sat on the couch opposite the artist.

"Have some anyone?" he asked as he opened the chicken box. Eileen hadn't bothered to teach her boy any manners but Mama Lo had seen to his proper raising.

Miss Clara Ann smiled. "You go on and enjoy, baby. We done finished up eating for the night. There's some pie on the counter though." She stopped rocking and sat up. "I can gets you a piece if you want."

"No, ma'am. You stay right there. I'll get it when I'm through here."

Miss Clara Ann continued her rocking. "Um hmm. Just like I thought. You got some home training. I told that Margaret you'd be a good catch."

"Your niece Margaret is a delightful woman, Miss Clara Ann. We engaged in a brief conversation just yesterday."

Miss Clara Ann rolled her eyes at Garrison. "You been watching too much of that public television, boy. You needs to learn how to talk right."

Wes glanced at Garrison and stifled a grin. The harumph from the wing chair could have been the other man's commentary on the conversation or his reaction to what he was reading. Wes really didn't care. He liked Miss Clara Ann. Sitting in her parlor reminded him of evenings in Mama Lo's kitchen. He and Marcus's brothers and sisters would sit around the table with cups of chickory coffee and talk about the big lives they'd have after escaping from the coal mining town.

As it turned out, only he and Marcus escaped. One of Marc's sisters left to go to college farther south but returned after she graduated to teach school at the town's only high school. Wes thought about Marc's brothers and sisters. He thought about Mama Lo. He hadn't seen her since the funeral.

Sitting in Miss Clara Ann's front parlor, Wes decided to go home again. He'd check on Mama Lo then come back to Serenity Falls.

His mind made up, Wes finished off the chicken.

"You awfully quiet tonight, Wesley. You thinkin' a man's troubling thoughts or you just enjoying our company?"

Wes smiled. "Just enjoying the company, Miss Clara Ann. I was wondering about the town though. Do you know a lot of people here?"

"Knows everybody who was born and raised here and even some who wasn't."

That's just what he was counting on.

"I met a young woman, Jan Langley, and a fellow by the name of Marshall." Wes tossed in the name of the deli owner so as not to draw undue attention to his interest in Jan.

Miss Clara Ann stopped rocking and her brow furrowed. "Jason Marshall opened up that little sandwich shop next to the bakery. That boy charge two-fifty for a piece of bread with some mustard on it. Gotta pay extra to get any meat. Spent too much time in the city and got too much education to have any common sense."

The old woman resettled the afghan about her legs then commenced rocking. "Now Jan Langley. Let me see, cain't rightly say I know that name. Oh, wait a minute. Langley. She be the pretty young thing what bought Mr. Tucker's old house. Girl paid cash money for it too from what I hear tell. Quiet thing. Keeps to herself. Miz Charleston over to the Garden Club been trying to get her to get active since she always in the lawn store buying dirt and flowers.

"Think I heard tell she'd been in some kind of accident and was laid up for a while. Word about town is she got herself a big insurance claim, too. That's how she bought Tucker's house for cash money. Folks say she just been taking it easy these days."

If Jan Langley had been injured in an accident recently, she'd had a remarkable recovery. Her flawless skin and athletic ability, not to mention her appetite for him, wore him out and gave not the least indication that she'd been laid up as Miss Clara Ann put it.

"You got a sweet on her, baby?" Miss Clara Ann asked.

That was one way to put it, Wes thought. He smiled. "Just wondering."

A loud guffaw was the elderly woman's answer. "I told you, boy. When you meets the right one you gon' be knocked over backwards and them footloose ways you was talking 'bout earlier gon' end. That Jan Langley's a pretty one for sure. Seen her at the grocery. She got old eyes though. Look like she done seen too much, more than a child her age ought to. Now my Margaret, she can be kind of bold for a woman, but sometimes that's okay. And her eyes ain't old," Miss Clara Ann added with a wink to Wes.

"I wouldn't call Margaret bold, Miss Clara Ann," Garrison piped in. "She has a refreshing outlook on issues of the day."

Wes looked over the slightly pudgy and definitely rumpled artist. His tan was even, that much Wes could give him. A pair of short, wire reading glasses balanced on his forehead. Wes wasn't sure if the man's bald pate was by choice or necessity. Whatever the case, he seemed to have an interest in Margaret. He could have her. The woman's voice was sweet honey, but that was about all that appealed to him. There was still something vaguely familiar about Margaret. It disturbed him that he couldn't put his finger on it. Maybe in some ways her airs reminded him of Eileen.

Wes grunted. He hadn't thought about Eileen this much in the past ten years. Jan had sure stirred up a hornet's nest with her innocent question about his allergy to chocolate. He'd noticed that she hadn't eaten any more of the M&M's after he'd told her.

He got up and dumped the trash leftover from his dinner. He cut a slice of the pie Miss Clara Ann left out and poured himself a cup of coffee. Carrying the items back to the front parlor, he took his seat on the couch.

The small group chuckled through a half hour sit-com and then Miss Clara Ann got up. Wesley stood as she did.

"Well, children. I gots to be getting me some beauty sleep abouts now. It takes those beauty fairies a little longer to work they magic these days. I'll see ya'll in the morning."

She looked at Wesley. "Yeah, boy. I see your mama sure done raised you right. Sit down, child. I'm just an old woman making my way to bed. Save yo' jumpin' up energy for the pretty young things."

"You obviously give the beauty rest angels all the pointers they need to help out the less fortunate."

Miss Clara Ann's cackle of laughter filled the room. Even Garrison smiled. A grunt issued forth from the wing chair.

"Ooh, boy," she said, patting Wesley's back. "Margaret missed out on a good one when she didn't turn your eye. Ya'll have a good one now."

Miss Clara Ann made her way through the parlor.

Wes figured her rooms were somewhere downstairs. All the upstairs rooms had discreet numbers on them.

"She's a pistol isn't she?" Garrison observed.

"Yeah. I like her," Wes answered as he took his seat again.

The lump in the chair offered no opinion. Garrison shrugged at the man then lowered his glasses and looked over the wire rim at Wesley.

"We didn't officially meet. I'm Garrison. I'm an artist letting out the third floor of Miss Clara Ann's residence as my working studio."

Wes shook hands with the man. "Nice to meet you. Name's Wesley."

"Do you have an interest in Miss Clara Ann's niece?"

"Oh, not at all," Wes answered, probably too fast to be polite. "Feel free." Something about Margaret told him she probably didn't do the interracial thing, but the artist could make a shot at it.

Garrison puffed his chest out. To Wes, he still looked like what he was, some wayward artistic type. Wes relaxed and folded his arms behind his head. He stretched out, his long legs crossed at the ankles.

"I will," Garrison declared, taking a critical look at Wes. "I plan to. Good to know you're not the active competition for her affections."

Wes was inclined to agree with Miss Clara Ann. This guy had been breathing too many paint fumes up on the third floor. They were starting to interfere with reality. Garrison needed to get in touch with the language patterns of the twentieth century. He talked like he just stepped out of some sappy historical novel.

Somewhere in the back of the house a telephone rang.

A few minutes later, they heard Miss Clara Ann holler out. Wes was through the door and down the hall in a flash with Garrison hot on his heels.

They found her sitting on the edge of her bed holding a phone to her ear.

"Lord, Jesus have mercy. Barbara Jean don't know 'bout this yet, do she? Lord, have mercy, Jesus. The news gon' send Barbara Jean into a heart attack. And poor Betty. Ain't she about seven months along. Lord, have mercy. What we gon' do?"

Wes and Garrison looked at each other. Whatever had happened, hadn't happened to Miss Clara Ann.

The old lady looked up and saw the two men standing, indecisive, in her doorway. "A tree done killed Jimmy Peterson," she told them then turned her attention back to the call. "Well, I be over to the house early in the morning. I bring some fresh made biscuits and my Mahalia albums. We gots to get prayed up cause dat family gon' need all the Jesus they can get."

Miss Clara Ann concluded her call and shook her head sadly. "Umph, umph, umph. Terrible thing. Terrible thing."

"Miss Clara Ann what happened?" Garrison asked.

"Are you all right?" Wes asked.

Still shaking her head, Miss Clara Ann pushed herself up from the bed. "Po, thing. Jimmy got killed. Ya'll come on with me to the kitchen. I gots to put out some extra for tomorrow to take over to the Peterson place."

Wes and Garrison looked at each other and shrugged. They let Miss Clara Ann pass between them then followed her to the kitchen.

"How does a tree kill a person?" Garrison whispered to Wes.

"I figure we'll find out in a minute."

Miss Clara Ann, still clucking about Jimmy's fate, poured each man a cup of coffee and pressed the mugs into their hands.

"Who is Jimmy Peterson?" Wes ventured.

"That poor child, bless his soul, is Barbara Jean Peterson's baby boy. He own that car store lot round the way from the Wal-Mart. That boy been tinkering with cars and trucks since he was a little kid. Nobody was surprised when he grew up to be selling cars."

"What happened to him, Miss Clara Ann?" Garrison asked.

"He was testing out a new car he had. Sitting at a stoplight up off Route 18 when a big, old tree fell on him and the car."

"Freak accident," Garrison concluded.

Yeah, Wesley thought. Freak accident just like the one where a marshal tripped over a garbage can and resulted in his own arrival in Serenity Falls. "How long ago did this happen?" he asked.

"Etta Mae say just 'bout an hour ago. There still be police at the scene," she said, accenting the first syllable so police came out poe-lease.

"Are you going to be all right, Miss Clara Ann?" Wes inquired.

She waved him and Garrison out of the room. "I be's fine. I'm gon' lay out everything I needs to make a coupla extra batches of biscuits then I'm gonna find them Mahalia Jackson albums to take over to the house. I'm worried 'bout Barbara Jean. Her heart ain't too good. And Jimmy's wife Betty, she be due soon with another young un. Lord, that girl gon' need some strength to see her through this."

Miss Clara Ann looked at the remaining piece of apple pie. She reached in a cabinet, pulled out a small plate and put the slice on the plate. Handing it to Garrison with a fork, she said, "Eat this boy. I'm gonna make ya'll some peach cobbler tomorrow."

Garrison patted his stomach. "Miss Clara Ann, I think I've already gained ten pounds since I moved in here."

"Ain't nothing wrong with that. Do some exercise

and you burn that fat you carrying around right off.
Eat the pie so I can wash the plate, boy."

"Yes, ma'am." Garrison took a bite of pie.

Wes made his excuses then left. He wanted to get to
the scene of the so-called freak accident to take a look
around. He quickly debated whether to take the truck
or the bike. In the end, he strapped a black leather case
to the back of the motorcycle and took off in the direction of Route 18. If need be, the bike could get him in
and out of some places the truck couldn't go.

It was close to nine by the time Wes got to the accident scene. It had happened, like Miss Clara Ann
said, off the busier thoroughfare so traffic wasn't a real
problem. Gawkers, however, were. It looked like every
resident of Serenity Falls had heard about the accident
and showed up to take a look at what was left of Jimmy
Peterson and his new show car.

Wes sat astride the motorcycle still wearing his helmet. He scanned the crowd looking for a nervous, anxious, or recognizable face. All he saw were curiosity
seekers. And Kenny Sheldon from the *Gazette*. Wes
frowned. Reporters were like vultures, always picking
over the remains of the fallen while waving the banner
of the First Amendment.

He scanned the crowd again, then froze. He zeroed
in on one familiar face, the face of the person who
had met him running early that morning. Wes unzipped the black leather bag attached to his bike. He
might need the firepower handy if things got weird.

Gunning the bike, he circled closer until he was
within ten feet of the witness.

Twelve

Amber Baldwin plucked Frank Jr. from the floor then picked up the ringing telephone on the kitchen counter.

"Hello?"

No one answered. "Hello? Is anyone there?"

After a pause a muffled voice came on the line. "Mrs. Baldwin? This is a friend. Tell your husband to watch his back. We'll be sending a sign." There was laughter and then the line went dead.

Amber, her eyes wide, stared at the telephone receiver. With shaking hands she returned the receiver to the cradle. Hugging Frank Jr. close to her, she made her way to the crate-style sofa.

"Frank, dear, God, Frankie. What kind of trouble are you in?" She hugged the baby so close to her that he began to fret. Amber put him on the floor and picked up a throw pillow. She squeezed it close and prayed for her husband.

Frankie had said he was working a double at the recycling plant. He said he worked a lot of double shifts, but Amber never saw any of the extra money he was supposedly making for them. She offered time and again to get a job, even a part-time job. But Frankie wouldn't hear of it. Now he was in some kind of trouble.

The man on the phone said they'd be sending a sign. What did that mean? A sign of what and to whom?

Amber rocked back and forth, bit her thumbnail and chewed on her lip. She glanced at the telephone on the end table. She looked around, then picked it up and punched out her mother's number. Her mama would tell her what to do. But before the line connected she slammed the telephone down. Frank Jr. jumped at the sound and started crying.

She handed him a pacifier from the table. "Shush, Frank Jr. I'm trying to think."

Frankie didn't allow her to call her mother. He'd said they had to cut all ties with the past, to forge their own way. Amber sighed and plopped back on the sofa. She didn't see how not talking to her mama helped them at all. She gnawed at her thumbnail and stared at the telephone.

If she just had somebody to talk to she'd feel better. Maybe the caller had been one of Frankie's buddies from work playing a joke on him.

Amber picked up the phone again. She had a friend she could call. She'd call Jan Langley.

Margaret Shelley touched up her lipstick and smoothed her hands over her full hips in the tight jeans. She'd gotten a lot done this night, more than she'd even anticipated. On the backseat of her car were several packages, her ammunition so to speak.

If that gorgeous Wesley Donovan thought he'd given her the slip, he had another think coming. She'd get him to notice her this time. She'd even taken Aunt

Clara's advice on the perfume and bought a lighter scent with earthy undertones.

Margaret smiled into her compact then snapped the case shut. Getting home had taken longer than necessary. She had to make a detour around an accident. She smiled again then dropped the compact in her handbag and opened the back door of her blue sedan to get her packages.

"It's best to get their attention with a big bang."

Amber got a busy signal when she tried Jan Langley's house. She briefly thought about taking Frank Jr. and just going over there. She glanced at her watch and thought better of that idea. If Frankie called and she wasn't home, he'd go nuts with worry. She couldn't do that to him. She'd try Jan again in a few minutes.

C.J. sat propped up in bed with a cup of chamomile tea in one hand and the telephone in the other. "What do you mean something or someone has obviously made you happy?"

"C.J. It's me, Rob. Remember, I know you. You sound positively giddy. It must be a man."

She chuckled at her brother's logistical arguments. "What if it is?"

"I can have a PI check him out. I need to make sure he's good enough for you."

"I thought you only had your wife's background checked out by private investigators."

"Ouch, C.J. That hurt," Robinson Mayview said. "She's talking about you," he said to someone in the background.

"That Nettie? Tell her I said hello."

"C.J. says 'Hello.' Toinette says get some rest and stop running up your long-distance bill."

C.J. smiled. Times hadn't always been as easy between her and the older woman her brother married. At one point, the lowest in her career, C.J. thought she'd lost her brother's love over Toinette and the center she ran for welfare mothers. That whole debacle had all been quite a while ago. Sometimes it still hurt like yesterday.

"Rob?"

"Yeah, sis?"

"I'm glad you and Nettie are happy."

"Me, too. Nice job at trying to change the subject. It didn't work though. Who's the guy, some southern gentleman with Old South charm?"

C.J. thought of the tall, powerfully built Wes Donovan, the black clothes, the easy French, the quick reflexes, the sexy motorcycle, his oh-so-slow hands. "Not exactly," she said. "This is new. So we'll see. I'll think about keeping you posted."

"You know you have a place when you're ready to come home again."

"I know."

"And what about the other part?"

She knew what he meant. "Fifty-three days and counting."

"Good girl. Be strong. You reading that material I gave you?"

C.J. leaned over the side of the bed and opened a small drawer on the night table. She pulled out the twelve-step handbook Rob had given her. "Everyday. I'm working on that moral inventory part. Tough stuff."

"You need to go to the meetings, C.J."

She shook her head no. On that point she'd steadfastly refused. Sitting around with a bunch of people talking about their drinking problems wasn't her idea of recovery. Rob had repeatedly made his case and even volunteered to go with her. But C.J. wouldn't budge on that point. She'd go this alone. She'd created the mess of her life by herself. She figured she'd find her way out by herself.

"You still there?" he asked.

"I'm here."

"You call me if you need me, C.J. Any time, day or night."

"I will. Love you. Tell Toinette I said 'Goodnight.' "

A few minutes later she sat in the bed finishing up her tea. She opened the twelve-step book and looked at the inventory of steps. She'd never been a real Jesus person so the whole God and Higher Power concept had been difficult to comprehend. It wasn't until she'd been able to view God as a spirit power as opposed to some omnipotent being that she'd been able to make some progress.

God was the spirit who gave sunsets and rain, the spirit that made flowers grow and the one who'd brought Wes Donovan into her life.

Their day together had been beautiful. C.J. spied the fishing hat on the bed post where she'd put it. She grinned. Maybe they'd find some more nature to explore tomorrow.

She glanced at the clock on the night table. Now that she again allowed herself TV she restricted it to one hour each day, national news only. She hadn't seen any today. She still avoided the local channels and newspaper. That part of her life was over. The folks back at the paper wanted to believe she was just taking an extended leave of absence but C.J. knew better.

The book in her hand weighed heavy, not so much in her hands but on her heart. She hated lying to Wes Donovan. She cringed every time he called her Jan.

Yes, it was technically her name but the spirit, if not the letter of truthfulness, was what mattered.

Would it hurt to tell him the truth?

The question that caused her greater pause was why was she going through changes over the man? She could honestly claim that the sex was the best she'd had, but sex didn't make a relationship. For a reason she couldn't fathom, if she wanted anything from Wes Donovan she wanted a relationship more than she wanted the sex. She wasn't about to give up the sex but she wanted more.

And that desire for more frightened her.

At the accident scene the protected witness spotted Wesley and gave a quick shake of the head to indicate everything was okay. Almost imperceptibly Wesley nodded but left his leather case unzipped. The cops weren't letting people near the tree that was already being cut into pieces to clear the roadway.

With a smirk Wes noted that ace reporter Kenneth Sheldon was making a nuisance of himself. But people were talking to the guy while pointing to the tree, gesturing, and describing what they saw when they first arrived.

The whole thing looked like what it was supposed to be: an accident. Wes figured there was nothing wrong with erring on the side of caution though. He parked the bike, zipped up his bag and took his helmet off. As if he were just another gawker, he eased his way into the crowd and toward the witness.

"What happened?" he asked a man two people away from the witness.

"Jimmy Peterson was test driving a new car and that tree fell on him when he was sitting here at the light," the man volunteered.

Wes had to give it to Miss Clara Ann. Her communications network was good. She hadn't left her house and knew as many details as the people at the scene.

He edged forward as if to get a better view as workers used chain saws to cut through the big tree.

"Sure is a big one," he said conversationally.

"They say it's about a hundred years old. Must have rotted from the inside," the protected witness said.

Wes leaned forward and turned his head slightly. Anyone watching would think, he, like everyone else was jockeying for the best roadside view. "This involve you?" he asked quietly.

"No. An accident," the Marshals Service's witness responded just as quietly.

"Call me."

With that, Wes straightened and moved around the circle of people. When he looked back a minute later, the witness was gone.

For someone who was supposed to be on an assignment getting his attitude adjusted, Wes had to admit he hadn't done much in that department. He lay in bed wearing just white jockey shorts in his room at Miss Clara Ann's and thought about the day. Propped up on a couple of pillows, he tucked his hands under his head. It had been a long day and a lot had happened.

He thought about Jan Langley then swore out loud.

Wes swung his feet off the bed and turned the television on to see what time it was. Eleven-thirty-two. Damn. Too late to call Scotty at home on a nonessential check. He'd do that first thing in the morning. He'd give Scotty her telephone number and see what, if anything, came up with that. Wes glanced at the pager he'd turned on and put on the night table. If the witness called, he'd get the message by pager.

He left the television on with the sound muted then got back on the bed.

Something Miss Clara Ann said came back to him. "She'd paid cash money for her house."

Not a lot of people could afford to do that. But the house was older and on the small side. Maybe Jan Langley had used savings. Wes frowned. "Yeah, right."

He had a savings account. The balance was healthy but not enough to buy a house and fully pay for it in cash. In the morning, he'd find the courthouse or treasurer's office and look up the deed for Jan Langley's property. If what Miss Clara Ann had said was true, and frankly, Wes doubted it, that accident settlement of Jan's must have been a big one.

With his plan for the next day in place, Wes pulled the sheet over him. With the remote, he turned the television off. When he closed his eyes, the vision of Jan's tight, firm body came to him. Fishing sure was a pleasure. In the dark room Wesley grinned. He lowered a hand and stroked himself. Maybe he'd take Jan Langley down by the riverside again.

A few hours later Wes sat up in bed, awakened by a noise that sounded like a car backfiring in the distance. He listened to the now quiet of the night. Nothing seemed to stir. Through his open bedroom window he heard crickets and nothing more.

And then the pager went off.

He flipped the sheet off and pulled his jeans and running shoes on. A check of the pager showed a local number.

For what was supposed to be a sleepy little Southern town there sure was a lot going on.

Wes thought about using the cell phone then

changed his mind. He grabbed his wallet, keys, and black bag then left the house with little noise.

He bypassed the pay phone closest to Miss Clara Ann's house and used one two blocks over. He dialed the number.

"This is Donovan. What's wrong?"

"You said 'Call me.' "

Wes looked heavenward. "What's the situation? It's like three o'clock in the morning."

"You Deputy Marshals are early bird types. That's why you always get the worms."

If the witness had been in front of Wes, he would have strangled the person. "Tell me what's been going on."

"How do I know this line is secure?"

"You don't. You can talk to me now. Or meet me in ten minutes."

"You know where the IHOP is?"

"I'll find it." He flipped through a phone book at the booth and got the street address.

Wes went back to the house, got the truck, and picked the witness up under a lamppost.

Wes turned toward Route 18. "Okay. The truck is clean. It's just you and me. What's the story?"

"I like it here," the witness said. "The people are nice. I have a good job. I'm tired of moving."

"But?"

"But for the last couple of weeks, I've been feeling like someone is watching me. It's unnerving."

"Have you seen anyone you recognize? Any car or vehicle that looks familiar?"

"No. I know the drill though. Then, when Jackson got busted up, it seemed like, well it seemed like just the kind of thing they'd do to send me a message or a sign."

Wes turned onto the open highway and headed

south. He, too, viewed the field inspector's accident as suspect but for a different reason. "Do you think you've been made or not?"

The witness sighed. "I don't know. Sometimes I just think my whole life is one paranoid move to another. Sometimes, you know, this really sucks."

"I know," Wes said quietly. Life for people in the Witness Security Program wasn't easy. That's why he wondered why Jan seemed so easy, so confident, and self-assured. Most of the folks he usually dealt with were paranoid, and with good reason. Most of the relocated witnesses had contracts out on them in their former lives.

"Do you want to relocate?"

The witness looked out the window and sighed again. "I don't know. Give me another week. Why are you staying at the old lady's boarding house?"

"Seemed easier. I applied for a job at the recycling plant, too."

The witness laughed. "What? You undercover or something? Your picture on the front page of the newspaper isn't any kind of undercover I ever heard of."

Wes had to admit to himself, he was wondering now why he'd applied at the plant. It had seemed like a good idea at the time. He needed a reason to just show up in a relatively small town. Looking for work seemed reasonable enough. He didn't expect it to be quite so easy to locate the witness. Usually they were real reluctant to open up to strangers, even strangers who were Deputy Marshals. It was that paranoia thing. And he sure could have done without that nosy reporter snapping pictures at the grocery store.

"Wanted to blend in," he told the witness. "This place is small."

"Not that small. There's more than twenty-five thousand people here."

Wes glanced at the witness and grinned. "What are you now, spokesperson for the Chamber of Commerce?"

The witness laughed. "I told you, I like it here. Would hate to have to leave."

"Your safety comes first."

"I know. Sometimes, here in Carolina, though, it's real easy to forget what life was like before."

Wes nodded. "You need anything?"

"No. I'm fine. The only thing I want is to be left alone. To live the rest of my life out in peace."

"It's my job to see that you do."

The witness nodded. Wes pulled into a roadside store got coffee and doughnuts for them both then headed back toward Serenity Falls.

By the time Wes got to Miss Clara Ann's place dawn was peeking over the horizon. He'd gotten all of three hours sleep. He shucked his jeans and shirt and got back in bed. Maybe, if he was lucky, he could get a another hour or two and cut his morning run short. He'd gotten a good workout with Jan Langley. Wes drifted off with a smile on his face.

Amber Baldwin tuned to the news on the radio as she fixed breakfast for herself. Frankie hadn't come home until real late, or real early in the morning. He'd been quiet when he got home, too. He didn't even kiss her, and he didn't look in on Frank Jr. like he always did.

What she heard on the radio made her worry more. She tuned the station in a bit more and adjusted the antenna.

". . . small explosion last night at the Woodsong Recycling Plant in Serenity Falls. Three people were slightly injured when a canister of what authorities believe was hazardous waste exploded about two-thirty this morning. Plant officials sent employees who work in the area near the accident home. Officials are investigating the incident. And in other news . . ."

Amber turned the volume down and looked at the bedroom door. Frankie lay sleeping behind that door. She glanced at the telephone on the counter and wondered if the explosion at the plant had been the sign the caller was talking about.

She'd been unable to reach Jan Langley. Her line was busy for a long time. Just as soon as Frankie left, she'd go to Jan's house. Jan was smart and confident. She'd know what to do.

Thirteen

Mulling over coffee at Miss Clara Ann's breakfast table Wes thought about what the witness had said the night before. He also thought about Jan Langley. What a woman. God, what a woman. Instinctively, he'd known it would be good between them, but he hadn't bargained on the surge of protectiveness he was feeling. The only thing that bothered him was the lingering worry that she was living under the auspices of the U.S. Marshals Service Witness Security Program; not much else could explain her vagueness on some things. If she turned out to be a witness he'd have a rough time justifying his actions.

"Didya read 'bout that explosion last night over to the plant?"

Alert now, Wes sat up. "What explosion?"

"Paper said last night. 'Bout two in the morning." Miss Clara Ann handed Wesley the morning edition of the *Serenity Falls Gazette* then topped off his cup of coffee.

"Thanks," he said.

"Sure is a lot of bad stuff happening around here in the last couple a days. First old Jesse's heart, then the accident last night. Now this."

Wes scanned the front page. Battery acid from a

drum full of discarded batteries had exploded. Three people were taken to the county hospital for minor lacerations. The lead story was short but promised more details in the next day's edition. Officials, according to Kenny Sheldon's story, were investigating the accident.

Wes filed the information as more small-town happenings. At least the reporter Sheldon had a decent topic to write about.

"Weekend starts today," Miss Clara Ann observed. "You got yourself some plans?"

Wes smiled. Not really up to Miss Clara Ann's matchmaking, he didn't want to sound too available. "Sort of," he lied. He had hoped to take a few hours off and drive up to see Mama Lo, but with the real threat of an antsy witness, he'd have to stay put for the weekend. As long as his plans included Jan Langley he'd be fine. Just fine.

"The Garden Club ladies having their annual picnic this weekend. Been telling Margaret about it. She got up and out early today. Said she had some thinking to do. Anyway, that picnic be tomorrow over at the town square. They always put on a nice show."

"That a fact," Wes said, noncommittal. "I'm not real big on flowers."

"But you likes to eat," Miss Clara Ann said while nodding toward Wesley's now empty plate. "The Garden Club always has a real nice spread. You put a hurtin' on them griddle cakes. You want some more? Garrison usually makes his way down 'bout this time. I'm gonna make up another batch."

"No, thank you. I'm full."

"Bet it takes a lot to fulfill a man like you," she said, clearing plates from the table.

Curious at her choice and tone of words, Wes looked up but Miss Clara Ann was already headed to the kitchen. "Now what did she mean by that?" Shaking his head in quiet bemusement, Wes flipped through the remaining pages of the newspaper.

A telephone rang in the kitchen. A few moments later, Miss Clara Ann popped her head through the door. "Call for you Wesley, baby. You can take it in the parlor. There's a telephone over next to my rocker."

"Thank you."

Curious as to who would be calling him, who knew he was at Miss Clara Ann's, Wes went to take the call.

"Did you see that story in the newspaper today?"

Wes immediately recognized the voice of his witness. "I saw it."

"That was a message to me. I just know it. There were a couple of, shall we say, interesting bangs in my former line of work."

"All right. Look, lay low. I'll get you out as soon as possible. You know the drill. It's going to take a little while to arrange things."

"No. I don't want to leave."

Wes shook his head and frowned. "You just said . . ."

"I know what I said. Maybe I'm just jumping at shadows. Look, I shouldn't even be on the phone with you. I think I'm just gonna disappear for the weekend. Maybe take a long drive, somewhere out of the way."

Wes got an idea. "I have a suggestion for you." He agreed to meet the witness in thirty minutes to go over the plan.

When he got off the telephone Wes smiled. If the witness went for it, he'd get to see Mama Lo after all.

Later that morning, confident that the witness was safe and secure and that his suggestion had been met with enthusiastic agreement, Wes made his way to Jan Langley's house. The information he'd dug up at the treasurer's office in town didn't make him happy and he really had no way to nonchalantly bring up the topic with Jan. But he was curious, real curious, about a woman who paid cash money for a house and two acres of land.

He found her in the backyard on her knees. A small boom box on the steps churned out Top 40 tunes from a local radio station. Faded denim curved across a tight rear end. Wes knew what that denim felt like, he'd been that close to her skin. And judging from what the sight of her was doing to him, he was going to need to get real close again, real soon.

From what he could see she was planting some kind of bush. But Wes had to be honest. He wasn't really paying that much attention to what she was doing in the front. That wiggling behind kept him riveted to the spot, mesmerized even. Jan was aggressive in bed— not that they'd actually had sex in a bed. Maybe she'd go for a few alternate positions. That thought brought a slow, knowing smile. He'd seen a hammock between a couple of trees out here and wondered if it would support their weight. She stretched forward and patted something on the ground then sat back and pulled out of her shirt. Wes completely lost his train of thought.

"Mercy." Wes gritted his teeth. He wanted her. Now.

The smooth brown skin of her bare back glistened with a fine light sheen of sweat. She wiped her brow with the faded white cotton shirt she'd taken off then spread her arms wide in a deep stretch. She leaned to one side and then the other, then with her hands at her waist she twisted around in a limbering motion.

"Wes! I didn't hear you come up." She rocked back on her heels and pushed herself up.

Wes swallowed, hard. Heat shot through his entire body and he could focus on just one thing: the way this woman filled out a halter top. He hadn't seen one of those things in years. Didn't even know women still wore them. Marc's sisters had pranced about in them back in the '70s, but they were girls then, just barely able to fill their training bras. There was nothing, not one thing, girlish about Jan Langley's halter top. The criss-cross design in a blue-jean-looking material separated and lifted and proudly showed off those fabulous wanna-be C cups.

He licked his lips and stared.

She dusted her hands off on her jean-clad thighs. The movement caught his eye. He couldn't claim to have ever been jealous of a pair of pants but Wes was jealous of those jeans. They hugged her thighs the way he wanted to. Those tight jeans and that halter made him want to howl. Wes knew exactly why a cave man would throw his woman over his shoulder and haul her off into a cave. Everything he was feeling now was positively primitive.

"Hey, Wes. You okay?"

Wesley licked his lips again and tried to swallow, tried to breathe. Down boy. Down boy. Keep your hands to yourself, Donovan.

"Hey," he finally got out, more grunt than greeting.

He reached up and took off the dark shades. C.J. gasped and took a step back. His eyes, his stare, everything about this man pulsated. She'd never seen that much desire in a man. Heat suddenly swirled through her, clenching her abdomen, making her knees weak. She would have stepped back again, more in self-preservation than anything else. But she couldn't move. She was rooted to the spot just like the rose bushes she'd been putting down would root in the ground.

His burning eyes held her still.

C.J. wondered at and marveled over the sheer, unleashed power of this man. His gaze held her captive and she wondered at the fates that brought her to this time, to this place, to this man. Had she been told a mere two months ago that she'd find herself in North Carolina, in a backyard that belonged to her, staring into the intense brown eyes of the man she loved, she'd have laughed out loud.

Her eyes widened, and this time she did take a step backward. Love? Impossible. Where that errant thought came from she couldn't imagine. Lust. She'd meant lust, deep, soul-wrenching, all consuming lust.

She swallowed and licked suddenly dry lips.

"I didn't hear you come up. Hi. Have you, uh, been standing there long?"

Wes slipped the handle of his sunglasses down the neckline of his white ribbed shirt. "I wanted to see you."

She answered with a small smile. "I wanted to see you, too."

"I've been thinking about what we talked about last night. I'm going to drive home for the day, probably stay over night and then get back here sometime Saturday afternoon or evening. Would you like to come with me?"

"To West Virginia?"

Wes nodded. "To meet Mama Lo and maybe Elizabeth, Hannah, Christopher, and Curtis."

"Who are they?"

Wes hooked one finger through a belt loop on his jeans. "They're like my sisters and brothers."

"And Eileen?"

The immediate scowl on his face made C.J. wish she hadn't mentioned the woman's name. The sensual tension in him suddenly replaced by an uglier tension wasn't difficult to see.

"What about her?"

With a shrug, she let it go. She wanted the other awareness back. Eileen wasn't important right now. C.J. advanced toward him until she stood right in front of him. She unhooked the finger at his jeans and placed his hand at her throat.

He needed no additional encouragement. He wrapped his other arm about her waist and pulled her to him. With one slow finger he caressed the smooth skin of her neck. That tantalizingly slow finger meandered its way down. C.J. closed her eyes and lost herself in sensation: Hot, like being too dangerously close to an out-of-control bonfire; cold, like the shivery coolness of a double chocolate milkshake on a parched throat. She moaned.

The soft touch of his hand at her neck and the hard length of his erection at her abdomen made her think of the rough smooth stone she'd plucked off the ground the night she left Baltimore. And then she didn't think about anything—except the soft rustle of fabric as Wes untied the straps of her halter top and bared her breasts to his gaze.

She opened her eyes and watched his own darken. The straps of her halter fell away. Wes took half a step back. Her breasts jutted out, full and proud.

He wet his two index fingers on the tip of his tongue then brought each finger to the tip of her breasts. Instantly her nipples puckered and turned into hard pebbles.

C.J.'s breathing came quickly.

Their eyes met. Wes smiled, slowly, knowingly.

He ran each finger over each nipple, around the areolae of her breasts. And then he fully cupped her, weighing and assessing the lushness of her breasts.

When his mouth finally closed over one, C.J. cried out and arched into him. "Wes!"

The sound from his throat could have been "Hmm?" It could have been "Umm," as in "Umm, this is good." But C.J. didn't really care. She pulled his head closer

and stroked the corded strength of his neck as he suckled her.

She looked down at him. With his eyes closed and
all his concentration seemingly centered on nothing
but giving her pleasure, C.J. wondered how it would
feel if he were suckling her breasts full to bursting with
mother's milk to nourish their child.

Startled, she gasped and quickly stepped back. Open-
mouthed, C.J. stared at Wes. He blinked several times,
clearly not sure what had happened.

"Huh? What? What's wrong, Jan?"

"My name's not Jan," she blurted out.

Damn, that wasn't what she meant to say. He'd gotten her so confused that she'd forgotten herself. But
her name wasn't as important as the thought she'd
had about her breasts. For her to have mother's milk,
she'd need to be pregnant—with his child. C.J. didn't
want any kids. She didn't even think she particularly
liked kids. The thought of being both pregnant and
pregnant with Wesley's child was enough to cool her
down and clear her head. Big time. Why was she thinking these things?

Focusing on Wes again, C.J. realized that something
about him had changed. He no longer looked at her
with passion-glazed eyes. He stood tall and strong, with
his arms folded at his chest.

"Cover yourself."

C.J. glanced down. Her bare chest looked incongruous in the now harsh light of day. She looked wanton
and felt cheap.

Turning her back to him she tied the halter straps
around her neck then picked up and pulled on the
white oxford shirt she'd been wearing. She buttoned
it all the way to her neck then tucked the flaps in her
jeans. Fully clothed again, she turned back to him.

His expression was hard, unforgiving, even cold.

With his arms crossed and his feet braced, he looked like a cop assessing a particularly gruesome sight. And the fact that he'd put those sunglasses back on bolstered the image.

"What's your name if it isn't Jan?"

C.J. hadn't liked lying to him but she definitely didn't care for the superior attitude he was taking now. She'd heard cops interrogate witnesses with friendlier tones.

"Jan isn't the name I usually go by. It's a shortened version of my middle name."

"So, what's your name?"

It was difficult to believe that the man standing before her was the same one who had just moments ago been lapping at her breasts like a sex-starved maniac. If he was going to cop such a cold attitude, he didn't deserve to know the truth.

"My name is Ja'Niece." She then spelled it for him.

Stoic, he stood before her, as if assessing the truth of it. "What's with the apostrophe?"

C.J. smiled then, for a moment. "My parents expressing their creativity."

"And Langley?"

C.J. blinked. "What about it?"

"That your real last name?"

"What is this, twenty questions? Do you normally meet people who run around giving you fake last names?" She hoped the question would startle him and get him off this path. She wouldn't be lying, exactly. Langley was on her birth certificate—as her mother's maiden name.

"As a matter of fact, I do."

C.J. reached for the gloves she'd dropped. "What is it you do, exactly?"

"I'm an Inspector for the U.S. Marshals Service."

Great, just great, she thought. She stared up at him.

It fit though. It also explained his quick reaction at the store parking lot yesterday and his vague description about being a government troubleshooter. He'd looked, smelled, and reacted like a cop, especially in the last few minutes. Of course, it had to be too good to be true to meet a man like Wes in a small town like this one.

She didn't like cops; she didn't particularly dislike them either. Federal ones though were a pain. She'd dealt with enough overly cocky FBI and DEA types to know she didn't want to get mixed up with one personally. A good roll in the hay was another thing entirely. She and Wes had had that. It was time to move on.

"Are you here in Serenity Falls working a case or vacationing?"

"Does it matter?"

C.J. looked him over from the top of his head to the tips of his feet. The ribbed shirt was some sort of cotton material. His jeans fit him the way jeans were supposed to fit a man. Boy, was this ever a setback in her personal recovery program.

She reached for the watering bucket and sprinkled water over the four rose bushes she'd planted.

Then, turning to face him again, she said, "No. It doesn't matter. Not in the long run. It wouldn't be a good idea for us to continue this."

"Conflict of interest?" he asked.

C.J. smiled a small, sad smile. "Something like that you could say. I told you I was here recuperating. One of the things I'm recuperating from is men like you."

"What does that mean?"

"It doesn't matter."

C.J. gathered up the boxes the rose bushes had arrived in. Wes picked up the other two and followed her to the area on the side of the house where her garbage cans were. She broke down her boxes and tucked them between the cans. Wesley did the same.

"Jan? Ja'Niece?"

When she ignored him, he grabbed her arm and pulled her toward him.

She tugged at him but to no avail. "What do you want, Wesley?"

"You," he said right before his mouth closed over hers.

This kiss was rough and ragged and punishing. He didn't want to want her. But he wanted her . . . and he needed her. His hard lips slanted over hers and his tongue boldly stroked the tender inside of her mouth. No gentle or even exploratory kiss was this.

For C.J. his hunger and his anger came through. She got the message as clearly as if he'd been shouting. She understood the hunger, wondered about the anger, and matched him stroke for stroke in aggressiveness. She kissed him back with pent up longing and heartfelt regret. If this was their last kiss, they'd both burn with the memory of it for some time to come.

When he finally pulled away from her mouth, C.J. touched her lips with a tentative finger. She knew they'd be swollen with his brand. She watched him pull off the wraparound shades. When she turned to leave he stopped her.

"Come to West Virginia with me."

Fourteen

When she didn't answer him, Wes caught her chin in his hand and turned her face toward him. His touch gentle, his eyes pleading, he asked another question. "Who are you running from, Jan? Tell me. I'll protect you."

Like images captured on film, Wes watched emotions move across her face: desire, pain, resignation, confusion, and this last one, the one that hurt him the most, anger. She had reason to be angry with him. He'd suspected all along that she was a protected witness. She didn't even blink when he'd told her he was a deputy marshal. Most people asked what it meant to be a Deputy Marshal—was the job like the ones shown in the movies. But not Jan, or rather, Ja'Niece. The nickname Jay seemed like it would suit her more than Jan, he thought as an aside.

Not only had she not asked him more about his job, she seemed resigned to the fact that he was a federal law enforcement agent. She asked if he was in town working a case. Not many people would have that as their first question to someone who'd just introduced himself as a Deputy Marshal. But witnesses would think to ask that question.

Wes didn't like feeling out of control of any situation. But that was the only way to describe what he felt right now. He lost control of himself when he was around her. All he could think about was holding her, being deep inside her, loving her and protecting her from the demons that haunted her physically and emotionally.

She jerked free of him and stalked back to the watering can. Lifting the can, she made her way to the raised platform near the back steps and then watered little sprigs of green in rich brown soil.

"What makes you think I'm running from someone? And why do you want me to go to West Virginia?"

Wes sat on the top step and watched her. She bent to pluck some offending item from the soil then flicked it away with her fingers. Patting the soil around the small plants, she steadfastly ignored him while waiting for his answers.

"I'm a Deputy Marshal, Jan," he said, putting emphasis on her name in a way that made her turn and face him. The look she gave him challenged him. Wes let it go—for now. "My specialty is Witness Security, WITSEC. I've been protecting federal witnesses for the last six years."

"And?" she said.

He ignored her caustic tone. "I can help you."

"The only thing I need from you, Wesley Donovan, is to be left alone. I think we've done enough damage already. If I need any help, I'll call a Boy Scout."

"You can't deny what's between us," he said quietly.

"Yes, I can. You're a step I thought I'd conquered. I can see now that I'm going to have to go back and work on it some more."

"What are you talking about?"

"I'm talking about addictions, Wesley. Pretty boys are a particular weakness of mine." She put a hand on her hip and assessed him. Wesley tried to keep still under the close scrutiny. When she walked toward him, he wasn't sure if he was going to be able to not touch her. But she solved his dilemma by reaching out to him.

Her small, smooth hand caressed his temple then soothed down the side of his face around his ear then over his neck. Wesley closed his eyes and shuddered.

"You see, Wes. All my life I've never denied myself pleasure. I believe in working hard . . ." she said, as her index finger traced the contours of his mouth. When he would have captured her finger in his mouth, she moved her hand and cupped his chin then eased her palm along his neck and to the rim of his shirt.

"And playing hard," she continued. "The pursuit of a hard body was as equally enjoyable to me as pursuing . . ." she paused. She'd almost said a story for the front page. "As pursuing other pleasures," she said after a moment. "I've had more men, more ways than I can remember." She ceased the teasing caresses and stepped back from him.

With her hands now folded in front of her and her eyes cast down, she looked like a small sorrowful child, about to do penance for a real or imagined wrong.

"More ways and more men than I'm proud of or could ever be sorry for," she said. She sighed then looked him in the eye. "I came here to get away. You asked who I was running from. I'm running from people like you, Wesley. You can't protect me. You can't protect me from me."

"Come with me to West Virginia."

She shook her head. "Have you been listening to anything I've been saying? What does West Virginia have to do with anything?"

Wes was hard put for an answer, particularly one that wouldn't make him look stupid. The only answer he had for her was that he didn't want to lose her, that her past didn't matter to him, that the connection he felt with her and for her was too strong to ignore.

He couldn't think of a suitable lie so he told her the truth.

"I don't want to lose you, Jan," he said. "I know this is new. It's likely to get me fired and you in trouble but that's the way it is. For too long now, I've lived on gut and instinct. Both are telling me right now that we're supposed to be together. I don't know for how long or how it'll work out in the end, but I figure a day and a half together will help tell us what's what."

She looked at him. In her brown eyes he could see her assessing and weighing the validity of his words. Wes held his breath as he waited for her answer.

C.J. looked deep inside herself for the answer to give him. Afraid to admit she felt the same way, she balanced the pros and the cons. All her life she'd been confident and competitive, a classic overachiever. If she targeted something as a goal, she went after it with a single-minded determination that won her many reporting and writing awards. She'd never looked a challenge in the face and said no. Except now.

It mattered now. Everything in her told her that if she turned her back on this man, she'd be saying good-bye to her future, farewell to any chance at permanent happiness. She was still shaken by the two earlier thoughts she'd had: love and babies. C.J. didn't think herself capable of handling either one. Love was for people like her brother Robinson and his wife, Toinette. And babies were for people who had patience.

Far outweighing any reasons to go with him, however, was the primary reason she had to say no, to take what they'd had together and live on sweet memories. She'd told him more of the truth than she'd ever admitted to her secret self: she thrived on sex with gorgeous men. She loved the chase and getting captured. She liked the feel and the smell and the weight of a man on her body.

And with each new encounter, she hated herself more.

She was always, always responsible. Safe sex was too important to leave to chance. But being protected did nothing for the way she usually felt the morning after. She hadn't felt that lonely, desolate feeling with Wes. But Wes Donovan would have to be the last of her one-night or one-weekend stands. Her life and sanity depended on it. The masquerade of her life had finally fallen away. She didn't like the person she saw clearly when the façade no longer shielded her. Her recovery from all the addictions that threatened to consume her back home was riding on this. She'd come too far, one day at a time, to blow it now.

A slow ballad on the radio caught her attention. C.J. stared at the boom box.

Wes followed her gaze and listened to the soulful crooner ask his lady for one more chance at love. Wes didn't know about love but he knew a whole lot about chances and gambles. He was taking a big one with this woman. He didn't know the why of it, but he easily recognized the how come—because his very life depended on it.

"Ja'Niece? What's your answer? Will you come with me?"

C.J. looked at him. She had to say no.

"Yes."

C.J. tossed a toothbrush and styling gel into a small floral-designed overnight bag. A black sheath that needed little ironing and just a strand of pearls to make it dressy was followed by the black high-heeled pumps she'd worn to dinner with Wes.

"It's not too late to tell him no. You don't have to do this," she told herself.

The chime of her door bell halted the internal argument. She glanced at the digital clock radio on her night table then dropped a package of pantyhose in the bag. A small pile of items that needed to go were scattered on the bed.

"You said we'd leave at one, Wes. It's just twelve-twenty now."

But when she opened her front door, Amber Baldwin with Frank Jr. on her hip greeted her.

"Hi, Amber. Come on in."

Amber smiled a trembly smile and hugged the toddler close to her. "Are you sure you don't mind?"

C.J. leveled an exasperated look at her friend. "What did I tell you about that?"

"Oh. Yeah. I forgot."

C.J. shook her head and followed Amber into the living room. She eyed the baby and looked around the room. Had this been her condo in Baltimore, no way would an infant be permitted to scramble about. But here, in the cottage she'd bought fully furnished, she didn't mind.

"Frank can play on the floor. I'll get a blanket to put down for him. Can I get you something to drink?"

"Some of your herbal tea would be great. Don't worry about a blanket though. He's used to going about without one on our linoleum floor."

C.J. shrugged and went to the kitchen to put water on for tea. "I don't have a lot of time. I'm headed out of town at one o'clock."

When the water boiled, C.J. made two cups of chamomile tea. She handed one to Amber and then followed her friend to the living room. C.J. sat in one

WE HAVE 3 FREE BOOKS FOR YOU!

(If the certificate is missing below, write to:
Zebra Home Subscription Service, Inc.,
120 Brighton Road, P.O. Box 5214, Clifton, New Jersey 07015-5214)

FREE BOOK CERTIFICATE

Yes! Please send me 3 Arabesque Contemporary Romances without cost or obligation, billing me just $1 to help cover postage and handling. I understand that each month, I will be able to preview 3 brand-new Arabesque Contemporary Romances FREE for 10 days. Then, if I decide to keep them, I will pay the money-saving preferred subscriber's price of just $12.00 for all 3...that's a savings of almost $3 off the publisher's price with no additional charge for shipping and handling. I may return any shipment within 10 days and owe nothing, and I may cancel this subscription at any time. My 3 FREE books will be mine to keep in any case.

Name _____

Address _____ Apt. _____

City _____ State _____ Zip _____

Telephone ( ) _____

Signature _____ AR0896
(If under 18, parent or guardian must sign.)

AFFIX
STAMP
HERE

ZEBRA HOME SUBSCRIPTION SERVICE, INC.

120 BRIGHTON ROAD

P.O. BOX 5214

CLIFTON, NEW JERSEY 07015-5214

of the chairs and Amber settled herself on the edge of the sofa.

"Watch that spring," C.J. warned. "I haven't reupholstered the sofa yet."

Amber grinned. "I remembered."

C.J. sipped from her tea cup and waited for Amber to meander into whatever it was she wanted to say. C.J. had learned soon after meeting Amber that you got more out of her if you waited and let Amber get her thoughts together.

Amber looked at Frank Jr., stirred her tea then looked at C.J. She put the cup on the coffee table and clasped her hands together.

"Jan, I need to confide in you about something. You're the only real friend I have here. Frankie and I have only been here a few months. I don't know who else to turn to."

"What's wrong, Amber?"

Amber glanced at C.J.'s front door as if checking to see if it were indeed closed. She leaned forward and whispered. "I think Frankie is mixed up with the Mafia."

"The Mafia? Why would you think that?"

Amber told C.J. about her life in Las Vegas, about the moves from city to city, about Frankie's strange behavior.

"Maybe he just owes someone some money," C.J. offered after listening to Amber's concerns.

Amber shook her head, then smoothed her straight hair held in place by a thin hair band. "I thought of that, too. Particularly since we never seem to have enough to get by on. And I know the recycling plant pays good. I'm the one who saw the ad in the paper and told Frankie he should try to get on over there."

"So what makes you think it's the Mob?" C.J. asked. "I mean, the Mafia," she amended. She hadn't seen any signs of organized crime in Serenity Falls but you never knew. Still waters run deep, she thought. For all C.J. knew, Serenity Falls could be the southeast headquarters. But she'd bet her grandmother's best pearls that that wasn't the case.

"The telephone call is what made me think that. A man called and threatened us. I didn't tell Frankie about it yet though. I didn't want to upset him. He already jumps at shadows and checks our apartment for hidden microphones every night."

C.J. sipped from her tea and nodded for Amber to do the same. "What did the caller say?"

"He had one of those scratchy voices like you hear on TV, you know, a gangster voice," she said, demonstrating. "And he said Frankie would be getting a sign soon." Amber reached into Frank Jr.'s diaper bag and pulled out a folded up newspaper. On her knees, she smoothed out the *Serenity Falls Gazette* then handed the paper to C.J.

"Is this the local paper?"

Amber nodded. "Don't you get it?"

"No. I'm allergic to news," C.J. said. She caught Amber's puzzled expression and waved the comment away. "Not important right now. What did you want me to see?"

Amber pointed to the top story. It was barely eight inches long. C.J. quickly read it then looked up at Amber.

"Okay. So there was a small explosion at the recycling plant. No one was seriously injured."

"Frankie was supposed to be there. That's the section where he works."

"So, where was he? What did he say about the explosion?"

Amber shook her head. "I don't know. He came home really late. Normally he always checks in on

Frank Jr. You know, kisses him goodnight even though
he's asleep. Then he always takes a shower and gets in
bed and pulls me close. This morning though, he
didn't do any of that. He just came home and fell in
the bed."

"That's it?"

Amber nodded.

"Amber, I think you're the one jumping at shadows.
Maybe Frankie just has a paranoid streak in him. Some
people are like that. The call could have been one of
his buddies playing a joke on him."

Amber chewed on her bottom lip. "I don't think so.
Frankie doesn't have any friends. He doesn't even have
any family but me and Frank Jr. All of my family is in
Nevada. They don't know we're here in North Carolina
so it's not them."

"What time do you have?"

"It's a quarter to one. Oh, I'm sorry. You said you
were about to leave. We can go."

"No, no. Just come with me so I can finish packing.
We have a little more time before my friend picks me
up."

In her bedroom, C.J. added a few remaining items to
her bag: perfume, panties, and the champagne-colored
teddy from Wal-Mart. On second thought, she pulled
that out of the bag.

"Ooh, that's pretty, Jan," Amber said while bouncing
Frank Jr. on her knee. "I wish I had pretty underthings
like that."

C.J. looked from Amber to the teddy. Lost for a minute in the moment when Wes had picked it out, she
didn't immediately answer Amber.

"No, Frank. You can't play with that."

Amber plucked from the baby's hands a box of condoms. Blushing, she handed the box to C.J.

"I'm thinking that maybe I won't need either of

these things with me." Then she thought about how quickly she and Wes fell into each other's arms. "Better safe than sorry," she said, dropping both the condoms and the teddy in the bag. She added a T-shirt and a pair of jeans then snapped the bag closed.

"We're going to have to have a girl's day out when I get back. When was the last time you had a manicure and a pedicure?"

Amber looked at her hands and smiled. Frank Jr. took the gesture as an invite to play patty-cake. Amber obliged the baby, then, laughing, answered C.J.

"Not since before I got married. There hasn't been the time or the money for that sort of thing since we left Vegas."

"Well, it'll be my treat. We'll find a sitter for Frank Jr. and spend the afternoon doing girl stuff."

Amber's smile transformed her face. C.J. saw all the possibilities in Amber and was glad she'd made the commitment to help her.

When the doorbell rang, the two women looked up.

"One o'clock. He's right on time."

Amber lifted the baby in her arms and followed C.J. from the bedroom.

"I'll call you when I get back and we'll make a date for next week to do our girls' day out. Okay?"

Amber smiled. "Okay."

"And, Amber, don't worry too much about your husband. If there was a real threat to you or to the baby, I think he'd let you know about it." Even as she said the words though, C.J. hoped they were true. She knew from countless stories about lying boyfriends, cheating husbands and domestic violence, that men could be liars.

Amber went to the sofa to get her diaper bag while C.J. opened the door to Wes. He grinned at her. They were dressed practically identically: blue jeans, white oxford, tan jacket. C.J.'s upturned shirt collar and jewelry, an intricate concentric metal pin and matching earrings, added a touch of femininity to her outfit.

Wes pulled off the shades and stepped into the house.

Holding the baby's hand, Amber walked to the door. She looked up at Wes and blinked.

"Amber Baldwin, this is my friend Wes Donovan. Wes, Amber."

Amber squinted up at Wes. "You look familiar. Have we met before?"

"I don't believe so. Pleased to meet you," he told Amber. Wes squatted down. "Hey, what's up little man?" he asked the baby.

Frank Jr. grinned. "Da."

Wes laughed. "No, I don't think so little buddy."

Amber smiled down at her son. "That's the only word he knows besides 'Ma' and 'moo' which means milk."

"He's a great looking kid, Ms. Baldwin."

Amber lifted Frank Jr. in her arms. "It's Mrs. and thanks. Well, I'm going to be leaving. Have a nice trip, Jan. Nice to meet you, Wes." She shifted the boy and looked up at Wes. "Oh, now I know why you look familiar. You remind me of a croupier back in Las Vegas."

All of a sudden, Wes knew exactly what his protected witness must be feeling. To have someone from the past recognize you, particularly when the past was thought long buried, could be scary. This Amber had a sharp memory. But he wasn't about to tell her that several years back he'd been working undercover as a croupier at a Vegas casino. Amber must have worked there, too.

Amber took her leave. Wes followed C.J. to the

kitchen where she made sure everything was turned off.

"Who is she?" he asked.

"Who Amber? She's a friend. We met shortly after I arrived in town. Her husband works over at the plant. Why?"

"Just asking."

But he filed the information away in his head as another so-called coincidence and definitely a reason to be even more on guard than he had been before.

C.J. turned off the lights and locked her front door.

At her curb sat a white Crown Victoria, the classic cop car. "What'd you do? Go out and buy a car for this trip?"

"It's a rental."

C.J. eyed the car then looked at Wes. "Yeah, right." He was already headed down the walk with her bag. "An armor-plated rental from Feds-Are-Us," she murmured to herself.

"We should get there about five."

"Can we stop at Bettina's Bakery. I'd like to get some croissants or something to munch on."

"First stop, Bettina's. Second stop, Interstate 40 East."

They walked into the bakery shop looking like identical twins. Yancey Yardley was at the counter chatting with Bettina. Her soft, round face was flushed with pleasure. She looked up when the bell twinkled signaling incoming customers.

"Miz Langley. Nice to see you again."

Yancey turned around, doughnut in hand. "Hey there, Jan. Good to see you." He nodded at Wes, said "Hello" then turned back to Bettina.

C.J. hurried to the counter to peer in at the sweet treats. "We came for croissants."

"Ah, then you're in luck," the baker said. "I have chocolate, lemon, and regular today."

C.J's eyes widened and she smiled. "Chocolate?" Then she remembered Wesley's allergy. She turned to look at him. "Is lemon okay for you?"

"Don't worry about me. Get the chocolate ones."

C.J. shook her head. "Bettina, I'd like three of the plain and three lemon."

"Coming right up. Ya'll sure look cute dressed like that."

"It was an accident," C.J. said. Then to Yancey, "I got those rose bushes in the ground this morning. I let them sit in water overnight like the directions said then grounded them this morning."

"I can't wait to see the results. About how long will it take for them to bloom?"

"I don't know. The box said a few weeks. We'll see. I'll let you know though."

"Here you go," Bettina said, handing C.J. the waxed bag with the baked goods. "That'll be nine sixty five."

C.J. reached in her pocket for the money but Wes stepped forward with a ten.

"Did you all hear about the explosion over at the plant? Yancey was just telling me that his delivery truck was right nearby where it happened."

"Yeah, I read about that in the newspaper," Wes added. "You were lucky. Maybe you should be more careful where you park your truck next time."

"Yancey, I'm glad you're okay," C.J. said.

"Me, too," Bettina added from the other side of the counter.

C.J. looked from Yancey to Bettina. She should have suspected that the talkative truck driver liked black women. He'd spent enough time chatting her up. Bettina looked happy and the soft glances in Yancey's direction confirmed for C.J. that there had been more

going on before she and Wes walked in than talk about
a plant accident. Since she genuinely liked both Bettina and Yancey, she silently wished them the best of
luck.

"Jan, we'd better get going," Wes prodded.

"Okay. Thanks for the croissants. See you both
later."

Wes nodded at Bettina and Yancey then held the
door open for C.J.

She walked out of the bake shop before him. When
they were settled in the car, Wes started the engine
and C.J. dug into the pastry bag.

"That's really sweet," she said, as Wes pulled into
the street.

"What?"

"Yancey and Bettina. They make a cute little couple."

Wes glanced at C.J. and looked back at the bakery
but kept his comments on the matter to himself.

Fifteen

A little more than four hours later, Wes pulled into an already crowded driveway of a small gray house.

The house reminded C.J of ones in working-class neighborhoods of Baltimore.

To Wesley, this house represented home, security, and most of all, love.

"Looks like everyone's home," he said. Wanting to surprise Mama Lo, he hadn't called ahead. But it looked like she already had a ton of company. For a Friday night, that was odd. But it didn't matter because Wes wasn't company. He was family.

C.J. opened her string purse and pulled out a tube of lipstick. She applied the color to her mouth then blotted her lips on a tissue. Wes came around and opened her door for her. He watched her step out of the car then tuck her shirt in her jeans and tug at her collar.

"Do I look okay?"

Wes leaned down and planted a small kiss on her mouth. "You look fabulous. Ready?"

She nodded then lifted a finger to smooth lipstick off his mouth. Wes grinned and kissed her again.

C.J. smiled and shrugged. "Well, some men do wear makeup."

Hand-in-hand they climbed the steps to the front porch. Wes ran a hand over his mouth, opened the screen door then rapped three times on the front portal before turning the knob. The door was unlocked, as he knew it would be.

"Anybody here! I'm home," he called into the house as he and C.J. stood in the doorway.

"Lord have mercy that sounds like Wesley," someone called from somewhere in the house.

C.J. looked up at him and grinned. And then they were overrun by people swooping into the room from all corners.

C.J. took a step back and watched as a small child literally leaped into Wesley's arms. He caught her and hugged her hard as another set of small arms wrapped around his legs. And then there were adults hugging him and slapping him on the back and grinning from ear to ear.

"Uncle Wes! Uncle Wes!"

"Hey, little man. I see ya down there. Let me give your sister a big fat kiss."

With loud kissing noises that made the girl giggle, Wes planted a big, sloppy wet one on her cheek.

"Are you my boyfriend now, Uncle Wes?"

Wes grinned. "Angelique, you know you stole my heart the day you were born."

"You weren't there the day I was born."

Wes rubbed noses with the little girl. "Was, too. You just don't remember."

He kissed her on the cheek again then put the girl down and squatted with open arms to the little boy. He hugged the boy hard.

Feeling somewhat like an intruder, C.J. took another small step back. She couldn't hear what Wes whispered to the boy. She smiled as she watched Wes interact with his family. Obviously a favorite son, he was welcomed with loving open arms and tears of joy. A pretty young woman with a bob haircut was in his arms hugging him, then a man about Wes's height and weight, then another woman.

It was odd seeing him this way. She'd never really thought of him as being connected to family, to people. It was as if their time in Serenity Falls was make believe . . . and this was real. This was what mattered.

C.J. watched the homecoming and wondered if she'd ever lay claim to one of these reunions. Her own family was small. Her brother Robinson and her sister-in-law Toinette weren't likely to be having any children but they were planning to adopt another child. Any of these joyful gatherings at her own parents' home would depend on her. She touched her flat stomach and wondered how it would be to feel a life growing there.

For the first time in her life, C.J. didn't shudder with just the thought.

She looked at Wes. He was tall and strong and committed. His was the best loving she'd ever had. When Wesley wrapped himself around her and in her she felt whole and complete. Just like she did right now—and he wasn't even touching her. That made her pause. She cocked her head to study him, to analyze what she was feeling.

At that moment, Wes turned and smiled at her. Something in C.J. flowered even as heat encompassed her. Not, she realized, sexual heat, but warmth and joy . . . and peace? She belonged here.

She'd been searching for peace for a while now. To find it in a living room in West Virginia seemed incongruous.

She smiled back at him and reached out to touch him, to connect with him in some small way.

"All right now. You all done seen enough of him. Let me take a good look at my boy."

The crowd in front of Wes parted. C.J. took a small step to the left, closer to the open door, so she could see who spoke with such a commanding voice.

Mama Lo.

The tall, big-boned woman was the color of sweet chocolate fudge. The green and white checked house-dress cloaking her large frame was covered with a cream-colored bib apron. Her hair, flecked with more gray than black was plaited on each side and coiled around the top of her head in a coronet.

She opened her arms. Wes closed the distance between them then wrapped his arms around the woman. It was difficult to see who leaned on whom. They hugged long and hard. When they finally broke apart, she reached into her apron pocket and pulled out a white handkerchief. But she didn't try to stem the flow of tears from her own eyes. She reached up to dry Wesley's.

"Wesley, child, dry your eyes."

He smiled down at her. "You're crying too, Mama Lo."

"That's because I've missed you. And I love you."

Wes hugged her tight again. "God, I've missed you, too. And especially Marc."

She rocked him in her arms. "Shush, now. We'll talk about that later. Introduce me to your pretty lady friend you left over by the door."

"Yeah, Wes. I've been waiting for that," one of the men said.

"I just bet you have, Curtis," Wes said.

"Don't pay him any mind, Wesley. He's been right steady these last couple of months with the new waitress over at the Lounge."

"I'm always looking out for, what do they call it, new

opportunities," Curtis said as his gaze wandered over Wesley's guest.

With one arm still around Mama Lo's waist Wes reached a hand out to Jan. She clasped her hand in his and Wes made the introductions.

"Mama Lo, I'd like you to meet Jan," he glanced at her, "Ja'Niece Langley, a friend of mine. Jan, this is Mama Lo who at one point in her life was known as Loretta Kensington."

C.J. extended a hand in greeting. "It's a pleasure to meet you, Mrs. Kensington."

The adults in the room chuckled.

"Who is Mrs. Kensington," the four-year-old Angelique asked.

The question brought more laughter from the adults.

"That's Mama Lo's other name," somebody answered her.

Mama Lo pulled C.J. to her bosom for a hug. "If you're a friend of Wesley's and he brings you to my house, that means you're family. And family calls me Mama Lo."

She smiled. "Yes, ma'am."

Mama Lo pulled back then situated C.J. next to Wes. Taking a careful step backward, she sized up the two. Then she nodded and smiled. "That's good. That's real good."

C.J. wasn't certain but she could have sworn Wes actually blushed before he turned to introduce her to the rest of the family. The fraternal twins, Christopher and Curtis, and Christopher's girlfriend Sheila; the children, Angelique and James, and the other adults: Hannah with the short bob haircut, and Elizabeth who looked to be late into a pregnancy. C.J. quickly attached names to faces.

"You all hungry?" Hannah asked. "We were just fin-

ishing up dinner and was going to have some dessert.
I can fix you up some plates, Star Gazer."

"Sounds good to me," Wes said.

C.J. turned a questioning look up to Wes at the nickname but he, with her hand clasped in his, had already
turned to follow the others into the dining room.

In no time, C.J. and Wes were seated next to each
other at the table. Brimming plates of collards, honey-
glazed ham, sweet potatoes, and stewed tomatoes were
put before them. Wes dipped a piece of cornbread in
a small honey pot and popped it in his mouth.

"I didn't see you say grace, Wesley," Mama Lo said.
"You have to remember to thank the Lord for what
He provides."

Before bowing her own head, C.J. glanced at Wes
who looked mildly chagrined. But he bowed his head,
muttered what had to have been the fastest prayer
she'd ever heard then dug into the food with gusto.
As C.J. picked up her knife to cut into the ham, she
realized she couldn't remember the last time she said
grace before a meal. She'd strayed far from her own
upbringing.

"What you doing up this way, Wesley? Didn't figure
we'd see you again for a while," Curtis asked.

The question may have been directed to Wes, but
C.J. felt Curtis's eyes on her, assessing and evaluating.
She looked up and stared him straight in the eye. With
a half smile, he nodded his head and turned his full
attention to Wes.

"I was thinking about Mama Lo and decided to drive
up for the day."

"Drive up for the day? Shoot, it takes about ten
hours to get from here to D.C. I hope you wasn't planning on driving back tonight."

"We came up from North Carolina," Wes said.

Hannah and Elizabeth shared a glance then looked quickly at Mama Lo.

"Marshals Service transfer you to North Carolina, Wes?" Elizabeth asked.

Wes chewed and swallowed a piece of sweet potato. "No. I'm still based in Washington." He looked at Mama Lo. "But I don't know for how much longer."

"Uncle Wes, you catching the bad guys like my daddy did?" James wanted to know.

An awkward silence fell over the room.

Mama Lo closed her eyes and shook her head. "Lord, Jesus, give me strength," she mumbled.

Hannah got up and put her arms around her mother's shoulders. "It's gonna be all right, Mama. It's gonna be all right." She pressed a paper napkin in her mother's hands.

"Yeah, Jimmy I'm still catching the bad guys."

"When I grow up I'm gonna be a cop like you and my daddy," James proclaimed proudly.

"Lord, Jesus!" Mama Lo cried out.

"Hey, come on you two. Let's go see what's on TV." Sheila whisked the two children away from the table.

"What about our cake?" Angelique asked on the way out the door.

"Elizabeth will bring some to us in the front room."

Elizabeth glanced at C.J. then took the cue from Sheila and got up to cut cake to take in to the children.

"Mama, Jimmy didn't mean any harm," Christopher said.

"I know. I know that," she said, dabbing at her eye with the napkin. "Lord, you'd think after these few months I'd have gotten myself together a little better. But it's just so hard, so hard. The thought of that baby growing up and being a policeman just scares me."

Hannah hugged her mother then returned to her

seat at the table. "There are worse things he could grow up to be, Mama."

"Yeah," Curtis said. "He could wind up being like one of them low-lifes that got Marcus killed."

"I know," Mama Lo said. She clutched her fist to her chest. "But that can't stop or lessen a mother's pain. He was my oldest child, my first born."

Elizabeth walked through with cake on paper plates for the children.

Hannah glanced at her mother who sat at the head of the table with her head bowed.

C.J. had a hundred questions she wanted to ask. Now, however, wasn't the appropriate time. Given what had transpired in the last few minutes, she wasn't sure when the right time might be.

She took a sip of iced tea from the tall glass in front of her. "This is wonderful, Mama Lo. I haven't had ham this good since I left my own mother's house," she said.

Mama Lo looked up and beamed at her. "Well, I can see that just like Wesley you like to eat. I can't stand people who pick at their food. I always say eat what you want, you can work it off later, right Wesley?"

Wes grinned at Mama Lo. "Yes, ma'am."

"Pardon my outburst Jan," Mama Lo said. "I, we, lost a son not quite six months ago. It's still hard for me to believe. My grandbaby James is the spitting image of his daddy, Marcus, who was killed. He was a police officer."

C.J. tried to remember the stories about cops being killed in the last few months. There had been a few so she couldn't pinpoint the case.

"I'm very sorry," she said.

Mama Lo nodded. "Thank you, child. I can see you mean that. Now, tell us where your people are from.

You been in North Carolina a long time? We have some second cousins down there near Raleigh."

"I'm on the other side of the state. Between Asheville and Winston-Salem," C.J. said. "But I've only lived there for a month or so. I'm originally from Maryland."

Christopher asked about the baseball team and the conversation steered away from the painful topic of death.

C.J. and Wes finished up their cake. Curtis got up and returned from the kitchen with three beers. He handed one to Wes and offered the other to C.J.

"No thank you," she said while looking at the can. "I have a tea bag. If I could get some hot water that would be great."

"I'll zap some in the microwave for you," Elizabeth offered.

Wes nudged Hannah. "She's always drinking that nasty tea. Stuff's too healthy for me."

C.J. stuck her tongue out at Wes then got up to help clear the table.

"Sit down, Jan. You're company," Mama Lo said.

"But I'll just help with the dishes."

"You can help the next time. For tonight, you're a guest."

C.J. sat back in her chair. Wes leaned over and draped an arm around her shoulders. "You better bask in it while you can. The next time she sees you she'll put you to work cleaning the oven or the bathrooms."

The folks around the table laughed.

"Wesley, quit telling tales out of turn," Mama Lo said, chuckling herself.

"I'm not telling tales. That's what you did with me. Second time I was over here I had to scrub the front porch."

Mama Lo's laughter filled the room. "Lord, I forgot

about that. Well, you sure enough are right about that. Jan, I won't make you scrub the porch when you come again."

"No. She'll probably make you clean the grout out of the bathtub."

Mama Lo chuckled as Elizabeth returned with a mug of hot water. "You all stop that before you send Wesley's lady running out the front door."

Elizabeth put the cup in front of C.J. who pulled a tea bag from her jacket pocket and put it in the water to steep.

"I'm glad Wes found himself a good sister. It's about time."

"Liz," Wes said in warning.

She ignored him. "Star Gazer was always so quiet I wasn't sure if he even knew how to talk to girls."

Wes laughed and playfully punched Elizabeth in the arm. "Yeah, well, you know what they say about still waters."

She rolled her eyes and laughed. "Um hmm. You trying to tell us something, Star Gazer?"

"Why do you call him Star Gazer?" C.J. asked.

Mama Lo grinned at C.J. from her chair. "When he was a boy, Wesley would sit on the porch step and just ponder the heavens. The kids took to calling him Star Gazer and teased him about it all the time. I always told my child to keep reaching for his stars."

"I did, Mama Lo," Wes said quietly.

"I know that." She nodded toward C.J. "And looks like you've captured yourself an angel."

Embarrassed, C.J. looked away. Wes took her hand in his and squeezed it.

"Mama, it's six o'clock. Want me to turn the news on?" Christopher asked.

Mama Lo shook her head. "Ain't interested in them lies those media people always telling. Go find me that new *Jet* magazine so I can look at the wedding pictures." She looked at Wes. "Maybe there'll be another one in there soon that I'll want to clip for my scrapbook."

C.J. pretended not to notice but couldn't miss the sly, smiling glances thrown her way by Wesley's sisters and brothers. But Curtis's look was a tad more predatory.

They sat around the table talking for another two hours before someone suggested going to a movie. Mama Lo begged off saying she was going to watch a little television. Someone found the movie listings in the paper. The group decided on an action-adventure film.

C.J. asked where the bathroom was and went to freshen up her lipstick. On the way out, Curtis cornered her in the hallway near a bedroom.

A nice looking dark-skinned man just a few inches taller than C.J., Curtis missed the mark of downright sexy. The arrogance stamped on him outshined everything else. C.J. met his gaze when he finally lifted it from the study of her breasts.

"Excuse me, please," she said.

Her attempt to move past him in the narrow shotgun hall was thwarted by one thickly corded arm across the expanse.

"That's not what I'd like to do to you, baby." Curtis licked his lips and nodded. "Wesley is kind of backward and what do they call it, anal, about some things. But he's a good judge of woman flesh."

C.J. folded her arms. "Is there a point to this?"

"You're wasting your time with Wesley." He lifted his other arm to caress her cheek. "I can show you what a real man is like."

C.J. slapped his hand away from her. "Don't touch

me, Curtis. You don't know me and I don't want to know you."

He smiled. "I like a woman who plays hard to get. Heightens the, what do they call it, sexual tension."

He wrapped an arm about her waist and pulled her to him. C.J. twisted to the side.

"Lay off pal or you're gonna get hurt," she said.

Curtis chuckled and reached for her again. "I'm not afraid of Wesley." He lowered his mouth to capture hers.

In a flash, C.J.'s knee connected with the sensitive part of him below the waist. Curtis swore and doubled over.

"It's not Wesley you need to be worried about," she said. C.J. stepped around Curtis and left him in the hall moaning and holding his crotch.

C.J. was worked up and turned on. Action films just had a way of doing that to her. She squirmed in her seat then took a chance. No one would see in the dark theater. Everyone's attention was riveted on the large screen while the squeals and sirens of a high-speed chase zipped by. As the film built to its final climactic end, C.J.'s hand edged into Wesley's lap. She stroked him and felt his entire body tense.

People in the movie audience yelled for the on-screen hero to watch out. Wesley grunted. C.J.'s hand grew bolder. She felt him grow hard and she smiled. Her hand worked him over.

He slid down a bit in his seat and C.J. angled herself. It looked as if she were getting a better view as a warehouse exploded and a car crashed through a line of orange construction barrels. She caressed him, toying with the inside of his thigh and the hard outline of his erection.

The action hero jumped from the car moments before it crashed into an ammunition supply shed. The car burst into flames. The movie theater audience yelled and applauded.

"Yes!" Wes cried out.

He and C.J. were the first up and out of the theater before the credits rolled.

Wes barely got to the car before pulling C.J. into his arms. With her back against the Crown Victoria's rear door, Wesley trapped her between his thighs. Grinding himself against her, his mouth slashed across hers in a kiss just as hot as the action on the film. He was full, aching, hard as a rock, and wanting her.

People from the theater began to spill out into the parking lot. Wesley's hand squeezed a full breast then smoothed its way down her body. C.J. moaned.

"Get in the car."

She fumbled with the door while Wesley went to the driver's side. She ignored the seat belt and slid as close to him as possible. When her hand inched its way to his lap Wes halted her.

"Don't touch me, Jan. I don't know if I'm going to be able to get out of this parking lot as it is."

She ignored his words and stroked him. Leaning into his arm, her breast a brand on his skin, she bit his ear.

Wesley swore out loud then pealed out of the theater parking lot.

In less than ten minutes Wesley had them checked into a roadside motel.

Wes locked the door behind him. C.J. was already coming out of her clothes. "I hope the sheets are clean," he said.

She knelt before him and unzipped his jeans.

"Who needs sheets."

Sixteen

Late the next morning they sat across from each other at a pancake house waiting for their breakfast orders to arrive.

"We should have gone to Mama Lo's for breakfast," Wes observed. "The food would be better and the company more to my liking."

C.J. looked around. Animated conversation, the clink of coffee mugs, and the smell of short-order food filled the air. "As late as it is, if we got to her house now they'd know what we spent most of the morning doing."

Wes grinned at her. "They're gonna know that already. The way we hauled out of the movie last night was a definite clue."

C.J. narrowed her eyes at him and then smiled. "Besides, there's nothing wrong with this place. It's clean. The waitress is nice. And look," she said, indicating the almost-to-capacity breakfast crowd, "it's a popular restaurant with the locals."

Wes looked around. The place was jammed with the faces of what he would have been had he stayed here. Men who lived life to the fullest while the black dust slowly killed them from the inside out. Wes had worked below ground one summer. He'd wanted to meet and greet the mistress who stole his father from him. What he'd found every morning when he emerged and squinted from the harsh glare of daylight, was a renewed sense that he had to escape.

In Marcus and Mama Lo he'd confided his dreams. Mama Lo told him to look beyond the stars he gazed at every night before going below ground and to reach for his dreams. Marc decided to follow him East to college and the big city.

Coal mining was an honorable profession. Generations of men in this community and others like it toiled day in and day out to earn keep for their families. But Wes had rebelled from the idea. His father's lot didn't have to be his own. And so he'd fled. And except for Mama Lo, he'd never looked back.

He didn't regret it. Until now. As he watched the faces of the miners, some off today and having breakfast with their families, Wes wondered what his life would have been like had he stayed and endured.

The soft touch of Jan's hand on his pulled him back. "Hey, are you okay?"

Wes smiled at her. Had he stayed, he never would have met this incredibly special woman. "This place is okay."

The waitress brought their food and they dug in. After finishing the meal, they lingered over coffee and hot tea.

Wes leaned back in his chair. If he inhaled deep enough he'd be able to catch some of the sweet acrid smoke he missed so much. Someone a couple of tables away in the smoking section was puffing on his brand. He tried to remember why he'd given up the smokes. Oh, yeah. A promise to Marc.

"So, what would you like to do today?" she asked.

"I was thinking we ought to rent a couple of action-adventure films and see what develops."

C.J. balled up a paper napkin and threw it at him.

Wes caught the missile and chuckled. He leaned forward. "Tell me something," he said in a conspiratorial whisper. "Do those kinds of movies always make you that hot? I wasn't sure if I was going to be able to walk today."

C.J. folded her arms and stuck her tongue in her cheek. "I just wanted to make sure you were paying attention."

"If you mean to the film I was trying to watch last night, I can assure you this, I'm going to have to go back, by myself, to see what it was about. At a certain point, I just sort of lost track of the plot line."

"That a fact?"

He grinned at her then leaned back when the waitress refilled his coffee cup and left more hot water for Jan.

"I was thinking about driving you around to see the sights. There's not much here but I can show you where I used to hang out as a kid."

"I was hoping you'd take me to your mother's house."

"I did. We were there last . . ." He looked at her, his mouth became a thin, hard line. "You mean Eileen?"

She nodded.

"Why would you want me to do that?"

C.J., for all her skill with words on paper, was having a difficult time coming up with the right words now. Family was so very important. Yes, Wes had a good relationship with the Kensington family. But blood was important, too. She just didn't want to see him live to regret not mending his relationship with his mother. C.J. knew from first-hand experience how important it was to mend fences. She'd almost lost her brother for a front-page byline.

"I don't want you to regret not having made peace with her. From someone whose been there"—in more ways than you can guess, she added to herself—"I know how important it is to make amends with family. Sometimes, when everything else falls away, family is all you have to depend on."

"Why do you care about this so much?" he asked.

C.J. chose her words carefully. "A while back, my brother and I had a falling out. His girlfriend at the time, now his wife, came between us because I did what I thought was the right thing to do. To make a long, painful story short, we came to realize that the dispute wasn't worth what we'd both lose in the long run. For us, forgiveness didn't come overnight. We had to work at it and work at it."

Wes was quiet for a long time. She desperately wanted to know what he was thinking and feeling.

Finally, he pulled out his wallet and dropped a twenty on the table. "Let's go."

C.J. didn't question him as she followed Wes to the door.

The neighborhood, old with a slightly run down feel to it, reminded C.J. of some of Baltimore's neighborhoods. Wes stopped the car in front of a house typical of its surroundings. What there was of grass in the matchbook-size front yard was cut low. A row of trimly cut box shrubs defined the yard on either side. The house, with its black shutters, could have used a coat of paint, but then, so could her own house in North Carolina.

C.J. glanced at Wes. He hadn't said a word to her since leaving the restaurant; he'd twisted and turned the large car through the streets until they arrived at this place. She knew, without being told, that this was

Eileen's home. His mother, whom he said he hadn't seen in years, lived in this house.

His expression was stony, and again, she wanted to know what he was thinking.

"When were you last here?"

Wesley's hands gripped the steering wheel and he stared straight ahead. "Here? On this street and in that house? Nine years ago."

C.J. hurt for him.

"The last time I talked to Eileen was about six years ago when I sent her money and she drank it up."

"Six years is a long time, Wes. Maybe she's changed," she said quietly.

Over the rim of his wraparound sunglasses he looked at her. His expression spoke volumes. "Don't bet anything important on it."

They got out of the car and walked hand-in-hand up to the door. At the foot of the steps were two tires that at one time may have held flowers. Specks of white paint about the tires looked like someone had tried to pretty the place up—a long time ago.

Wesley knocked on the door.

When after three seconds passed and no one answered, he turned to leave.

"Wes, come on. At least give it a try."

C.J. knocked on the door.

A few moments later a light-skinned man with a day's growth on his face answered the door. He was tugging a white T-shirt over a pot belly that hung below the waistband of his pants.

He opened the door wider and squinted through the storm door at Wesley and C.J. He pushed the storm door open. "Oh, hey, thanks anyway but we don't need no Bible tracts. We got all the religion we need."

C.J. smiled to herself. She'd never been mistaken for

a holy roller. "We're not evangelists," she told the man.

"I'm looking for Eileen Donovan," Wesley said.

The man opened the door a bit wider and shielded his eyes from the sun's glare—except it was overcast outside.

"Hey, you Eileen's boy? She got a picture round here somewhere that looks like you."

When Wes nodded, C.J. wondered what it cost him to admit he was his mother's son.

The man waved them in. "Come on in. We had a little party last night so the place is kind of a mess. I was just getting ready to run down to the store to grab a coupla things. Eileen! Hey, Eileen! Get yourself out here. You got some company."

C.J. and Wes followed the man then came to a halt. The place looked like lots of parties had been hosted in the room and no one had bothered to clean up between the occasions. Beer cans and bottles overflowed from several small trash cans as if someone had tried to straighten up a bit but then tired of the notion. A couple of half empty bowls of pretzels and cheese doodles were on top the television and coffee table. The stained carpet may have once been beige. A matching sofa, loveseat, and chair all carried myriad cigarette burn holes visible from where they stood near the door. The room reeked of stale cigarettes, cheap wine, and old sex.

Wesley gripped C.J.'s hand in a vise. She glanced up at him but said nothing.

"Eddie, didn't I tell you to get rid of 'em. My head hurts and I don't feel like talkin' to nobody. Hurry up and go get the aspirin."

The man grinned at C.J. and Wes. "Guess you figured. My name's Eddie. Me and Eileen sort of stay together." He sized Wesley up and took a respectful step backward. "Uh, that all right with you?"

"You don't need my permission," Wes said dryly. "You're both adults."

C.J. squeezed his hand in warning. He didn't need to pick a fight with this man.

Eddie looked unsure for a moment. He scratched his stomach through the T-shirt that barely covered his gut, then hollered for Eileen again. "You all find a seat. I'll go get Eileen."

Wes looked around the room. "No thanks. We'll stand."

Eddie, already on his way to the bedroom, cleared off the edge of the loveseat and tossed the debris into a trash can. Then, looking back at C.J. and Wes, he grinned. "Go on, make yourselves comfortable."

When he disappeared, Wesley took off the sunglasses and looked around the room.

"If you're wondering," he said, "yes, the place still looks the same. The furniture is new though. But it's taking the same kind of beating that all Eileen's furniture gets. Sometimes, after my father died, I'd lay awake at night afraid to go to sleep because I was afraid she'd fall asleep on the couch with a cigarette and burn the house down. First my father looked after her. When he died, the job fell to me. Eileen always was one for appearances, outside that is. At home, she didn't give a damn."

A few minutes later, Eddie came back out into the living room. He hadn't shaved but he'd put a shirt on over the T-shirt.

"I'm gonna go get some beer and cigarettes. And some aspirin for Eileen. You all want me to bring you anything back?"

C.J. smiled at Eddie. "No, thank you. We're fine. But thanks for asking."

Eddie glanced up at Wes, whose expression remained stony. "It's a pleasure meeting you, Wesley. Your mama's told me some nice things about you."

"That a fact?"

C.J. elbowed Wes in the side.

Clearly not sure what to make of the chilly reception, Eddie shrugged. "Well, I'll be back. Don't want to intrude on your homecoming. Eileen'll be out in a minute."

Eddie left them standing in the living room.

"You don't have to be rude," C.J. hissed at Wes. "He was being nice."

Wes said nothing. He stared at the woman who stood framed in the doorway between the living room and the kitchen.

C.J. turned and followed his gaze.

Eileen wore a pair of leopard print leggings with high-heeled mules. A short-sleeved cream-colored blouse with ruffles around the collar completed the ensemble. Her face, however, stopped C.J. cold.

Time and hard living had taken its toll. A long time ago this woman was a beauty. C.J. could clearly see where Wesley picked up his Mediterranean features. But there the resemblance ended. Where Wesley's short hair was thick with a high gloss and healthy sheen, Eileen's hung long and dank. Wesley was a dark, golden brown to Eileen's light complexion.

With lipstick smeared outside the outline of her mouth, Eileen had obviously put her makeup on in a rush and without the benefit of a mirror. Or maybe, C.J. thought, what she was looking at was the remnant of last night's face. The woman, thin as an anorexic, teetered forward, careful to keep a steadying hand on a chair here, the sofa back there.

"Well, well, well. Look who's here. The prodigal son returns."

Wes stood tall and stoic in front of Eileen but C.J. was almost knocked backward by the woman's alcohol-laced breath. The party may have been last night, but Eileen and Eddie clearly had started up again early today.

"Hello, Eileen."

"Call me Mama, Wesley. Show some respect. I'm your mama."

Wes stared at her. C.J. squeezed his hand in hers, silently encouraging him to do as Eileen bid.

Wes looked at her then at Eileen. "This is my friend, Jan."

C.J. extended her hand to Eileen. "It's a pleasure to meet you, Mrs. Donovan."

Eileen laughed, the sound harsh and bitter. "It might be for you. But I can see here that Wesley disagrees. He's still as talkative as he was as a boy."

She turned and carefully walked into the kitchen. "You all come in here. I need to make myself a cup of coffee. Where are my cigarettes?"

Wes stood stock still in the living room. C.J. tugged on his arm until he followed her.

In the small kitchen, Eileen tossed a couple of pizza boxes in the general direction of what looked to be a large green garbage bag. She then rummaged through a drawer until she found a half crushed pack of cigarettes. Tapping one out, she turned on a burner at the stove and leaned into the gas flame.

C.J. gasped, half expecting at worst for the place to explode, at least for Eileen to catch her hair or face on fire. But neither thing happened; the woman apparently was proficient at lighting her cigarettes in this manner.

Eileen turned off the burner and took a deep drag on the cigarette. She then exhaled the smoke in

Wesley's face. She chuckled when he merely waved the smoke away.

"You still running around pretending to be a cop?" she asked. "Couldn't get on at a real police department like your old friend, huh? I heard about him getting himself killed. It was in the paper and on the news here. Saw you on TV at the grave, too. You was in town for that black boy's funeral but you didn't come by to see your mama."

When Wes didn't respond, C.J. glanced up at him and tried to fill the awkward silence.

"I'm sure he would have stopped by if he'd had the opportunity, Mrs. Donovan."

Eileen laughed then turned and reached into a cabinet for a jar of instant coffee. "That a fact, you say, Jan. Wesley ain't never been too busy for them Kensingtons. But his own flesh and blood he treats like dirt."

C.J. looked at the stoic Wes. He seemed nonplussed by any of his mother's words.

Eileen poured instant coffee straight from the jar into a mug. She ran hot water at the sink, stuck her finger in the stream to test the temperature, then filled the cup. "You want some coffee, Jan?"

"Uh, no thank you, ma'am."

"Ain't no need in me offering any to Wesley. If it don't come from his precious Mama Lo's kitchen, he don't want it."

Eileen opened another well-stocked cabinet. She pulled down a fifth of whiskey and poured two fingers' worth into her coffee. She stirred the concoction with a pink plastic drink swizzle stick.

With two hands she brought the mug to her mouth and greedily drank.

She topped the cup off with more whiskey then screwed the cap on and put the bottle away. After her third long sip from the cup she seemed calmer—and more caustic.

"You ain't sent your mama any money in a long time, Wesley. This place needs some fixing up. Your daddy's check from the mine company don't go as far as it used to. Eddie and me don't have the resources to do this place up right."

Wes stood near the table with his arms folded, C.J. at his side. "I'm not giving you any money, Eileen."

She slammed the mug on the counter top and tottered toward him. C.J. reached a steadying hand out to Eileen when it looked like the woman would fall over.

"I bet you send lots of money to that cow Loretta Kensington. You been trying to pretend I wasn't your mama for too many years now Wesley. I'm sick and tired of it."

Eileen saddled up to his side and reached a bony hand to his face. He turned away from her.

"Look at you, you even trying to look different than me." She held a thin arm next to his. "You used to be just a shade or so darker than me. Now you look nearly black as your daddy."

Sorry she'd instigated this meeting, C.J. looked from mother to son. From the stillness in Wes, she guessed he held onto his temper with iron control.

Eileen stepped around and got in his face.

"You too good to answer me, boy? You just like all them nigra Kensingtons you used to run with. That's where you picked up such a uppity attitude."

C.J.'s eyes widened at the slur. She never would have expected to hear anything like that. She moved closer to Wes.

"Answer me, dammit. You been sending money to Loretta Kensington?"

C.J. looked at Wes. He refused to be baited. Eileen

lifted a hand as if to slap him but Wes caught her wrist in his fist.

Eileen tried to twist free. "Ow, dammit. You're hurting me, Wesley."

"Wes . . ." C.J. said.

He looked at C.J.

"Let her go," she said quietly.

Wes opened his hand and released Eileen. She shook her wrist and then slapped Wes across the right cheek with all the force she could muster.

C.J. jumped between them and pushed at Wes before he did something he might regret. His eyes darkened. She recognized the rage in him and feared for Eileen.

"Don't you ignore me, Wesley Donovan," Eileen railed. "I brought you into this world. I'm your mama. You ought to be taking care of me."

Eileen's shrill screams about neglect came louder and uglier as C.J. continued to move with Wes through the kitchen and living room.

"Don't you turn your back on me, you ungrateful bastard," Eileen screamed. "What'd you come here for anyway!"

Eileen chased them to the front door. "You found yourself a little ethnic piece did you, Wesley? You always did have something about them dark-skinned Negroes. When I see that old Kensington woman in town every now and then she looks at me as if I wasn't even there. Bunch of uppity nigras, that whole family. Never did understand why you ran with them. You're no good just like the lot of them."

C.J. wanted to get as far from the house and Eileen Donovan as fast as she could but Wesley's steps were measured and slow as he walked to the car.

Eileen stood at the front door screaming obscenities at them.

Wes opened C.J.'s door for her. She hopped in the

car and wanted to scream in frustration when he took his time walking around to the driver's side. When he finally got in the car and started the engine, C.J. was crying.

"I'm sorry, Wes. I never should have insisted we come here. I'm so sorry."

Wesley, silent, pulled away from the curb. He drove to Mama Lo's house, the only home he'd ever really known.

C.J. gave up trying to talk to him. His one word answers to every comment made her feel even worse for putting him through such an ordeal. She hurt for Wesley, for the pain he must have suffered growing up with Eileen. She glanced at him as he put the car in park in Mama Lo's driveway. She reached a hand out to touch him then pulled away, not sure if he'd welcome her touch.

He seemed unfazed—almost as if he'd been in a trance the entire time they were at Eileen's.

"Wesley, talk to me please," she pleaded.

He looked at her. "There's nothing to say. You wanted to meet Eileen. You met Eileen."

He opened his door. C.J. scrambled out of the car. "Wes, I'm sorry. I didn't know."

"There was no way for you to have known. Besides, I gave her the benefit of the doubt like you wanted."

Wes climbed the steps to Mama Lo's front porch then walked into the house without knocking.

Hannah sat in the living room watching a religious program on television.

"Hey, we looked for you but you two pulled a disappearing act after the movie last night. Mama asked where you were at breakfast this morning."

Hannah got a good look at C.J. She pressed the mute button on the remote control and got up. "Jan, what's wrong? You look like you've been crying."

C.J. shook her head and wiped at her eyes.

Mama Lo walked into the room then.

"Wesley, Jan. There you are. I was expecting you to come for breakfast this morning."

Wes turned and looked at Mama Lo. "I'm sorry. We went to the pancake house."

His dull, flat voice made Mama Lo look at him closer, and then at his girlfriend. Hannah had her arms around the shoulders of Wesley's lady. Mama Lo's gaze made its way back to Wesley. She sighed and came to him.

"You went to see your mama didn't you?"

Wesley closed his eyes.

She folded him in her arms and hugged him close. "Come on, baby. We'll go talk. Hannah, make some tea for Jan. Jan, sweetheart, I'm gonna go have a talk with Wesley. You going to be all right?"

C.J. looked at Wes. He refused to meet her eyes. Her mouth trembled but she nodded.

"Okay then," Mama Lo said. "Hannah, stop standing there and go get the tea."

"Yes, ma'am. I'll be right back, Jan. Here, take the remote."

C.J. watched Mama Lo lead Wesley from the room. The old woman seemed to be supporting the virile young man.

C.J. prayed Wes would forgive her for forcing him to face Eileen.

Seventeen

"She told me some little story about having a falling out with her brother. They eventually kissed and made up. I guess I was supposed to take that and apply a fairy tale mist to my own relationship with Eileen."

Wes sat on the edge of a wing chair in Mama Lo's bedroom. She sat from her bed watching him and listening.

He got up and paced the area between the chair and Mama Lo's big sleigh bed. "It was worse than I imagined and exactly as I expected it to be. Eileen was sloppy. It's barely noon. She had on some leopard costume and looked like a Las Vegas show girl on crack. She's hooked up with some guy named Eddie."

"That would be Eddie Galatian. He's an above ground supervisor over at the mine."

"I wish them much happiness," Wes said caustically.

Mama Lo caught his hand when he walked by again. He stopped and stared down at her.

"Why'd you go, Wes?"

He ran his free hand over his face then looked heavenward. Swallowing hard, he then looked away. Get a grip, Donovan, he told himself.

"I don't know."

"Wesley, it's me, Mama Lo, you're talking to."

He sank to his knees on the floor next to her. With his hands folded on the coverlet of her bed, he faced away from her as he spoke.

"Listening to Jan, I guess. I don't know. When she talked, it was as if I owed it to myself, to my daddy, even to Eileen to give it one more try. Jan pointed out that a lot could have changed in the six years since I last talked to Eileen. The only thing that's changed is that she looks worse than before and she's shacking up with a slob."

Mama Lo ran a soothing hand over Wesley's head and then his back. "In her own twisted way she probably loves you."

Wes looked up at her. "Spare me."

She smiled sadly. "Well, maybe that is pushing it for Eileen. Tell me how you feel about her."

"Who? Eileen or Jan?"

"I meant your mother but you can tell me about Jan, too."

"You're my mother."

Wes put his head in Mama Lo's lap. She held him and comforted him like she'd done so many times when he was a child. She wondered at the miracle that had brought this boy, this man, into her family.

When she heard him sob, she closed her eyes and hugged him closer. It took a lot to make a man cry. It took even more than that to make Wesley cry. He had so much bottled up inside him. She knew Marc's death still weighed heavy on his heart. And to add Eileen to the mix . . . she felt his pain to the marrow in her bones. She rocked him and held him close and prayed that her love—and the love of a good woman—would be enough to heal him, to make him whole again.

"I hate her. I despise her. I loathe her. I'm sorry I even carry the same name she does."

"Hush, Wes. Don't let Eileen's poison eat at you. Most of the time with her it's that bottle talking, not Eileen the real woman."

Wesley looked up. "Don't you understand, Mama Lo. They are one in the same."

He got up, wiped at his eyes and resumed pacing. "Eileen's been living in liquor for so long, to tell you the truth, I was surprised to see her still alive."

"What are you going to do now that you've seen her?"

Wes shook his head. "Try to forget I did."

"Your lady is going to want to know details."

"She won't get them. The past is dead and buried." He paused and then looked at her. "Just like Marc is."

Mama Lo pressed her lips together.

"Just like there's nothing I can do to help him now, there's nothing I can do for Eileen. But unlike Marc, with Eileen, there's nothing I'd rather do more than dance on her grave."

"Hush up, Wesley. I've been telling you for the last twenty some years that each person on this earth is responsible for his own destiny. You got good genes in you and your daddy's work ethic. That's carried you too far to let this set back knock you down. You've been fighting too long."

"Sometimes you have to concede defeat."

"Is that what you're doing? Are you going to turn into an alcoholic now and let yourself go like Eileen and Eddie Galatian?"

Wesley whirled around. "I'm not an alcoholic. I drink a couple of beers now and then but I know when to say when. There's only one thing I hate more than alcoholics."

Since Mama Lo knew what that one thing was, she didn't question him on it.

"I didn't say you were, Wesley," she responded quietly. She rose from the bed and went to him. "I'm asking you if you're giving up on life and living. If you are, you need to take that woman out in the living room back to wherever you found her. She represents life and living, Wesley. She looks like she's already more than half in love with you. If you feel the same, you need to do something about it. If you don't, I can give you the papers to your spot over in the Kensington family plot at the cemetery. You can just climb right on in next to Marcus and call it quits right now."

Wesley looked at her. A small smile slowly turned into a wide grin. "Must you always be so dramatic?"

Her answering smile was just as broad. "Come give an old woman a hug, Wesley."

In the living room, C.J. anxiously watched the arched doorway Mama Lo and Wesley disappeared beyond. They'd been gone a long time. Try as she might, she wasn't able to follow the conversation Hannah tried to have with her. Eventually, the other woman lapsed into silence and waited with C.J. for the two to reappear.

"He might take a walk," Hannah said. "Star Gazer used to do that sometimes when he came over from his mother's house. He and Mama would talk for a long time and then he'd go for a walk. Usually it was nighttime though. We'd eventually find him on the porch looking at the stars."

Now this was a line of conversation C.J. found interesting. "What was Wes like as a boy?"

Hannah shrugged. "A lot like he is now. Quiet, reflective, intense. When he feels, he feels deeply."

She paused for a moment then peered closely at C.J. "Jan, do you mind if I tell you something. I don't want you to take offense or anything."

After surviving Eileen Donovan's tirade, C.J. didn't think she'd take offense at much else.

"What is it?" she asked.

"Well, we, meaning me, Christopher, and Elizabeth, and Curtis, too, we were all kind of surprised when Wes showed up with you yesterday. We talked about it after the movie last night."

"Why?"

Hannah paused, clearly embarrassed.

"I won't be upset by whatever you say," C.J. assured the woman.

"We've never seen Wes date anybody as light as you."

"Excuse me?" Was everybody in this town color struck? C.J. looked at her skin. It was far from being light.

"Wesley's mother, Miss Eileen, well, she always had this thing about light skin and dark skin. She used to run around pretending she was white. Wesley kind of took the opposite tack and he only went out with real dark girls. Like even darker than me. You know, 'the blacker the berry . . .' "

" 'The sweeter the juice,' " C.J. finished the old saying.

"What do you mean?"

Hannah frowned. "Well, it's difficult to say. It wasn't a secret around town Miss Eileen had a preference for lighter skin tones. Now why and how she got hooked up with Star Gazer's father I don't know. But Wes, well, since he just talked to dark-skinned girls, I always figured it was his way of getting back at Miss Eileen. You know what I mean?"

C.J. nodded. "I suppose so. It seems awfully calculated though."

"He may not have even been aware he was doing it. Don't get me wrong. Wes is a good judge of character. He doesn't like people who are phony or who put on airs." Hannah laughed. "Maybe that's why he's fit in so well with our family."

C.J. looked at the beautiful brown woman Wesley considered his sister. Her flawless dark skin glowed with reddish-orange undertones. C.J. didn't consider herself dark, but she wasn't what some people called high-yellow either. In actuality, she and Wes were about the same complexion.

"He's been gone from home for a long time though," Hannah continued. "He and my brother Marcus went east as soon as they graduated from high school. I don't know what Wesley did or who he dated over there but here, well, he was always real clear on where his allegiance was, in terms of color I mean."

"Color shouldn't matter," C.J. said.

"Yeah, I know. But if you grew up in Eileen Donovan's house, you'd probably have a color complex too, one way or the other."

C.J. didn't have anything to add to that. She'd heard enough of Eileen's invective to agree with Hannah.

The one thing she planned to do as soon as she got back home though was find out all she could about the death of Marcus Kensington. Everyone talked around it and about it as if she knew all the details. Wes hadn't shared many details of that part of his life with her. But C.J. knew an easy way to get all the information she needed.

Mama Lo appeared in the arched doorway.

"Jan, Wesley went for a short walk. He'll be back in a little bit. Can I get you something to eat?"

C.J. looked at Hannah.

"Told you," she said. "Some things just don't change."

Wes was glad that some things didn't change—like the woods out beyond the end of Mama Lo's street. He'd expected that developers would have built it up by now like some other parts of the mining town. His woods were still the same, yet somehow smaller than he'd remembered. Half-hidden trails through the underbrush told him that other people, probably little boys looking for adventure, made their way through here from time to time.

He breathed in the fresh scent of the early summer day. He let the chatter of birds and scampering squirrels surround him.

When he looked within himself, he was both surprised and upset to see that Eileen still had the power to hurt him. He'd been angry and embarrassed that Jan had seen and been subjected to Eileen's rages. More years ago than he could remember he'd learned to turn inward, to block out the rage and the pain and find shelter in a calm place deep in the core of himself. He'd gone there today while at Eileen's, but part of him remained on the surface to protect Jan. In doing that, he'd laid himself open to actually absorbing what Eileen said. He'd taken each barb like a physical beating.

As a child, on more than one occasion he'd gone to Mama Lo battered or beaten with little recollection of what had happened. She'd tended his physical wounds and loved him past the emotional ones.

He came to a small clearing, paused, and took off his shoes. Taking a deep breath, he relaxed all of his physical being. Blocking out all sound and all thought, he concentrated on breathing, then slowly worked through the graceful meditative tai chi he'd taken up in college.

When he finished, he stood in the clearing and let the sounds of the woods and his surroundings come to him one at a time. He breathed deeply and heard birds. He exhaled and recognized the rustle of a small creature, of a dog barking in the far distance, someone cutting grass. Slowly, he opened his eyes. Blinking twice he took in all that was around him. The green of leaves, poison ivy growing near the base of a tree. He took it all in then looked within himself and found he was whole.

Only then did he make his way back to Mama Lo's house—back to Jan.

Hannah had told her to wait on the back porch. If Wes followed the habits of his childhood, he'd come back to the house and pause on the porch.

C.J. saw him approach and wanted to run to him and throw her arms around him. But something stopped her. Maybe it was the purpose of his step or the set of his shoulders. He was too far away to see his eyes, and besides, he had again donned the wrap-around sunglasses. Maybe he wore them to shield himself from the harsh realities of both the sun and life. She rose from the caneback chair and stood at the top of the steps waiting for him.

She watched him and then she knew. Someway, somehow she'd fallen in love with this man. He was hard and unforgiving; gentle and loving. C.J. gripped the banister for support. She'd never been in love before. She'd never had time for anything as mundane as an emotional attachment to a man. Relationships, she'd always believed, were simply for achieving a means or an end to something. She'd collected and discarded men as easily as she did panty hose. But Wes Donovan broke that mold.

Asking herself the tough question, she wondered if what she felt was pity, not love. After all, through the years she'd written about a lot of families just as dysfunctional as Wesley's. She wrote their stories and felt a gamut of emotions, sometimes sorrow, sometimes pity, at other times empathy or sympathy. But it was never personal.

Never had she felt like this. Grounded. Sure. Anxious about tomorrow and the day after that. She wanted to hold him and love him, and not a single one of the things she felt had anything to do with his mother.

He reached the bottom of the steps. "Hi."

"Hello." She reached out a hand to him. He climbed the three steps then sat down with her on the top one. He pulled the sunglasses off and tucked them down the front of his shirt.

C.J. wrapped her arms about his waist and hugged him to her. "You okay?"

He nodded.

"Mama Lo told me you went for a walk."

He nodded again. "I needed to clear my head."

She rested her head on his shoulder. "I'm sorry, Wes. Had I known what a bad scene it would be at Eileen's I never would have harped on you."

He looked down at her then kissed her head. "You didn't harp, and you have nothing to apologize for. If anything, I should apologize to you for even exposing you to that. Eileen is . . . Eileen. She'll never change."

For a long time they sat together on the steps enjoying the silence of the warm afternoon.

Wes held out his right arm and indicated a faint but visible inch-long scar on his arm. "I'd gotten an A+ on my geography test. Geography was hard for me. I don't know why since I spent a great deal of time thinking of all the places I could escape to. I was so excited about the grade on the test that I forgot one of the cardinal rules at our house: Don't wake Mom up out of a drunk. She was slumped over at the kitchen table and I woke her up to tell her about my class and the test. She grabbed the first metal object she could get her hands on and sliced me with it. Blood spurted out everywhere, all over me, the table, my bookbag and my test. I grabbed my arm and ran to Mama Lo's house."

C.J. hugged him tight as he spoke.

"It wasn't the first time," he said.

He placed both palms behind him and leaned back. C.J. let him go, tucked one leg under the other and faced him.

Nodding back to the door, he said, "This house, with this family is where I found out that not all people lived like we did. Things weren't so bad when my father still lived. But after he got sick and died, it was like my mother had no self-control. My guess is that he controlled her as much as was possible when he was living. But all I remember is their fights and her nagging, constant nagging and yelling."

He smiled a small, bittersweet smile. "There was a deaf kid at our school. I always wanted to be like him. He talked with his hands. If he didn't feel like being bothered with you, he turned his back. If you yelled at him, he couldn't hear. Every night when I went home, I wanted to be deaf like that kid at school."

"How did you meet Mama Lo?"

Wes smiled then, a real, honest to goodness feel good smile.

"Mama Lo was an angel God sent down to watch over me. I was seven, maybe eight years old. At this point, I can't remember what I'd done or said that set Eileen off. It was pretty bad though. All I remember is that everything hurt, I mean everything. I ran away and was hiding in some bushes in those woods out there," he said, indicating with a nod of his head the direction in which he'd just recently come.

"I don't know how long I was there but it had gotten dark. I wanted to go to sleep but it hurt too bad every time I tried to lay down in the grass and brush. Then I heard somebody coming. I started crying because I thought it was Eileen. I thought she'd found me. My ribs hurt from where she'd been kicking me. My arm hurt where she'd tried to put a cigarette out on me, but I tried to ball myself up as small as possible to hide."

He sat up and dropped his hands between his knees. "It was Marcus Kensington who found me huddled up like an animal. He helped me up and half carried and half dragged me to his mother's house. The last thing I remember was him hollering for his mama and then strong arms lifting me up. Those strong arms, I later found out, belonged to Mr. Kensington. He died a few years back."

C.J. put a hand on his thigh. Wes closed his own hand around hers and brought it to his mouth. He kissed her hand then entwined his fingers with hers.

"It didn't take them long to figure out what was happening. There'd been talk all over town for years about my mother's drinking and her temper. I didn't know about that until later though," he added. "Marc and I were inseparable after that. He never told a soul about what he'd found in the woods. I'd come here as often as I could and stay as long as I wanted. By the time I got too big for Eileen to beat me, I was part of this family."

Wes turned and looked at C.J. She offered him a trembly smile. He leaned forward, wiped the single tear from her face, and pressed his lips to hers in a soft, quiet kiss. Then he pulled back and stared into the space that was the Kensington family's backyard.

"My father and Eileen gave me the middle name Lamont when I was born. When we were fourteen, Marcus and I took this blood oath that we'd be brothers forever. When I turned eighteen, I legally changed my middle name to Kensington. We were blood brothers as well as brothers in name."

C.J. wrapped her arm through his. "Thank you for sharing that with me."

Wes shrugged. "I wanted you to know."

They sat on the step holding each other.

His pager going off broke the quiet between them. Wes pulled the pager from the waistband of his jeans and looked at the number. No digital message came after it.

"I need to go answer this."

C.J. nodded as he got up.

When the back door shut behind him, C.J. wrapped her arms around her legs and rested her head on top her knees. In all her own months of darkness, she hoped and prayed that she'd never sunk as low as Eileen Donovan. C.J. knew that when she was drinking she drank to numb the pain, she drank in a fruitless attempt to forget what she'd allowed herself to become.

Sobriety was sobering. There were few things she could think of that supported sobriety as much as the sickly, vindictive and drunk sight of Wesley's mother. C.J. shuddered and thanked the God she didn't necessarily believe in for one more day of being clean and sober.

A few minutes later, Wesley popped his head out the back screen door. "We need to hit the road."

"Okay."

They said their goodbyes to Hannah and Mama Lo.

Mama Lo hugged C.J. tight and whispered in her ear. "That boy needs some good loving, Jan. You're the one to give it to him."

"I'm trying my best," C.J. answered back.

Hannah and Mama Lo saw them to the car. The older woman tucked a cooler on the backseat.

"That's lunch for you," she said. "Wesley, you two call and let me know you got home safely."

"We will," he answered. He hugged her again. Then held the door for C.J.

They waved to the two women and Wes backed out of the drive. Before he got to the street, his pager went off again.

He muttered an expletive. C.J. looked at him then pulled her seat belt on. "Uh, have you been working or on-duty or whatever you Deputy Marshal types call it, while we were here?"

He looked at her. "What do you think?"

C.J. was thinking maybe she needed to go get a rental and drive herself back to North Carolina.

Wes pulled the pager from his waist and read the message. This one wasn't a telephone number.

Watch your back. These are strange days with bad blood flowing. 007.

Wes frowned. The cryptic message was from Ann Marie Sinclair at headquarters. The joke that had started between them twelve years ago as they filled out paperwork on their mutual first day with the service remained.

Ann Marie had said she really wanted to be James Bond but the only listed opening was for a temp so she settled for that. He'd called her 007. In the years since, as they both rose through their respective ranks, Ann Marie had paged him just twice. Both times she'd signed the message as 007. Both times, his life had depended on heeding her warnings.

Eighteen

"Wes, are things about to get weird?"

"Not any weirder than normal," he answered with a grin.

"That's so very reassuring," she said.

Wes reached for her hand and kissed it. "I'd never put you in any physical danger."

C.J. stared at this man she knew she loved and wondered at his choice of words. She was already deeply entrenched in the emotional danger zone.

She took a look at their hands, joined on the seat, then glanced at the dash of the car. If the Crown Victoria was a cop car like she'd first suspected, the car was working undercover. It looked like your basic vehicle—except she'd never met a real person who drove one.

"Is this a cop car?"

Wes looked at her but didn't answer.

To C.J.'s relief, they arrived back in North Carolina without any high-speed chases or any defensive driving. Her relief was short-lived though. About twenty miles outside of town, blue and white lights flashed from several police squad cars. Flares along the road and the red flashing lights of two ambulances heralded an accident. Wes slowed as they approached the scene.

He carefully watched a blue sedan in front of them

ease its way beyond the two officers working traffic detail. Wes followed the sedan and the cop's hand signal directions. He slowed up some more and rolled his window down.

"What happened, officer?"

"Wrong way, driver. Had a head-on collision here. Keep it moving, pal."

Wes eased around the accident scene but kept a close eye on the progress of the sedan in front of him.

"Oh, my God. That's terrible," C.J. said. She'd turned around in her seat to rubberneck and get a good look at the scene.

The twisted metal and scrunched car bodies left little to hope for in the way of survivors. The roof of the smaller car lay in the middle of the roadway and a child's car seat dangled from the popped open rear door of the other vehicle. Glass was everywhere.

In her earlier days of reporting she'd done the cop stuff and had worked many an accident scene. This was one of the worst she'd ever seen.

As Wes cleared the scene, the siren from one of the ambulances fired up. The emergency vehicle sped past them. C.J. faced forward again.

"That makes you wonder why and how we so readily put our trust in these tons of steel and plastic that hurtle so recklessly down these paved over horse and buggy trails."

"Stagecoaches with actual horses and buggies were just as dangerous in their day."

"I know," she said quietly.

"What do you drive?" he nonchalantly asked.

"Just your basic transportation. I walk most places I need to go."

Wesley sighed inwardly. So much for trying to get some answers out of her. Now that they were back in Serenity Falls, the reality of their situation hit him. He knew his job was on the line with this woman. And unless Scotty had had any better luck at pulling up her background, he could think of just one way to find out if she was a protected witness. If she was, he'd need to start looking for a new job.

He thought about how much of himself he'd revealed to her in the past twenty-four hours. It was more than people he'd known for the last twelve years knew about him, more than he would have thought just last week, that he'd ever want a woman to know about him.

He turned onto her street and pulled up in front of her house.

"Jan, there's something I need to ask you."

C.J. unbuckled her seat belt and leaned over the back seat to grab her string purse.

"What?"

Wesley's eyes narrowed at the sight of her behind pushed up in the air. He reached up a hand to pat that sweet temptation then caught himself.

"Are you in the U.S. Marshals Witness Security Program?"

C.J., clutching her small bag, sat back down with a plop. She looked at him and grinned. "You mean like wiseguys and gangsters using the feds to hide out from their buddies they informed on?"

Wiseguys? Feds? Either she watched a lot of television or she knew exactly what he was talking about. Regular people weren't quite that familiar with the lingo.

Wes nodded.

C.J. chuckled and patted his cheek. "What do you think?"

Wes grabbed her arm and pulled her body against his so she was half kneeling and half laying on him.

"I think you're an addiction I need to give up cold turkey," he said right before his lips covered hers.

The hot embrace fast turned into something more.

Their breathing was erratic, their heartbeats accelerated when Wes finally let her come up for air. But he didn't let her go. Not yet. He wanted her too much.

"Do you want to come inside?"

"More than you know, Jan Langley."

She smiled when she caught his meaning then rubbed one smooth palm over his chest. "I meant into the house, my bedroom."

Wes twisted his hips and brought her hand down to feel his erection. "Actually, what I'd really like is to do you on the backseat." If he was going to lose his job over this woman, he might as well make it memorable.

"Well, that certainly is a retro idea. But there's one problem."

When he raised his eyebrows in question, C.J. sat up and tugged her shirt down. "It's still broad daylight outside. Someone, like a little kid, would walk by and see us."

"Where's your sense of adventure? Don't you like to flirt with danger?"

"I've been hanging out with you for the last couple of days. I'm getting a good dose of it." She paused and looked him over. "Along with some of the hottest sex I've ever had in my life."

"I want to make love to you," he said.

C.J. looked up quickly. She'd been thinking the same thing. It surprised her that he'd distinguished between the two. After their first wild coupling at the river, they'd made love . . . on the ground. A part of C.J. wanted to be seduced, the old-fashioned way. No quickies in the car, standing up, or in cheap motels. For once, she wanted to make love with and be loved by a man. There was only one man for her. But she knew she wasn't worthy of love, particularly not the love of a man like Wes. She'd seen and done too much to be worthy of a pure love.

She leaned toward him and kissed him on the cheek. "Thank you for inviting me to day trip with you. I enjoyed meeting your family. Mama Lo is a terrific lady."

"I'm glad you liked her. She definitely liked you."

"I better go," she said quietly.

"Okay. I'll get your bag from the trunk."

C.J. let herself out her door, glad that Wes understood what she'd meant about meeting his family, the Kensingtons. Eileen Donovan didn't merit counting as family.

He carried her bag to her front door.

"When can I see you again?" he asked.

She caught herself before she answered "Never."

"Want to come over for dinner tomorrow? I can't promise to make you a meal like Mama Lo's, but I'm sure I can find a box of something to feed you."

Wes frowned. "A box of something? Tell you what. I'll come over. I'll bring the groceries. I'll cook."

She grinned. "Sounds like a plan to me."

"And what are you going to provide?"

"Dessert."

Wesley's head lowered to hers. "I do love a good dessert."

She watched him walk back to the car and drive off. C.J. dropped her bag in a chair and went to the telephone. It had been more than a month since she'd dialed any numbers at her old newspaper but she remembered the extension.

"Hey David, it's C.J. Mayview," she replied when she got an old friend on the line.

She small talked with the reporter and then got to the point of the call.

"David, I need a favor, an overnight mail or FedEx type favor."

"Whatever you need, C.J."

"Would you go to the library and pull all the clips you can find on these two names: Marcus Kensington and Wesley K. Donovan." She spelled the names to make sure he got them down correctly.

"Don't stop at our clips, do the entire region. D.C., Virginia, Maryland, even West Virginia. I want anything and everything you can find. Copies of any photographs, too, if you can swing it."

"How fast you need this stuff?"

"Like yesterday."

The reporter chuckled. "You always were a demanding diva. Can I ask a question?"

"That's what they pay you the big bucks to do," she answered, smiling.

"Are you really on leave of absence or are you working some top secret investigative assignment like the rumors around here have it?"

C.J.'s eyes widened. Top secret investigative assignment? Why didn't anyone believe she'd just tired of doing what she'd been doing for the last ten years of her life.

"You're a reporter, David. Figure it out."

C.J. grinned. She knew the answer was oblique and would only add fuel to whatever rumors were already making the rounds in the newsroom. But it was better than revealing why she really wanted the clips.

She gave him the address to send the material then rang off after he caught her up on some of the latest newsroom gossip.

C.J. took her overnight bag to her bedroom, changed into a pair of shorts and a tank top then went to the kitchen to brew a cup of tea. The telephone rang just as the tea kettle whistled.

"This is C . . . Uh, Langley residence," she amended. She still wasn't used to answering the telephone. Years of responding to ringing phones by stating her name was hard to alter overnight. Besides, no one ever called her here in North Carolina. Few people even knew where she was. David might be a problem but she'd worry about that later.

"Jan, this is Amber. Please, you've got to help me. I think Frankie is trying to kill me."

"Amber calm down," C.J. said. Her friend sounded on the verge of hysteria. "Where are you? Where is Frank Jr.?"

Amber had started crying. "I'm at the pay phone outside the apartment building. Please, help me. Tell me what to do."

"Amber, where's the baby?"

"He's right here. I have him. Frankie's got a gun, Jan. He's going to kill me."

"Okay. Listen to me, Amber. Are you listening?"

"Uh huh," she sniffled. "Please hurry."

"Does Frankie know me? Do you think he's ever seen me?"

"No. He doesn't allow me to have any friends. I've never told him about you."

"Okay, listen. I'll be at your place in about five minutes. Can you hold on that long?"

"Uh huh. We'll hide in the bushes."

"Amber, I'll be driving a blue and silver Cherokee with Maryland tags, okay. Don't get in the car until you're sure it's me."

"Okay. Please hurry."

C.J. rang off, turned the burner off under the kettle and grabbed her string purse.

The stuck garage door took several pulls and tugs before it lifted. She hadn't used the four-wheel drive since she'd arrived in town. C.J. turned the ignition and prayed the vehicle would start. When it kicked over, she breathed a sigh of relief and backed out of the garage.

As she took off down the street, a blue sedan followed her. "Well, well. This is an interesting turn of events," the driver said. The driver passing by noted the house number and the open garage door then stepped on the gas so as not to lose the woman in the Cherokee.

Nineteen

Less than half an hour later, C.J. whisked Amber and the baby into her house. She locked up the Cherokee and pulled the garage door down and locked it.

Amber was a wreck. For the first time in a long time, C.J. wished she had some alcohol in the house. Amber needed something to calm her down. As it was, all C.J. could do was offer herbal tea.

Frank Jr. was irritable and agitated, probably more a response to his mother's mood than what he was really feeling. Amber had run out of the house without her diaper bag. C.J. had made a fast dash into a convenience store for milk and disposable diapers. She didn't have any baby bottles in her possession. She poured milk into a paper cup and set it on the table. Amber could figure the rest out.

Except she was in no shape to do any creative thinking. The woman's hands shook and her eyes constantly darted to the two doors of the small cottage.

C.J. got her to sit down on the sofa. Frank Jr. started crying. C.J. looked at the kid.

Scrunching up her face she lifted the boy under his arms. She didn't do kids and wasn't sure how to deal with this crying one. Carrying him well away from her body, like a sack of foul smelling garbage, she handed him to Amber who clutched the child to her breast and rocked.

C.J. brought the tea into the living room and sat in the chair closest to the sofa. She sat fascinated as Amber quieted the child with soft coos and comforting.

"Okay Amber. Start at the beginning. What happened? What did Frankie do?"

"I, I told you yesterday how he came home from work and just went straight to bed."

C.J. nodded. "You said he didn't look in on Frank Jr. or follow his usual routine."

Amber sniffled and wiped her nose. The baby settled in her arms and dozed off. "That's right. Then the explosion over at the plant I told you about. Well, when he finally got up, and he didn't sleep as long as he normally does, he said he had some business to attend to and left. That's when I came over here."

C.J. nodded and sipped from her tea, anxious for Amber to hurry it up and get to the point. "So what happened that made you think he's trying to kill you?"

"He came home with a gun and pointed it at me and Frank Jr."

C.J. sat up. "Tell me more, what happened, exactly."

"I was fixing lunch when he came tearing into the house. He told me he needed me to keep alert, that 'they' were close and watching."

"Who is 'they'?"

Amber shook her head. "I don't know. He won't ever say. Whenever I ask him about it, he just says the less I know, the safer I'll be."

"The gun," C.J. prompted.

"Frank Jr. was in his high chair while I was mixing up some tuna salad. Frankie came out of the bedroom with this big steel gun. He aimed it at me and Frank Jr. I said, 'Frankie, what are you doing with that thing? You might hurt somebody.' "

Amber shifted the baby in her arms and held him close. "Then he told me to shut up and sit down. I sat on the sofa just like here and he was in the chair about where you are."

Amber started crying again. C.J. handed her a tissue. "What happened then, Amber?"

"He was going on and on about no place being safe and he had to think. I don't know what all else he said because I just kept my eyes glued to that gun he was waving around. Frank Jr. started crying and he told me to shut the kid up. I gave Frank Jr. a bottle and put him in bed. Frankie told me to hurry it up and get back in the living room."

Amber looked down at her son and kissed his forehead. "I was so scared I didn't know what to do. My hands were shaking, my legs were shaking. I didn't want to do anything that would set Frankie off, not as long as he had that gun in his hand. When I got back to the sofa, he pushed me down and put the gun to my head. I heard it click like he was getting ready to shoot me. I was crying and begging him not to kill me. He told me not to move, not to even breathe and that when he got back I better be there."

"What'd he do then?"

"He picked up a small bag and left. I didn't see him again until a few minutes ago. He came in and was acting like nothing had happened. His clothes were rumpled up and he hadn't shaved. I was still sitting on the sofa. I had Frank Jr. in my arms. I didn't move, just like he told me, except to get Frank Jr. when he woke up and started crying. I sat there all night scared out of my mind that Frankie was gonna come back and kill me."

"You should have called the police, Amber."

The young mother shook her head. "No police. Frankie says the police lie and can't protect you."

"Yeah, well, someone needs to protect you from

Frankie." C.J. got up and pulled out a telephone book. "Amber, I'm going to try to find some help for you, a safe house." She flipped to the blue pages in the directory. "There ought to be a shelter around here somewhere. If not, I can get you to Winston-Salem. Or maybe Charlotte. That's a bigger city and . . ."

"Jan, I can't leave him," Amber said.

C.J. looked up from the directory. "What do you mean?"

"He's my husband. I can't leave him."

"You just sat here and told me he's threatened you. What do you mean you won't leave?"

"He needs my help," Amber whispered.

"You need help, Amber. What makes you think that the next time he won't kill you?"

The tears started down her face again. "I can't leave him, Jan. He needs me."

Frustrated with Amber, C.J. decided to forgo working in her garden for a walk. Maybe she could get her head cleared. She slipped her housekey and a few dollars in the pocket of her jeans then slipped out her front door. Still light out, the summer evening was perfect for a stroll. She shut her gate and decided to head toward town.

Amber had refused to go anywhere except back home to Frankie. C.J. had hated covering domestic violence stories back at the newspaper because what many women did was the same thing Amber did—rationalized away the sick behavior of the men who assaulted them. Amber, just like so many other women, needed counseling and a safe haven, not a return for more punishment.

C.J.'s pace was slow, meandering. She waved as she passed people on their front porches, kids playing in the street. She wasn't out to exercise and had no real purpose except to enjoy the evening. Except her thoughts wouldn't let her. She worried about Amber.

Then it hit her. Wesley! Frankie Baldwin. She paused and thought about the two men. It all fit. Amber's husband was probably in the Marshals Protected Witness Security Program. Amber had described constant moves. The couple had crisscrossed the country, and, according to Amber, the Mafia was after Frankie. From the little she knew about the U.S. Marshals Service, dealing with people hiding from the Mob was one of their specialties. Wes had to be in this small town on some sort of assignment. Serenity Falls was too off the map to justify anything else. She'd just met his family and they all lived in West Virginia. Could there be some other reason for his presence here?

She started walking again, layering the pieces of the puzzle over each other just like she did with the news stories she used to write. One action led to reaction, which led to action, and so forth. When woven together, the pieces created a tapestry that, depending on the merits of the case, would land her on the front page, on a section front, or as one story did, on a platform accepting a Pulitzer Prize.

One part didn't fit though, the puzzle piece at an odd angle. People in the witness protection program got new identities, new names, and from what C.J. knew, they weren't supposed to talk about the past. Amber had never given any indication that she or Frankie had had other names. And she knew their background, at least their background according to Amber: They'd met in Las Vegas, then moved to Florida and now North Carolina. Maybe the pressure of the constant moves was getting to Amber and she needed to unload on someone.

C.J. filed the information away. Just because the puzzle piece didn't fit right now, it didn't mean the odd piece was something to discard.

When she looked up she was in the center of town. It just took about five minutes to get there from her house. Main Street bustled with activity, as far as small-town bustling went. Traffic was pretty heavy and all going in the same direction—toward the old armory for Saturday night bingo. C.J. thought about going, then discarded the idea. A room full of cigarette smoke, conversations, and people yelling didn't quite appeal to her now. But a chocolate croissant did. She hoped Bettina's Bakery was still open.

She stopped at a corner then stepped into the street to get to the side where the bakery was. She waved to someone who waved to her in one of the slow-moving cars.

Tires screeched.

C.J. whirled around and instinctively jumped toward the center of the street. A blue sedan whizzed by in the opposite direction of the traffic.

Her breathing came hard and fast. She clutched her chest and stared at the place where she had been standing. A second or two longer and she'd have been hit by that careless driver.

"Hey, lady, you okay?"

C.J. turned and looked at the man who called to her from his car window.

She nodded. "It just scared me."

The man shook his head. "I tell you. These young kids get their driver's licenses and act like they own the road."

He waved for her to safely finish crossing the street.

She did, then waved at him as he slowly made his way down the street in the bingo traffic. C.J. looked in the direction the blue car had gone then shook her head. "You'd think this was Baltimore."

Another block put her at Bettina's. C.J.'s mouth dropped open. The façade of the bakery was completely knocked in. Small bits of concrete and glass littered the sidewalk. Orange construction cones and yellow tape cordoned off the area.

C.J. peered through the front door that remained in tact. Bettina saw her and waved her in.

With one more look at the front of the store, C.J. went into the bakery.

"Bettina, what in the world happened? We were just here yesterday."

The chubby baker shook her head. "It wasn't too long after you left. I was in the back fixing to decorate a couple of cakes for the Garden Club's annual picnic when there was a crash. The building shook. I heard glass breaking. I thought we were having an earthquake or something. I came out to see what had happened and there was a car, big as day, sitting in the place where my front window used to be."

C.J. followed Bettina to take a closer look at the mess. C.J. picked up what used to be the plastic top tier of an elaborate wedding cake. The groom was missing a leg and his top hat.

"Don't even bother with that mess, Miz Langley. The insurance man just left. It's gonna cost a pretty penny to get this fixed up."

"What happened?"

"Well, that's the darnedest thing. It didn't take me but a minute to get out here from the workshop in back but by the time I did, whoever was in the car that crashed through the window was gone. The place was a wreck, the car was still running with the driver's side open."

"Do you know whose car it was?"

Bettina shook her head. "Police are checking but so far they've come up empty."

C.J. didn't believe in coincidences. Everything in life

happened for a reason and all events were in some way connected. Did this constitute two more pieces to the same puzzle or a separate but interlocking, interrelated puzzle? She thought about the car that had almost run her down a few minutes ago. Could this have something to do with Frankie and Amber Baldwin? It seemed far-fetched, but stranger things had happened.

"Do you know Amber Baldwin?"

Bettina looked up from her perusal of the damage. "Scared looking woman with a toddler?"

C.J. nodded.

"She comes in here for one-eighth of a pound of chocolate-covered strawberries every now and then. I usually slip an extra one or two in her bag. She always looks so pitiful. I just want to help her. What put you in mind of Miz Baldwin?"

"The hard pretzels on the counter looked like something the baby would like." The lie out of C.J.'s mouth came easy. Too easy.

She blinked back sudden tears. After carefully guarding herself and her actions, how could she so easily slip back into the persona of the person she wanted to forget?

It's only been a month, C.J., the voice of her conscious told her. *It'll take longer than that to break habits and behavior that you've cultivated over more than a decade.*

But C.J. didn't pay attention to that voice because she knew who and what the real culprit was. Wesley Donovan.

"Miz Langley, you all right?"

C.J. looked up. She'd just about forgotten where she was. She nodded to Bettina. "I'm fine. Do you need any help around here? Is there something I can do for you?"

Bettina shook her head. "Nope. I'm just here trying to go about my regular business. The contractor can't come until Monday. Mr. Anderson over at the hardware store is gonna secure a tarp over this in," she glanced at her watch, " 'bout half an hour or so. Thanks for offering, though. Can I get you anything?"

C.J. grinned. "I came for a chocolate croissant."

"You're in luck."

Bettina went to fetch the pastry. C.J. turned to assess the damage again.

It reminded her of her life. She'd taken a wrecking ball to her own façade and was starting over. Except Wesley Donovan had stepped onto the stripped canvas and was wreaking havoc on the carefully plotted and meticulously serene landscape she'd created.

He didn't leave her feeling cheap or emotionally shattered like all the other half-developed relationships she'd had over the years. He left her wanting more, always more.

Like an addict.

"Here you go," Bettina said, coming up with a pastry bag.

C.J. pulled money from her blue jeans pocket and handed it to the baker.

Bettina shook her head. "No charge."

C.J. tried to hand her money again but Bettina folded her arms over her ample bosom and shook her head. "Everything's free today to friends."

C.J. laughed. "Okay. If you need me to help with anything just let me know."

After leaving the bakery, C.J. picked pieces off a croissant—Bettina had put two in the bag—and thought about Wesley. She thought about him being an addiction and came to a conclusion as she slowly walked down Main Street.

She could yield as she'd always done in the past, capitulate to the desires and demands of her body. Or she could be strong, stay focused on her recovery goals. The only way to do that would be to get away from the temptation. Her will power was nil. She recognized that character fault for what it was and just went on with her life. She was the spoiled baby girl in a very well-to-do family. As far back as she could remember she'd always gotten what she wanted. If her parents said no to something she wanted, she just worked harder and longer to attain it. That's how she'd gotten her first BMW at seventeen years old.

All of her friends thought that rich, little C.J. Mayview had asked her parents for a Beamer and had gotten the car lickety split. But Genevieve and Robinson Mayview had said no sixteen-year-old with a fresh driver's license *needed* a BMW. If she wanted a car to drive, her parents said, she could drive the station wagon that sat unused in the garage. C.J. had turned her nose up at the car then gave up Friday, Saturday, and even some Sunday night dates in favor of extra baby-sitting and housesitting jobs. With the extra work and the money she already had in her savings account, within a year she had enough to buy the used Beamer she wanted.

Proud of her accomplishment, she'd taken snapshots of the car and sent them to her brother who was in college at the time. Robinson sent her a card telling her that he was proud of her. She still had the card. And even though she was now a grown woman, she still wanted her big brother to be proud of her.

C.J. wanted to be proud of herself. Then she thought about how easily she'd shed her convictions and joined Wes for his quick trip to West Virginia. She couldn't ditch all her hard work, all the soul-searching she'd done so she could be the person she'd been three months ago.

When she looked up, she found herself at the end of the sidewalk. In front of her, just across the street, the armory's parking lot was jammed with the cars and

trucks of Saturday night bingo players. To her right
was the last store on the block.

She put the remaining bit of the chocolate croissant
in her mouth and stepped up to the store window. She
swallowed the pastry and scrunched the top of the bag
in her hand. Her mouth watered, but she knew it had
nothing to do with the sweet treat she'd consumed or
the remaining one.

The business at the end of the street was a liquor
store.

Fifty-five days. She'd been clean and sober for fifty-five
days. As she stared in the window, she got a mental image of Eileen Donovan. C.J. had never been a sloppy
drunk. Like a lot of journalists, she drank too much.
Her favorite after-work hangout was a sports bar most
folks from her newsroom congregated to after hours.
She'd never gotten a DUI. No one had ever had to drive
her home or call a cab for her, but C.J. knew she'd been
dependent on the liquid courage, the sharp smooth
edge of the liquid fire to soothe her at the end of a
rough day. She'd had a lot of rough days.

Like a child longing after a mountain of toys in a
Christmas store window display, C.J. stared in the window of the liquor store. For just a moment she thought
to move on, away from the temptation.

"You can run but liquor will always be in your face,"
she said aloud. What better way to prove she was capable of handling alcohol than to have it readily available and still say no?

"You're strong," she said. "You can do this."

Determined to prove to herself that she was indeed
strong and that she could overcome and pass this test,
she pushed the door open. Minutes later she departed
with a small brown bag. It held a bottle of her favorite
smooth Kentucky bourbon.

Twenty

Margaret Shelley tired of the cat and mouse game. It was time to stop dallying around and get down to business. Her ploy hadn't worked quite as effectively as she'd planned. That sexy Wesley slipped out of town on her. But he was back now. And Margaret was ready. She sashayed into the dining room, the open splits on her car wash style dress showing flashes of shapely leg. Her makeup, expertly applied, was flawless.

Margaret frowned. The place where Wesley sat at the table was empty.

Miss Clara Ann harumped. Garrison glanced up, then scrambled from his seat to assist Margaret.

"Girl, you gots the most awful timing I done ever seen in my life," Miss Clara Ann said. "If you all prettied up for that there Wesley, you done missed him again. He come in, got himself a quick bite, cleaned up, and headed back on out the door."

Margaret stomped her foot in exasperation.

"Miss Margaret, may I have the singular honor of seating you next to me?"

She rolled her eyes.

"How long ago, Aunt Clara?"

"Oh, 'bout ten, fifteen minutes."

Margaret's shoulders slumped. Garrison held out a chair for her. She gave him a weak smile.

"I'll be right back," she said.

There was no need in chancing that she'd spill something on the expensive dress. Margaret dashed back upstairs to her room, took off the dress, scrubbed her face clean, and pulled on a pair of baggy gray sweatpants. She tugged on a raggedy T-shirt and slipped her feet into a pair of rubber flip-flops. Figuring that her bad timing served her right for not focusing on business, she stomped downstairs.

When she arrived back in the dining room, Miss Clara Ann took one look at her and laughed out loud. "Margaret, you are something else. You trying too hard, baby."

Margaret tried not to let her exasperation and frustration show as the artist Garrison helped her into her seat. Then he passed her a platter of meat loaf. Margaret sighed as she selected a slice for herself.

Half an hour later, the small group at the dinner table greeted Wesley when he poked his head in the door. Margaret's mouth dropped open. Miss Clara Ann's bark of laughter filled the room. Even Garrison grinned.

"What's the joke?" Wes asked.

"Missed opportunities," Garrison replied.

Wes shrugged, bid the group "Good night" and went to his room.

"Don't either of you say a word," Margaret threatened.

Garrison and Miss Clara Ann shared a look and smiled.

C.J. unpacked the overnight bag she'd dropped in her bedroom earlier in the day. The champagne teddy caught her eye and made her pause. Lifting the delicate garment from the bag, she took it to the mirror over her bureau.

She held the lingerie up to her chest and imagined how Wesley would respond if he saw her in it. Reflective now, she went to her bathroom, teddy still in hand, and started drawing a bath. Sprinkling lavender and rose bath salts in the water, she watched the tub fill and the water swirl. She ran the silky smooth material of the teddy over her cheek and wondered what it would be like to live on memories.

She'd never wondered what love felt like. It was, in C.J.'s opinion, an emotion for fools. But now she knew what it felt like. And she knew love was something she couldn't afford to feel.

"Telling him goodbye is going to be the hardest thing you've ever done," she said out loud.

But you'll have good memories, glorious memories, she reminded herself. And besides, he never has to know how you really feel.

Turning to face the mirror in the bathroom, C.J. stroked the piece of lingerie then folded it and placed it on the vanity. With both hands on the vanity she leaned forward and critically studied her face.

"You look old and tired, C.J. Mayview, not young and in love." She thought about the fake name she'd been running around with. Jan Langley. Ja'Niece Langley. No one had ever called her Jan or Ja'Niece. No one had even ever called her by her first name, Cassandra.

"You're supposed to be in love and the man you love doesn't even know your name." C.J. shook her head in disgust, at herself more than anything else.

She brushed her teeth then turned off the running water in the tub. Coming out of her clothes, she left them in a pile on the floor then slipped into the soothing bath. It had been a long, emotionally exhausting day. She thought about Eileen Donovan. She thought about Mama Lo Kensington. She thought about Amber and about Bettina, about Wesley and his brother Marcus Kensington, about children forced to grow up before their time, about violence and fear and about love that was so often intricately woven into the fabric of destructive behavior.

C.J. sighed, closed her eyes and sank deeper into the water. Sometime later, she woke with a start. She shivered from the cold water. With her toes she unstopped the tub then got out, dried herself off and moisturized and powdered her body. The teddy went into the top drawer, the dirty clothes she dropped in a hamper then fell into the bed. Her sleep was fitful and troubled.

In his own room at Miss Clara Ann's place, Wesley stared at the ceiling for a long time. Hours later, he closed his eyes and eventually slept.

C.J. slept late, much later than usual. But when she woke up Sunday morning, she felt like a new person. After dressing and grabbing a bite to eat, she called Amber. The young mother assured her that all was well even though she couldn't stay on the telephone to chat. Refusing to let the frustration of Amber's situation ruin her day, C.J. counted the hours until she'd see Wes for dinner.

With about eight hours to kill she figured she could get the sofa reupholstering project underway. But instead she opted to putter in her garden. It was too beautiful a day to stay cooped up in the house. The rich soil and the process of helping something grow had a soothing effect on her psyche. Four short days ago she'd met Wesley Donovan. He'd managed to wreak havoc on her senses and turned her carefully orchestrated world upside down. She would be able to put things into perspective while she gardened.

She made a pitcher of herbal iced tea then picked up her gardening gloves and the boom box. She tuned the radio to a cool jazz station then went to inspect and try to resurrect the petunias the toddler Frank Jr. had trampled.

Humming along with the jazzy tunes on the radio, she worked all afternoon on the living things that grounded her. After heaving fifty-pound bags of mulch and ringing every tree in the backyard with the stuff, she drank long and deep from the pitcher of tea. Then, deciding to rest for a while, she sank into the sturdy hammock hoisted between two of the older trees. Before long, she drifted to sleep.

That's how and where Wesley found her.

He looked at the sleeping woman and smiled. He didn't know what her yard looked like before but she obviously spent a lot of time out here. Protected witnesses were strongly encouraged to steer clear of their previous occupations once they secured their new identities. So he doubted that Jan Langley had been a gardener or florist in her former life. He had a pretty good inkling of what she'd been though.

He'd spent the better part of the previous night analyzing everything he knew about her, everything she'd said and had not said. She'd admitted, bluntly, that she had been with men, lots of men. He couldn't particularly hold that against her, not when he himself had been with lots of women. The last thing he needed or wanted in his life was a naive virgin who would have to be schooled every little step of the way.

The only lessons Jan needed were in how to cast a fishing rod. Wes grinned.

She shifted in the hammock. He watched her move,

sensuous even in slumber. His smile faded as the reality of his situation hit him. In a worst case scenario, he was falling for a former prostitute or the ex-girlfriend of a drug lord or Mafia boss. They'd eventually stop using condoms and would have to have regular HIV and AIDS testing done. She could very well be on the run for the rest of her life, constantly hiding, always looking over her shoulder. While most people in the Witness Security Program followed the rules and lived out their lives with just one new identity, some, like the other one he was working with here in Serenity Falls, had to constantly move. Sometimes through no fault of their own.

Wes thought about that life and wondered if he'd be able to deal with it. He'd finish up this case, turn in his resignation, and then get to live out his life with Jan.

Was it worth it?

He studied her. Jan was a beautiful woman. But beauty faded over time. Would he love her when she was old, if she got sick, if she put on fifty pounds, if an old lover tried to claim her?

"Yes."

Wes blinked, momentarily surprised by his answer. Then, it settled in him, warm and tender, a realization he'd never thought he'd have.

"Hmmm?"

He'd awakened her but her eyes weren't open. Jan turned again in the hammock and almost rolled out of the netting. Wes was there though, to catch her, support her; like he wanted to do for a long, long time to come.

"Wes?"

"It's me, sweetheart."

Sweetheart? He had never called anyone that. If falling in love meant turning mushy, he'd have to guard

against that part. There were few things as disgusting
as watching two adults cooing at each other.

Jan rubbed her eyes and swung her legs over the
edge of the hammock. He held her around the waist
as she rose.

"Hi. You're early. I think. I fell asleep."

"Hi, yourself, beautiful."

Jan ran a hand over her face and grubby clothes.
"I'm more a mess than anything else. I got everything
done though. For now."

Wes held her about the waist with one hand and
with the other he smoothed a knuckle down her
cheek.

"You're beautiful to me." His mouth lowered to
hers.

But Jan turned her head and twisted away from him.
"No, Wes."

He let her go.

"What do you mean 'no'?"

She stepped away. "No as in we shouldn't do this."

"Have dinner?"

Jan huffed then folded her arms. "This, this sex
thing between us. I let you talk me into . . . no, I ignored my own better judgment and went with you to
West Virginia but that doesn't mean I've changed my
mind about us. I can't afford to be with you, Wesley.
Can't you understand that?"

He could. She was probably having the same doubts
and worries he harbored himself. But he also knew
how to overcome those problems. Every relationship
wasn't like the one between his mother and father.
Mama Lo and Mr. Kensington had shown him how a
loving couple interacted. They'd had problems but
every couple did.

Then he paused as a thought hit him.

"It's Eileen isn't it?"

C.J. turned from picking up her gloves. "Eileen? What does she have to do with this?"

"Nothing. That's my point," he said.

She shook her head. "Wes, let's just have a nice dinner and then we can go our separate ways. Okay?"

No. It wasn't okay. But he wasn't going to argue the matter. He had a better plan. He'd show her that she was wrong. He'd prove to her that they could overcome their pasts and make a future together. And he would start right now.

He smiled. "I'm going to impress you in that kitchen."

She grinned. "Oh, really? Well, I'm going to go get cleaned up so I don't smell like soil and mulch at the table. This better be good, too. I'm hungry."

Wes helped her carry gardening tools to the porch, then hefted up the brown paper bags of groceries and supplies he'd left there and followed her in the house.

She didn't know it but he even had a necktie to change into for dinner. If she knew how much he hated ties, she'd know how serious he was about her. Before this night was over, he planned to make sure she knew exactly how he felt.

C.J. closed the door to her bedroom and leaned against it. Her resolve had a tendency to melt whenever Wes Donovan was near. She couldn't think straight, half the time she could barely get her well-reasoned thoughts out in a semi-articulate manner.

Wesley was just the latest in a long string of headed-no-where, for-a-good-time-call-me relationships.

Stop lying to yourself, her conscience scolded.

She pushed herself from the door and stripped off her grubby sneakers and grass-stained jeans. By the time she made it to her tiny closet, she was naked ex-

cept for the panties she wore. She looked in the closet
and for the first time since moving to North Carolina,
she wished she hadn't been so rash in giving away all
her nice clothes. She'd carted off boxes upon boxes
of things to the Salvation Army and a women's shelter.

With her new life, she knew she'd never have need
for the sequined dresses and matching high-heeled
slings she had needed to attend country club events
with her parents. All that frivolous stuff that her
mother insisted she own got shipped to the needy. She
wasn't going to report another story from City Hall
and had no need for suits and blouses. She'd held
onto her jeans, all of her expensive lingerie, and one
or two semi-dressy outfits.

The black sheath would have to do. She quickly
pressed the dress she'd taken to West Virginia but
hadn't worn. A pair of sheer black hose and the black
high-heeled pumps would have to be it. She then studied what she'd kept of her jewelry and selected a jazzy
brooch that she would wear just off her shoulder. Her
dinner outfit selected, C.J. made her way to the shower.
With the water on as hot as she could stand it, she put
a shower cap on and got under the spray. She let the
hot water cascade over her and she rehearsed what
she'd tell Wes at dinner.

Basically, she needed a relationship about as much
as she needed a hole in the head. She'd tell him about
her addictions to stress and to work. She'd tell him
about winning the Pulitzer, about her years of reporting and living by her wits and her love of journalism,
of the writing prizes she'd won and things in her life
she was proud of.

He'd have to understand why this sojourn, this period of self-discovery and healing was so important to
her—so very vital to her existence and her peace of
mind.

All she'd ever wanted was peace.

C.J. held her face in the water and let it beat her up. The hot stings of water hit her like so many pin pricks. She took it until she winced, then turned around and let the soothing stream massage her back.

Wes had been rude to that reporter the other day, she thought. But she remembered as she reached for a loofah sponge and lathered it up with scented body wash, he was after all a Deputy Marshal, a cop. Cops and reporters had a love/hate relationship when it came to information. Wes had implied but hadn't confirmed that he was working on a case, so being in the local newspaper, small as it apparently was, was probably the last thing he wanted.

C.J. could tell him about notoriety and dealing with the press. It could hurt sometimes—a lot. She knew that firsthand when she inadvertently found herself in the news. Someone had implied that she got a great front page story about a welfare program when her brother leaked her the information. The charge had been ludicrous, of course, but the damage to her credibility and to her relationship with her brother had already been done by the time everything was cleared up.

She sighed as she lathered her legs. Then she frowned and reached for her razor. She quickly shaved her legs and arms then proceeded with her shower.

One bad experience with the media was all some people needed to forever bad mouth the entire profession. Look at what Mama Lo Kensington had said at the dinner table Friday: "Ain't interested in them lies those media people always telling."

C.J. turned so the shower spray would rinse her body. She then moisturized herself with her favorite body moisturizer. When she stepped out of the shower and dried off, she was surprised to discover how much time had passed.

"Better hurry or he'll be in here knocking the door down."

She waved her hair up. C.J. had never been one for a lot of makeup. A touch of color at her cheeks and a bit at her lips finished off her face.

At the bureau, one of the pieces of furniture that had come with the house, she reached for a pair of silky panties and matching bra. She paused when her gaze fell on the champagne-colored teddy Wes had bought at Wal-Mart. She turned and glanced at her closed bedroom door.

"He'll never know."

Smiling to herself, she donned the teddy then opted for sheer black thigh-high stockings instead of the pantyhose.

Her mother's advice came to her as she secured the hose at her thigh: "You can look good and feel good about yourself even if you're facing a bad situation. No one has to know what you have on under your clothes." C.J. smiled as she thought of her mother.

She reached for a bottle of cologne in the same earthy scent as her bath moisturizer, then, at the last minute, changed her mind, opting instead for the perfume of the same essence. After putting on her dress and shoes, C.J. stood in front of the bureau mirror wishing the house had a full-length mirror. She smoothed her hands over her hips. The form-fitting sheath hugged her shape. It was one of her favorites because of its versatility. Tonight, she'd dressed it up.

And tonight, she'd tell Wes Donovan goodbye. She'd worry about getting through tomorrow later on. One day at a time would be the way she'd deal with this.

Funny, the prospect of goodbye had never hurt before, she thought. She had embraced just about every previous farewell with a joyful relief, not this unforgiving ache.

She sighed.

"You can't have him, C.J. Not that way. Be grateful for the pleasure you've found in his arms and let it go."

She sighed again. "Just let it go, girl."

With that advice to herself, she turned the light off in her bedroom and went to see what Wes had cooked up.

"I hope whatever you made is good because . . ."

C.J.'s voice faded away to nothing and her mouth fell open. Wes had transformed her tiny dining area into a romantic setting for two.

The beat up table she wanted to strip down and refinish was covered with a pristine white lace tablecloth. A low arrangement of fragrant yellow and red tulips served as centerpiece. C.J. knew she hadn't brought any china with her to North Carolina, yet two beautiful place settings adorned the table.

"Where? How?" she got out.

From the kitchen with his back turned to her Wes answered. "Did I forget to tell you that magic is also one of my specialties?"

C.J. smiled. "Yes. You forgot that part."

He pulled something from the oven and placed it on the counter on top of folded dishcloths. When he stepped around the counter, C.J. looked at him and her mouth dropped open for the second time. He wore a crisp white shirt with a blue and gray tie. Her gaze traveled down the rest of him and took in the dress slacks and shoes. Either he'd had the clothes tucked in one of those bags or she'd been so busy staring at his face earlier that she'd missed the rest of him.

He cleaned up real well, but with a bit of wonder

that actually surprised her, she realized she liked him better dressed in bad boy black. With the way he looked now, like a newspaper editor or publisher about to meet with stockholders, it would be too easy for her to forget that the man standing in front of her was the very one who threatened the foundation of her existence.

He lifted a suit jacket from the back of a chair at the table and shrugged into it. "You look fabulous."

C.J. swallowed. "Thank you. So do you."

Wes advanced a step. C.J. retreated two steps.

"Actually," he said, "you look better than fabulous. You outshine the stars in the heavens."

Oh, boy. "Wes . . . there's something we need to get clear about. Something I need to tell you."

Wes reached for her arm and pulled her into his embrace. "Save the serious talk for later. Right now, I just want you to relax and enjoy the evening."

He hummed a slow tuneless melody and slowly twirled her about in the small space. C.J. thought he was bending to kiss her but he instead smoothed one large hand across and down her hairline. His touch light, his voice low, C.J. felt her resolve melting away. He slow danced her to her chair then helped her into it. Brushing a light kiss on her cheek, he left her and went to the kitchen.

C.J. took a deep breath.

"The table is beautiful, Wes."

She was dying to know where and how he'd come about this stuff: crystal stemware, white china rimmed in a gold leaf motif, linen napkins. While all were staples in her former life, she'd abandoned most of the evidence of conspicuous consumption for the less complicated, healthier lifestyle she'd adopted in Serenity Falls.

He smiled and held up a bottle of wine. "Would you like a glass?"

"No, thank you," she said, and meant it. She thought about the bourbon she'd bought and made a mental note to throw it out. She was strong, but she realized now that she didn't have to have temptation in the house to prove that she was strong.

Wes simply nodded. "I've already put water on for your tea. Dinner will be ready in about five minutes."

A few minutes later he placed before her marinated chicken breasts, almond glazed baby carrots, and au gratin potatoes. C.J. opened her mouth in question.

Wes leaned over her, placed a quick kiss on her lips. "Before you even ask the question, the answer is Mama Lo. She made sure all her boys knew how to fend for themselves in the kitchen. There's one thing I haven't quite mastered though. I hope you don't mind my substitute."

"What's that?"

"I never quite got the hang of rolls and biscuits. I make a mean pan bread though."

C.J. got up and went to the kitchen. It wasn't trashed, but there was evidence that real cooking had been going on, an open box of cornmeal, brown sugar, an opened package of almonds. She looked in the waste can for the tell-tale red and white box of a Kentucky Fried Chicken restaurant or foam takeout trays from a restaurant.

Wes chuckled.

C.J. looked up at him and grinned. "You amaze me."

Wes grabbed a potholder and overturned the pan bread from a small cast iron skillet onto a small napkin-covered plate.

"Dinner is served."

C.J. looked at him and shook her head. "You're really something else."

"So are you."

They shared a quiet meal together, talking about inconsequential things, getting to know each other's likes and dislikes. As each minute ticked by, C.J. found it more and more difficult to bring up her concerns about their relationship. How could she tell him she couldn't see him again when she felt she was being slowly, deliberately and delicately seduced into submission. She'd never seen this side of Wes, gentle, loving, ever considerate of her every wish and need. There was no way he could know she'd actually been missing some of the trappings of her other life. She hadn't even dared admit that to herself.

When they finished dinner, Wes cleared their plates. "Dessert's coming right up."

"You're spoiling me, Donovan," she said.

"That's what I'd like to do for a long time to come," he answered quietly.

C.J. looked up and caught her breath. He was there, so close she could see the whiskers from his sexy five o'clock shadow, so close she could pick up the faint citrus scent of his aftershave. So close she could feel his breath mingle with her own. Heat swirled in her abdomen as desire snaked through her. But she had to be strong.

She kept telling herself there was nothing special about this man, nothing out of the ordinary that made him different from any other man she'd been with.

Nothing except the way he makes you feel, the warmth he brings to you, and the fire you share, her heart's voice challenged.

C.J. closed her eyes. His kiss, light, easy, and flirtatious as it was, held an undercurrent of barely leashed passion. She knew he wanted her just as much as she wanted him. He pulled away then, and when she heard a soft rustle she knew he'd stepped away. She sighed. "Wesley, there are some things I need to tell you."

"Not now," he murmured. "Open your eyes."

She obeyed the husky command. The sight before her was a treat to behold. Wes sat close by holding the tip of a strawberry dipped in chocolate at her lips. Not sure which she wanted to nibble on more, the man or the chocolate, she eyed both with equal amounts of desire. Each promised to be sinfully delicious. Without thinking, she captured his hand in hers then opened her mouth and bit into the sweet delicacy.

She licked first her lips then his fingers. Wesley cleared his throat.

"I cheated on dessert. I stopped by Bettina's. She said that next to her brownies, your favorite is chocolate swirl cheesecake."

C.J. followed his gaze and noticed the slice of cheesecake garnished with sliced strawberries on a small plate with a small bowl of uncut strawberries beside it.

She smiled and ran his finger over the contour of her lips.

"Jan, I'm trying to be a gentleman tonight."

"No you're not," she said. "You're trying to seduce me."

It was his turn to smile. "Is it working?"

Twenty-one

"I think you know the answer to that question."

He fed her the rest of the juicy fruit. "I want to hear your answer."

C.J. swallowed the strawberry. "I think you're a man who knows what he wants and goes after it."

He smiled. "You're right about that." His gaze dipped to the scoop neckline of her bodice. "Did I tell you you're putting a hurtin' on that dress?"

"Not in those words."

He cut a small piece of cheesecake with the tines of a fork and held it to her mouth. Accepting the morsel and the fork with a smile and a "Mmmm," C.J. released his hand long enough to slice off a bit of the creamy dessert and offer him a taste.

He shook his head, took the fork from her and fed her the cheesecake.

"But . . ." she protested. Her eyes widened when she remembered. Wes was allergic to chocolate. That explained the bowl of plain strawberries. She took the fork, dropped it on the table and wrapped her arms around his neck. "Oh, Wes."

The man cared enough about her wants and desires to buy and then feed her chocolate, the one thing that he had to deny himself.

She rained tiny kisses along his face then plucked a piece of fruit from the bowl. She put the wide end in her mouth and offered to him the juicy tip. They nibbled until their lips met.

A small giggle escaped when a tiny trail of juice from the succulent fruit escaped her mouth. Wes caught it with one well-defined finger then brought that finger to her mouth.

Fire raced through C.J. Wes moaned.

And then they were standing, holding each other, slender arms draped around broad shoulders, her soft woman's body pressed close to his tall, hard one. Their dessert forgotten, Wes first kissed the tip of her nose, then her eyes. When his mouth finally slanted over hers, C.J. pulled him closer and moaned the satisfaction she found.

His tongue danced over hers first lightly, then with a passion that made her knees buckle. Wes supported her.

He tore his mouth from hers long enough to bury himself in her neck. "God, woman, you make me burn."

Too dazed to speak, too involved with the way she was feeling, light and airy, explosive, hot, hungry, C.J. simply threw her head back to give him better access, then slid her hands over his back. She loved the muscular strength of him, the honed physique that let her know he cared about his own physical well being.

And then she stopped thinking at all.

Wesley's tongue rimmed her ear and she let out a shuddering exclamation . . . of need, of fire and desire.

Wes moved and she followed. When he made to sit on the sofa she stopped him.

"Not there. Bad spring."

"Um hmm."

She wasn't sure if he comprehended what she meant to say but he shifted and settled in one of the chairs. With an "Oomph!" she landed in his lap.

C.J. grinned. "Hope I didn't break anything."

She felt his deep chuckle before the sound issued forth. He ran a hand down her thigh. "It'll take more than that . . ." his voice trailed off.

His hand paused then inched back up her thigh over the sheer hose. He eased the short hem of her dress up a bit.

"Mercy." It was a curse and an exultation.

C.J.'s breath came in short gasps. "Wes?"

His hand eased up her thigh exposing the lacy edges of her stockings. "No garter belt?"

She shook her head. "They stay up by themselves."

"Not if I can help it."

His large hand left the exploration of her thighs and legs just long enough to turn her face to his. Their lips met in a fierce battle of need. She wrapped her arms around his neck.

A crash, almost like an explosion ripped through C.J.

Then the lights went out.

"What the . . . ?"

She sat up. "It sounded like something crashed in the yard." If the lights hadn't shut off at the same time, C.J. would have sworn the earth moved when Wes kissed her.

He stood her up. Wes went to the back door while C.J. headed to the front door.

"I don't see anything," he said.

"Oh, my God. Oh, my God."

She snatched the door open and Wes dashed to where she stood. Street lights were out all up and down the street, but clearly visible in the early evening light was a small plane and the path of destruction leading to where the plane precariously balanced on its nose in the front lawn of a house three doors down.

In a sprint, Wes shot out the door. C.J. ran back in the house kicking off her high heels. She called 911, changed into some flats, and looked for a slim reporter's notebook. Adrenaline pumped through her. She quick-scanned the counter, the coffee table. She knew there were at least a dozen of the things around, she always kept some at home just in case she needed to hit the street from home.

Then she stopped. Who she was, what she was, and where she was hit her with a staggering force. She sighed. It would take longer than a month to break habits ingrained for so long that they were reflexive actions. "You're not a reporter any more, C.J.," she said aloud. "You don't carry press credentials and don't have to call news in to the city desk. You don't have any reporters' notebooks around here, either. You live in North Carolina, not Baltimore."

She glanced around her house, taking in the small kitchen, the tiny dining area, the sofa that needed to be repaired. "Definitely not Baltimore."

The pretty table with the cheesecake and strawberries reminded her of the other important thing. "You have to let him go."

The shrill cry of a siren startled her. C.J. ran to the front door, and like the rest of the neighborhood, gathered at the crash scene.

The small-engine plane rested in a front lawn less than three feet from the side of a house twice the size of C.J.'s. Sod kicked up and whacked off shrubbery gave testimony to the plane's path. Downed power lines trailed behind it.

Mothers held back curious children. Two police cruisers rolled up and officers shooed people away from the power lines. From where she stood with the gathering crowd, C.J. could see Wes and another man helping the man in the plane.

A fire truck, ambulance, and hazmat van all screeched to a stop at the same time. Red, blue, and white flashing lights backlit the crash scene.

Someone knocked into C.J.'s side. "Ow!"

When she turned, she saw someone shoving through the crowd and toward the street. C.J. frowned. The guy had either elbowed her or hit her with something. Shaking her head, she put a hand over her side where pain still throbbed and turned her attention back to the crash.

A shadow of memory made her turn back to the fleeing man but the crush of people all clamoring for a better view was all she saw.

First someone tried to run her over, now this. Serenity Falls, North Carolina, was more dangerous than Baltimore.

And there sure was a lot of weird stuff going on for such a small place. But then she had to admit, cars crashed and people had heart attacks all the time.

Almost an hour later, the crowd began to disperse. The ambulance, long gone, had taken off for the hospital. Wes found C.J.

"Hey."

She wrapped an arm around his waist. "Hey, yourself. You sure you weren't a dragon slayer or a knight of the realm in a former life?"

Wes chuckled. "Why do you say that?"

"Always on the scene to rescue the distressed. Maybe that's why you're a Deputy Marshal. Sort of like the Old West, huh?"

"That pilot kept his cool the whole time. That saved his life and his wife's. She's a little banged up and has some scratches. He walked away though."

"What did he say happened?"

They followed hangers-on around a police cruiser. Power crews were already working on the downed lines strewn across the sidewalk and yards. C.J. saw the town reporter interviewing someone and smiled.

Wes waited for a woman with a stroller to pass by them, then steered C.J. to the middle of the street for the short walk back to her house.

"He said the engine just quit on him. He was trying to aim for a field about three hundred yards away but when he realized he wasn't going to make it, he said he was aiming for the middle of the street."

C.J. shook her head. "That was really close. Someone could have been killed."

Tires screeched. The woman with the stroller shrieked and frantically pushed to get out of the way. Wesley's pager went off at the same moment the car gunned toward them.

He whirled around. The mother frantically worked at the straps to free her baby. Wes grabbed the stroller and the woman's arm, dragging them to safety. When he turned to look after Jan his heart stopped beating.

The car was going to hit her.

The woman with the stroller screamed. Wes sprinted and dived. Tackling Jan about the waist he dropped and rolled, his own body shielding hers as the car sped by.

He held her close, not sure if the trembling he felt came from her or from him. A moment later and he'd have been too late. A moment later and she'd have been hit, injured, maybe killed.

His heart beat frantically. But as Wes held her close he realized with a start that he loved her. Right or wrong he was in love with Jan Langley. The prospect of losing her shook him to the core. He'd never imagined loving someone, feeling this way—particularly about one woman. But in the moment he thought he'd lost her, he knew. She was his destiny.

The siren from a police car squawked.

Wes hugged Jan close then helped her up.

With her baby tucked securely in her arms, the woman who'd been pushing the stroller ran over to them. "Oh, my God. Are you all right? That guy must have been nuts. He tried to run you down."

With Wesley's steadying hands at her waist, C.J. dusted off her knees then her rear end. "I'm fine. I'm fine, really."

Wes looked her over, then, with his hands scanned her body in a modified frisk. Her eyes were wide with shock probably setting in. Her elbow was scraped but otherwise she looked okay.

"Does anything feel broken, Jan?"

She shook her head. "I'm okay. Really. I just . . ." Her voice trailed off and she looked at him.

Wesley folded her in his arms. She shuddered and then pushed him away. "I, I need to go home. I've got a run in my hose."

"Jan, you're in shock. It'll take a little while for your heartbeat to settle. Why don't you stay right here? I need to go talk to that cop."

C.J. shook her head. "I need to go home," she mumbled.

"One of them took off after that driver," the woman with the baby said. "I can't believe he tried to run us all down. People are just crazy today."

Wes looked in the direction the blue car had taken. He hadn't had time to make the plates. All that registered with him before he dived for Jan was North Carolina tags with a T and a 2. The nondescript blue sedan looked like a hundred other cars he'd seen in the same make and model. Jimmy Peterson must have had a fire sale on the model before he got killed by that tree.

Wes looked the woman and baby over. "Are you all right, ma'am?"

The woman cuddled the now fretting infant then kissed the baby's forehead.

"Yes. Thanks to you," she said. "I don't think we'd have made it if you hadn't jumped and snatched the stroller up. I owe you my life and my baby's life. How can I thank you?"

"Did you happen to get a look at that driver or get the license plate on that car?"

The woman shook her head. "I'm sorry. I wasn't thinking about that. Maybe those policemen over there saw something."

"Yeah," Wes said.

He turned to check on Jan. But she wasn't there. He saw her walking through her front gate. She was home. She'd be okay for a few minutes. He wanted to talk to the cops.

In a daze, C.J made it to her front door. Was someone trying to kill her, injure her? She would bet cash money that the driver had been the same one who almost ran her over on Main Street yesterday.

She shut the door and without purpose or reason went to the kitchen.

She had no enemies in North Carolina. For God's sake, she didn't even know anyone here. She made it to the sink and turned the water on, surprised to see that her hands were shaking. She ran cold water over a cloth then pressed it to her elbow. Wincing at the sudden sting, she stared at the still running water.

Was someone trying to kill her? Injure her? Send some sort of obscure message?

She dropped the cloth in the sink and reached up to open a cabinet. What she needed was there, there right next to the few glasses she had. With trembling hands she broke the seal on the bottle of Jim Beam and shakily poured a generous amount in a juice glass. She twisted the bottle's cap back in place.

Someone had tried to run her down. Twice.

She stared at the rich amber bourbon. She liked her liquor neat. No chaser. Someone in a blue car in North Carolina wanted her dead or injured.

She raised the glass. Closing her eyes, she took a shuddering breath and wondered who had a grudge against her. Maybe it had all been an accident. Maybe it was just a coincidence.

C.J. didn't believe in coincidences and hadn't for some time. Everything that happened in life happened for a reason. She could smell the pungent whiskey. Kentucky produced the best there was. Her mouth watered.

She opened her eyes and stared at the glass. Then she brought it to her mouth, anticipating the warming fire and the calming effect the drink would have on her. Maybe the car had something to do with Wes, maybe the case he was working on.

The thought of Wes brought Eileen Donovan to mind.

C.J. shuddered. She lowered the glass and looked at it, then looked at the bottle on the counter.

Eileen Donovan was a drunk, an alcoholic.

So are you, the voice of her conscience taunted.

C.J. raised the glass to her mouth again. One taste wouldn't hurt. One sip wouldn't make any difference. Jesus, she'd just narrowly escaped being run over by a car. She needed something to calm her nerves. Paralyzed with fear that the woman pushing the stroller was going to be hit, she'd paid no attention to her own safety. Wes had knocked her to the ground seconds before the car would have struck her.

Her hand shook. Drops of the bourbon sloshed over the rim of the glass. She breathed in the smell of it, rich, pungent, welcoming. She'd been dry a long time. One drink wouldn't kill her.

She closed her eyes. Eileen Donovan's face swam before her. The skewed lipstick, the liquor breath, the morning coffee more alcohol than java.

C.J. slowly lowered the glass from her mouth then turned it upside down. The amber liquid hit the metal sink and trailed down the drain. She turned the faucet on and let the clear water wash away the bourbon and the corner in the glass. Unscrewing the bottle, she poured the remaining contents down the drain, then carefully rinsed the bottle.

Her hands continued to shake.

"That took a lot of courage."

C.J. whirled around. The Jim Beam bottle fell from her hands and crashed at her feet. Running water, her heavy breathing and the sound of shattering glass echoed through the kitchen.

"I'm proud of you," he said quietly.

She turned away from him. "I didn't hear you come in."

Wrapping her arms about herself, she leaned forward toward the sink and rocked. "Somebody tried to kill me, Wes."

"I know, baby. I know."

She heard the crunch of glass and knew he'd come up behind her. Leaning over her, Wes turned off the faucet.

She turned, staring up at him. He enveloped her in his open arms.

C.J.'s mouth trembled once, and then she wept.

Twenty-two

When she woke a while later, C.J. was in her bed and naked except for the teddy. Normally she slept in the nude. A sheet and a lightweight blanket covered her. She opened her eyes to glance at the alarm clock on her bedside table. A single lamp cast warm shadows in the room.

Her gaze locked with Wesley's.

For a few moments neither of them said anything. They simply stared at each other, the silence a communion of spirits rather than an awkward space.

"How did you know it was a problem for me?" she quietly asked.

Wes unfolded his long, athletic frame from the chair he'd brought in from the living room. Sitting up, with his hands dropped between his knees, he watched her.

"I didn't really. Not until just now. There were signs though. Signs I should have recognized. At Mama Lo's your eyes tracked the beer I had from the moment Curtis brought them in to the time I belted the first one back. You asked for water for tea but you watched me. Tea, that's all I'd ever seen you drink. You watched me and it just seemed too intense, almost sexual."

C.J. closed her eyes and sighed. "My whole life has been too intense."

"Do you want to tell me about it?"

Opening her eyes again, she looked at him. "Yes."

The first thing she had to tell him was her name. The next thing would be why she'd run to North Carolina. The one thing she couldn't tell him, not now, not ever, was that she'd fallen in love with him, fallen in love with the one addiction she couldn't afford to deal with.

C.J. sat up. When his eyes tracked to her chest, she unconsciously tugged the sheet up. She scooted over a bit on the bed, silently offering him the space next to her.

Without a word, Wesley accepted the invitation, settling himself on top of the blanket. C.J. propped pillows at her back and braced herself against the bed's headboard and took in the picture they made: she, barely dressed, looking wanton with her hair flying in a hundred directions, yet modestly clinging to a sheet that shielded what he'd already seen and had. He, a bronzed dark warrior come to life from another age, indolently stretched out on his paramour's bed. He'd ditched the tie and slipped his shoes off.

With his feet crossed at the ankles and his arms folded behind his head, he looked as if he didn't have a care in the world. He was a hard, lean warrior who had mapped out a seduction for the evening that had been spoiled by a plane crash, a crazy driver, and her insecurities.

C.J. sighed as she tried to smooth her hair down with one hand. He'd still managed to get what he came for, he was in her bed. She knew, just like she knew that she'd always fight the temptation of "just one drink," that they'd have sex before this night was done. Then it would be over, done, and finished like every other relationship she'd had. In the morning she'd hate herself, but she'd still love him.

First she folded her hands together, then she drew up her knees and wrapped her arms around her legs. She rested her head on the top of her knees and looked at him.

Wesley's heart constricted. She was his sun, his moon, his stars. Mama Lo had been right about him catching an angel. With an inward smile Wes thought his Kensington brothers and sisters had had some sort of psychic vision when they nicknamed him Star Gazer. This beautiful, strong woman could only have been sent to him from some heavenly being.

He loved the small waves in her. While she slept, he'd run his hands through the softness. He'd watched her sleep and yet again marveled at her capacity to touch him so deeply in such a short span of time.

Yeah, he was curious about her past. But its importance paled when compared to their future together. She sat in bed staring at him. He wanted her, but more than desire he felt a surge of protectiveness that overpowered every other longing. She looked so fragile, so beautiful. Her eyes held secrets though. Miss Clara Ann said she had old eyes. Jan's eyes held the secret longings and secret dreams of strong black women through the ages.

He brought his arms down then reached out to her, unable to resist not touching her. One well-defined finger traced her hairline, smoothed its way to her full mouth.

The light touch sent ripples of heat through C.J. Desire welled within her. She sat up and blinked back sudden tears. She couldn't control anything, not even her body's willful reaction to this man.

"Tell me, Jan," he said quietly. He sought her hand then laced his fingers through hers.

"People call me C.J. That's my name. Not Jan."

He squeezed her hand encouragingly.

"As a matter of fact, until I moved here, that's the only name I've ever answered to. I came here to get away. Too many things in my life were pressing in on me. My job, my personal life. Stress was killing me. Even the stress caused by good things happening to me."

She looked at him, and then at their hands clasped together. She tried to pull away, but Wes just held her hand tighter, stronger. Like an anchor in a storm.

"I can't remember the first time I needed, really *needed* something to help me cope. My doctor was accommodating. He'd known me and my family for years. Pretty soon I was depending on those little white pills to get me to sleep at night, the blue ones to calm me down during the day when the assignments got to me."

She shrugged and glanced at Wes. "When the family doctor became suspicious about my need for refills, I simply went to another physician. It was easy. I pushed myself, more and more. I wanted to be the best, the absolute best. Long hours, bad food, and a bag full of legal drugs to keep me going. As for the alcohol, well, that's legal, too. Sometimes I couldn't wait to call it quits for the day so I could stop by a bar and get a drink."

Wes lifted their clasped hands and pressed a kiss on the top of her hand. C.J.'s answering smile was sad.

"I told you about my brother. His name is Rob. After the falling out we had I lost three days in a drunken haze. The only reason I know for a fact that I drank nonstop was because of the credit card bill."

"The what?"

"Apparently I was calling the liquor store and having them deliver straight to my apartment. I don't remember going out. I may have. God, I hope not. I just don't remember. When I got that charge card bill and realized I hadn't had a big party or anything at my place, not one that I remembered at least, I got scared. I couldn't physically or financially afford drunken binges like that."

C.J. shuddered. That time remained a blank spot in her memory. The only thing she could figure was that the housekeeper who took care of her place had cleaned up after her. She'd been too embarrassed to ask. She'd simply enclosed an extra one hundred dollars in the woman's pay envelope and prayed that she never again lost control that way.

"I cut back on the liquor. I had to be able to keep my head together to do my job. I attacked it with a vengeance. My boss and coworkers thought I was possessed. I figured if I kept myself busy I'd be too busy to drink or to rely on pills, that when I finally fell into the bed at night it would be in pure exhaustion and not supplemented by a little pill."

A little laugh, of derision and of wonder, escaped her. "I did some of my best work then. It's amazing, here I was living the total dream, racking up praise, getting big raises and bonuses. Hell, I was employee of the month six out of eighteen months. And on the inside, I was falling apart. I was a shell. I'd even lost about twenty pounds. One day I woke up and I knew. I couldn't keep at that pace any longer. So I left. Just walked away from it all and came here to lick my wounds, to heal myself."

Wes shook his head. "Wait a minute. So you're not in the federal Witness Security Program?"

C.J.'s face scrunched up. "What? I told you the other day I wasn't. Why did you think that?"

He ignored the question and asked one of his own. "Then what do you do?"

C.J. looked up at him. Her radiant smile dazzled him.

"I garden. It's peaceful."

An eighty-pound weight fell away from Wes. She wasn't a potential felony or a firing offense! He could keep his job, keep her. They'd be able to find a place to settle, if not in this little town, maybe someplace near D.C. or Baltimore. They could always go to West Virginia. Working the coal mine was no longer his only employment option. He'd put in for a permanent transfer. He'd turn his whole world upside down to make this woman happy. She needed peace and he needed an anchor.

He wrapped his arm around her and snuggled her close. Her soft curves pressed into his chest, his midsection, his thigh. He felt himself harden, lengthen, for her, only for her. She had to feel it, too. He couldn't hide—didn't want to hide—his physical reaction to her.

Wes buried his head in her neck and kissed her in the tender place behind her ear. C.J. moaned then snaked a hand around to stroke his leg.

"Kiss me, Wes."

She sighed when their lips met. Lingering, she savored each moment, each not so gentle swipe of his tongue against hers. She loved the taste of him, the feel of him. Quivering at the sweet, hot tenderness, she turned. She wanted to feel her breasts, aching for his touch, against the hard strength of his chest.

In a moment, she found herself on her back. Wesley's gaze burned into hers. Like a moth attracted by the dazzling flame that would consume it, she came to him, reaching for the buttons on his dress shirt.

"Make love to me, Wes."

He stilled her hands. "Jan . . . C.J., I want to make sure you understand something."

The edge to and command in his voice shamed her. She lowered her hands and lay back, ready for him to throw her past in her face. She lay still, waiting for the conditions he'd set. She'd willingly given him weapons with which to hurt her.

Maybe, after all she'd told him, he no longer wanted her for anything except what she had so freely and carelessly given to so many others. How could she convince him that this time it was real? She closed her eyes against the pain. How could she explain to him something she couldn't quite grasp herself?

With his voice calm and his gaze steady, he studied her. "Open your eyes, C.J."

The lace edge of the—what did she call it?—a teddy, beckoned him. The rush of desire that hit him when he'd undressed her and seen the scandalous bit of clothing now assaulted him even stronger than before. His fingers shook as he reached for her.

Like he did in the store when they'd bought the silky piece, his finger rimmed the lacy edge. This time, however, her soft, radiant skin, not a hanger, filled the garment. She arched into his touch and a soft moan escaped her. That small sound almost broke him.

"What I want you to understand," he said, "is that I want to make love to you and with you."

"I . . ."

With a flick of his thumb over her nipple he silenced her. She cried out and again arched toward him. The bud hardened under his hand. Through the fabric of the teddy, he gently fondled her breast, tracing small curliques, teasing her, and, he hoped, making her as hot for him as he was for her.

"I want to make love to you. Not sex. Not screwing or bumpin' and grindin' or doing the nasty. I want to make slow, sweet love to you."

He lowered his head to her breast. His intense gaze never left hers while his tongue lapped over the fabric to scorch her skin.

C.J. sank into the mattress. "Yes."

She stretched her lithe body, giving him access. He caught her hands and held them over her head, then continued the exquisite sampling, soft skin here, a full breast there. The feast before him promised an endless buffet of delight. And he had all night long.

His mouth closed over her breast.

"Oh, God. Yes, Wesley, yes!" She pulled his head in a vain attempt to get closer, closer.

He had all night to show her with his actions and tell her with his words how much he cared, how very much he loved her. This night, her pleasure constituted his solitary goal.

He lifted his head then slowly stripped the tangled sheet and blanket from her body. He kissed every bit of skin exposed along the trail of the sheet. C.J. His woman. Wes worshipped her with his mouth, with the slow stroke of his hands, with everything in him he had to give her.

C.J. shuddered and sighed when his mouth kissed her knee. Her other leg lifted and stroked his. The cloth of his trousers frustrated her, she wanted to feel his hot skin next to hers. She'd been holding back her feelings for so long, so very long. Tonight, she'd give to him. She wanted to tell him but she couldn't speak to form the words. Every part of her was focused on what he did, how he made her feel. Cherished, lost in a sea of sensation.

He lifted her leg and flicked his tongue over the tender flesh at the back of her knee.

C.J. cried out.

Wes smiled. "Do you like that?"

Incapable of speech, she merely shook her head back and forth on the pillow.

"What? No, you don't like that? Well how about this?"

His big hand stroked down her leg and then slowly back up. He bent low to again lick the area behind her knee, then he moved up and over to kiss her inner thigh.

"Don't want any part to feel neglected now."

Had anything been funny C.J. would have laughed. As it was she merely moaned his name. Then his hand covered the core of her. Opening her legs to him, she knew she'd died and gone to a place where only pleasure existed.

"These snaps are awfully convenient," he observed while undoing them. He unfastened the last one and lifted the lacy edge of the fabric away from her. C.J. lifted her hips to him.

"Thank you," he murmured. "How'd you know that was one of my favorite things in the whole world?"

His head lowered and she lifted her legs. He positioned them over his shoulders and loved her with a maddening slowness. C.J. writhed beneath him. A storm raged in her, heat and flame and a desire she never suspected even existed.

The first trembling spasms shook her.

"Wesley!"

"Let it come," he murmured.

Wes lapped her sweetness then made his way up her body. Stradling her with a knee braced on either side, he stared into her eyes as his hands closed over her breasts.

His breathing came ragged, uneven, as if he'd run the 100-yard dash.

"Let me love you, Wes."

He smiled. "Tonight is for you."

C.J. reached for the erection in his pants. She stroked him. "I want you deep inside me."

His tormented groan spurred her. With her free hand she brought his head to hers. The kiss, deep and powerful, promised more rapture, if either of them could stand it.

Wesley's weight settled on her. C.J. wrapped her arms around his neck. He rolled over so she was on top of him.

She could feel the blunt hardness of his erection through his trousers. C.J. rocked back and forth, savoring the feel of him, loving the way his eyes had darkened. He gripped her thighs and thrust upward, seeking the release they both wanted.

While kissing him in short, greedy spurts, she worked at the buttons on his shirt. Finally exposing his rippled chest, she broke away from his mouth and kissed each of the taut male nipples. He groaned again then crushed her to him, his mouth slashing over hers. But she wasn't finished with him. Unbuckling the slim leather belt at his waist, she glanced down at him, a wicked suggestion in her eyes.

"Jesus." Wes pushed her hands away and in short order came out of his pants and briefs. Then he pulled the lacy teddy over her head. "Wal-Mart is always going to have a fond place in my heart."

She did laugh then. On her knees in the middle of the bed she stretched languidly and watched his eyes track her every movement, then, like radar, settle on her full breasts. "There are other places to be fond of," she said.

His mouth curved in an unconscious smile. C.J.'s heart flipped even as she watched him draw near.

"I can see a few worth endless exploration," he said. He pulled her to him. They fell together on the firm mattress.

"Show me."

He did.

Twenty-three

She woke with a start. It was light out and she knew she was alone in the bed. They'd made slow sweet love before dawn. The last thing she remembered before drifting into a well-satiated sleep was being snuggled spoon fashion next to his big, warm body. His large hand covered and caressed her breast even in sleep. She'd felt secure, loved.

But his warmth no longer comforted her. He'd left without saying goodbye.

She waited for the guilt to kick in, for the self-recriminations to do their usual number on her. But nothing happened. Except for the pounding on the door.

Realizing what had awakened her, she flung the sheet to the side and dashed to the closet for her robe.

A quick glance at the clock told her it was . . . she couldn't see the clock. A piece of paper propped against it obscured the face. She smiled. He'd left a note.

The knocking on her front door continued.

"Coming."

When she opened the door, a Federal Express driver thrust a clipboard at her.

"Good morning," she cheerily greeted him.

The man smiled. "It's afternoon, ma'am. Sorry to disturb you."

"Not a problem. I'm expecting this." She accepted the package sent from her reporter friend. David had really done a scramble to get this to her so quickly.

The driver turned to leave.

"What time do you have?" she asked.

"One-thirty-three, ma'am. You have a good day."

C.J.'s mouth dropped open. It couldn't be that late.

She closed the door and ripped open the package as she made her way to the kitchen. She put water on for tea then remembered what had almost transpired in her kitchen last night.

"First things, first," she said, reaching for the telephone book on top of the refrigerator. She looked up the listing for Alcoholics Anonymous and dialed the number.

"Hi. My name is Jan Lang . . ." She paused and took a deep breath. "My name is C.J. Mayview and I'd like to know where I can go to an AA meeting." She wrote the time and day down then got directions. Robinson had been right. She needed to attend the meetings. She could try to go it alone, but would her will be strong enough to overcome the next temptation and crisis? Not likely.

She looked around the kitchen and in the trash but couldn't find either the shattered pieces of the bourbon bottle or the bottle of wine Wesley had brought with their dinner. As a matter of fact, her kitchen was spotless, cleaner even than it had been before Wes had arrived the night before. He must have cleaned while she'd slept.

In a crashing wave, she remembered why she'd thought she needed a drink, why she'd cried in Wesley's arms, why he'd put her in bed. Someone had deliberately tried to run her down. There were no ifs, ands, or buts about it. And she'd be willing to bet it was the same driver as the one on Main Street.

The kettle whistled. C.J. poured hot water over a tea bag of her favorite, chamomile. While the tea steeped she finished opening the FedEx packet. Then she remembered the note in her bedroom. She pulled a file folder from the packet then left it on the counter and went to her bedroom.

Sitting on the edge of her bed she plucked up the note Wes had left propped against her alarm clock.

You are my life, my sun and moon and stars. Thank you for giving to me the wondrous gift of yourself. There are some things I need to do today, but I'm counting each moment until we can be together again.

Yours,
W. Donovan

C.J.'s mouth trembled. The man was sheer poetry and she loved him beyond reason. She clutched the short note to her breast and closed her eyes. His bronzed image came to her. The strength in his face, the power in his hands, the undiluted maleness of every part of him. He'd opened his heart to her in West Virginia. C.J. knew that the experience of seeing his birth mother had taken its toll on him. But he'd been willing to give the woman the benefit of the doubt.

She thought about his niece and nephew then spread her hand over her stomach. She glanced back at the rumpled sheets on the bed. They'd forgotten about protection last night. She had never, *ever* done that before. They'd loved through the long, dark hours and into the dawn of the new day. She could be pregnant even now.

C.J.'s mouth blossomed into a smile and then a huge grin. Pregnant. Not only did she fail to cringe at the thought, she embraced the possibility.

When she'd awakened, she hadn't been beset with doubt, anger, or self-directed loathing. Maybe, just as she'd come to the realization that she needed to accept Alcoholics Anonymous, maybe, just maybe, she also needed to accept that Wes was different from the other men. Different in ways that mattered. For the first time, her heart was involved. She loved him. It was just that simple.

She reread the note from Wes then carried it to the kitchen. She added a touch of sugar to the tea then picked up the packet from David and carried the tea, the folder, and Wesley's note to the living room. Smiling, she read Wesley's note again then put it aside. Sipping from the cup of tea, she pulled off a yellow sticky note from David: "Here's what you asked for C.J. I want research credit in the tagline of your story. David."

C.J. shook her head. Apparently, she was the only person who believed she left journalism for good.

Mindful of the bad spring in the sofa, she settled on the edge, opened the file and quickly scanned through it. It was pretty thick, some of the stories dating back more than ten years. David had found a lot of clips on Wesley Donovan. Clipped together at the end were black and white photocopies of pictures and one color photocopy of an official-looking mugshot.

"Marcus Kensington." She recognized him even though she'd never met him. He looked just like his brothers. In his eyes she saw compassion, and she wondered what kind of man he'd been. He'd left behind two small children, and, C.J. presumed, a wife. His family still grieved for him. Wesley still grieved for him.

Not sure where to begin, C.J. spread the clips out on the coffee table. The photograph of one in particular caught her eye. The somber picture was at a gravesite. Black umbrellas and dark suits dominated the photo. She read the cutline: "Law enforcement officials from eight states gathered Friday for the funeral service of slain police officer Marcus Kensington."

C.J. took a sip of tea then settled back to read the funeral story. What she read made her uncomfortable. About an hour later she finished reading everything in the file. She tossed the clips on the coffee table.

She pinched the bridge of her nose and rubbed her eyes. "Oh, God. Now what?"

Mama Lo's words came back to her, the meaning now painfully clear. *Ain't interested in them lies those media people always telling.*

Just like Mama Lo, Wesley probably wasn't interested either. So many things made sense now. Wes Donovan probably didn't just dislike the Serenity Falls reporter as a person, most likely he despised all journalists in general.

From beneath the stack of newspaper clips about him and Marcus Kensington, she pulled out the note Wes had left for her. Would he feel the same way about her when he found out what she did for a living?

Wes made two telephone calls. The first to his pal Scotty at headquarters to thank him for running the make on Jan, or rather C.J. He didn't know what she'd done for a living before arriving in Serenity Falls but it didn't make any difference. The important thing was she wasn't in the Marshals Service's Witness Security Program.

The Serenity Falls witness who was, however, was in trouble. Wes had put the witness in a safe house, one secured by Scotty and signed off on by Casey and Holloway. The page that had come while a car was trying to run him and C.J. over had been from the witness who swore up and down that a maid at the motel looked a whole lot like a contract killer. The witness had slipped out a back window and run hard and fast to the first phone.

Wesley's second call had been for backup. In less than two hours he'd have the witness tucked safely on a plane headed for a new identity, a new life on the run.

A lot could happen in two hours. Wes didn't like the odds. Too many weird things went down in this town for him to feel secure about anything. He shifted, the weight of the Kevlar vest he wore under a lightweight jacket reminding him that danger lurked everywhere, even in little southern towns like Serenity Falls. The witness had gone to ground, as safe as could be under the circumstances.

Ace reporter Kenneth Sheldon's big story of the morning had been heralded by a huge headline: "Town under siege by calamities." The reporter's main story was about the plane crash on C.J.'s street. Then every little blip and sneeze that had happened up to that day was recounted: first the old man who collapsed at the grocery store; then Jimmy Peterson, the car dealer, got snuffed out by a falling tree; and battery acid caused a small explosion at the local plant. According to Sheldon's story, a car had crashed through the front window of the little bakery he and C.J. had stopped in before leaving for West Virginia Friday. A head-on collision on the interstate right outside town came next, followed by a plane crash. Wesley added an incident the reporter didn't have in his story: the car trying to run C.J. down.

Wes didn't care for Sheldon but he couldn't ignore the fact that all the town's bad luck had started the day he rolled into Serenity Falls. Coincidences were rare. He sorted through each incident looking for a common link, any common denominator. In some fashion or another he'd managed to get himself embroiled in a couple of the incidents. But he hadn't been around for the plant explosion, and Jimmy Peterson's accident with the tree didn't seem to have any link to anything. But Wes didn't discount those things.

Mentally, he carefully reviewed his protected witness's lengthy dossier.

He rubbed his chin in frustration. "God, it could be anything, it could be nothing."

He had just one priority: Keep the witness alive and safe. He'd left a lot open with C.J. but he felt secure that what they had was real. They'd been on fire for each other the previous night. She'd shared her past with him, and he'd loved her beyond it.

Then he remembered something, something important. *Dark Warrior.* She'd called him that when they first met. In the midst of passion she whispered it just last night. He'd let his guard down and had been too caught up in the silken feel of her to make a deal out of it then. But he remembered now. He remembered and he wondered if somehow, someway he'd been played for a fool.

Amber Baldwin threw clothes into a small particleboard suitcase. Frankie had called and said they had to move again. This time they had to leave everything except what she could fit in one bag. Amber started crying as she stuffed Frank Jr.'s favorite rag doll in the bag. She was tired of this life, tired of running. Maybe she'd just leave him and go home to Las Vegas. Her legs still looked good. She could easily get work.

She slammed the suitcase closed and pressed the latch down. A sudden pounding on her front door made her squeal. She snatched the baby from the couch where he dozed and stared at the door.

She didn't know who or what was on the other side of that door. She glanced at the phone, picked it up to call 911 then remembered Frankie's warning.

"Don't use the phones. They're all bugged." With wide eyes she backed away from the door.

"Please don't kill me. Please."

"Amber! Amber are you in there?"

A voice penetrated Amber's fear. She recognized the voice.

"Amber, come on now. If you're in there, please open up."

Jan! It was Jan Langley, not some hired killer or Frankie gone completely crazy.

Amber ran to the door and unlatched the four locks Frankie installed when they'd moved in.

"Oh, Jan. Thank God it's you. I was so frightened."

C.J. walked into the small apartment and looked around. The toddler fretted in Amber's arms until she placed him on the sofa. Amber then turned and quickly locked the door again.

C.J.'s eyebrows lifted. "I haven't seen that since I left Baltimore," she said, nodding toward the multiple dead bolts and chains securing the door.

"Frankie . . ."

C.J. waved her hand. "Yeah, yeah. Frankie. By the way, where is he?"

"I don't know," Amber responded. "He called about thirty minutes ago and told me to pack. We have to leave again. We're going to Texas this time."

C.J. eyed the suitcase on the crate coffee table. "How long are you going to run and how many times are you going to let him threaten you before *you* leave?"

Amber looked at the floor. "He's my husband, Jan." Her gaze lifted to C.J.'s. "We'll be okay. *I'll* be okay. I'll send you my address when we get wherever it is we're going in Texas."

There was little use in arguing with Amber. C.J. well knew the statistical chances of Amber leaving Frankie.

She also knew how many women eventually found themselves in emergency shelters and safe houses after running for their lives with just the clothes on their backs and their children in tow.

She sighed.

"Here," she said, handing Amber a white business-size envelope.

"What is it?"

Amber peered into the envelope. "Jan, I can't take this. It's money." Her eyes widened as she took in just how many crisp fifties were in the envelope.

"Look, you never know what might happen down the road. Take it. There's also a telephone number on a card in there. It's for a national hotline. If you ever need someone to come get you, if you're ever in trouble and think you have no way out, someone at that number can get help for you. Understand?"

Amber nodded, then stepped forward and hugged C.J.

Uncomfortable with the show of affection or gratitude, whatever it was, C.J. patted Amber's back then stepped away. Amber wiped her eyes.

"I'm sorry I didn't get right back to you," C.J. said. "I had company yesterday and I'd turned the ringers off and the answering machine down. I didn't get your message until about an hour ago."

Amber picked up the baby and bounced him in her arms. "I don't know where we're going to be in Texas. Frankie never tells me anymore. I was surprised he told me that much. We just get in the car or whatever and wind up some place. I've been thinking about what you said though. I've been thinking maybe I should just go home. My mama can take care of Frank Jr. while I work. People talk about Vegas and sometimes it gets a bad rap but Las Vegas is home for me."

C.J. kept her opinions about the city to herself. "Maybe home will be good for you. Can I help you finish packing?"

Amber shook her head. Her straight hair, as always held back with a head band, barely moved. "That's all I can take. Frankie said just one bag. He wants to start fresh. I'm taking a big purse though. I can fit lots of extra stuff in there."

C.J. didn't know what else to say or if anything else could be said. "May I hold him for a moment?"

Amber blinked, obviously surprised by the request. Then she smiled and handed the toddler to C.J. "I didn't think you liked kids."

So, it was that evident, C.J. thought. Frank Jr. reached for the spiral triangle earring dangling at her ear. "I used to think the same thing. Now, well, let's just say, I'm re-evaluating my position."

Cooing at the baby, she captured his little hand when he tugged on the earring. "This one is mine. Maybe when you grow up a little more your Mom'll let you get your own earring."

Amber laughed. "Frankie would have a fit if any son of his came home with a hole in his ear. He says that's a mark of fairy boys and sissies."

"That's not true," C.J. said. "Some of the most sexy straight guys I know have earrings, a couple of them even have holes in both ears."

C.J. sat on the sofa and played patty cake with Frank Jr. who laughed and gurgled at her.

"I know," Amber replied. "Frankie can be so traditional sometimes."

There wasn't anything traditional about a man physically and emotionally threatening his wife, but C.J. again kept her thoughts to herself. Amber didn't need a sermon, she needed a solution—and a divorce. But that decision would have to spring from Amber, not from C.J.

Hugging the baby to her one last time, C.J. kissed his forehead. "You take care of your mom now, okay?"

"Ma!"

C.J. laughed then hugged him close again before handing him back up to Amber.

"Well, I better leave. If there's anything else I can do for you, you know where to find me."

Amber smiled. "In your garden."

"I'll plant petunias for Frank Jr. and a rose bush for you," C.J. said with an answering smile.

Amber quickly hugged her again. This time, C.J. didn't recoil from the embrace.

"Jan, don't worry about me. I was just overly emotional the other day. I'll be fine. We'll all be fine. Thank you for the gift of your friendship. It's meant a lot to me."

C.J.'s smile was sad when they stepped apart. Then, a moment later, standing outside the door, C.J. heard Amber redo all the locks on the apartment door.

The only thing Margaret Shelley disliked was lying to Aunt Clara. She'd outdone herself this time though. In a blind stroke of luck mixed with providence, her quarry had landed in little Serenity Falls, North Carolina.

Margaret could kill a man, woman, or child without flinching, had done so many times. Her work generally took her far, far from her North Carolina roots. This time, however, she couldn't do the job. She'd let a personal issue distract her from her main purpose. She'd managed to spook her quarry while enjoying a cat-and-mouse flirtation with the man sent to protect her prey.

Everything in her protested the necessary act of returning part of her substantial fee. As a professional, she prided herself on a clean, quality hit. If she got a little playacting in at the same time, so much the better. Margaret had always wanted to be an actress. Contract killing paid better.

But a job undone remained a job undone. She couldn't put Aunt Clara in danger. So far she'd managed to remain a peripheral shadow for her quarry, just enough to make anybody nervous, edgy, and looking over the shoulder at every turn.

She could take out the witness but didn't like the odds. He may have talked and given that Wes Donovan enough information to actually work with. How Donovan had ended up at Aunt Clara's remained a troubling mystery—just the sort of loose end coincidence that always caused trouble.

Margaret packed her last bag. She'd come up with a plausible story for Aunt Clara, an out-of-the-blue work assignment she couldn't possibly turn down.

She laughed. Twice now, Donovan had looked at her as if they'd met before. Funny what losing fifty pounds, changing hair and eye color, and having a little nip and tuck done on a face could do to alter appearance. She'd even gone so far as to use her real name on this job. That had been a mistake.

It wouldn't take Donovan or his buddies in D.C. long to figure out what was what if she took out the witness and left all the peripherals walking around. Following him had been a stroke of genius. Calling in an associate to take care of the rest had been a necessity, even if he was an incompetent idiot, failing twice now to do an easy hit-and-run.

She'd like nothing better than finishing up this job and giving herself the added bonus of striking out at Wes Donovan through the little piece he'd gotten himself in this town. But she couldn't risk any harm or the notion of guilt by association to Aunt Clara. Besides, her original prey could be stalked to another town, another day.

"Ah, well. It was fun while it lasted."

Twenty-four

Wes gunned his bike toward Miss Clara Ann's house. He saw Margaret hug Miss Clara Ann then wave, get in her rental, and drive off. By the time Wes parked the Harley around back and made his way to the front parlor, Miss Clara Ann was coming in the door.

"Wesley, baby, there you are. You just missed Margaret. She got called back to the city for her job." Miss Clara Ann shook her head. "Never did understand just what that girl does for a paycheck. That ain't important though. You done missed lunch again. I gots some leftovers if you hungry. You hungry, baby?"

"No, ma'am. I was just coming in to gather my gear. I'll be on my way soon and I wanted to say goodbye."

"Goodbye? Boy, you just got here the other day. I'm gonna have to give you a refund on your money."

Wes smiled. "No, you keep it. I've enjoyed my stay with you."

"I tell you, all you young folks pulling out at the same time. First Margaret, now you. And that Garrison, I ain't seen hide nor hair of him in a while. All his artist stuff still upstairs though so I reckon he'll be back for it. You younguns keep some busy lives."

Wes kissed Miss Clara Ann on the cheek.

"I'm gonna make you up a bag. I knows you said you ain't hungry now but that don't mean you won't be later."

Wes smiled. "Yes, ma'am."

"Well, you get on up there and get your stuff together."

He did. It took less than five minutes for Wes to toss his gear in his bags. His immediate problem consisted of too many vehicles on hand. The truck Casey secured for him was just a truck. Maybe Ray Bob over at the service station would buy it. Wes grinned, wondering if he'd get any brownie points with Holloway if he turned a profit for the Marshals Service.

"Not if your witness winds up dead," he reminded himself.

He looked at the ceiling in the room he'd called home for the last few days. "Never did get to see the artist's studio set up up there."

He thought about taking a peek now but discarded the idea. It didn't matter now.

The pager at his waist beeped. Wes pulled it off the waistband of his jeans and stared at the number. Two exclamation marks followed ten-digits. Wes recognized the long-distance number and swore. The simple code at the end meant call ASAP and don't worry about a secure phone line.

He checked the bathroom then glanced around the room one last time. He clipped the black pager back on his jeans then checked the gun he shouldered and grabbed his bags.

In the hallway a moment later, had he not been looking down at the pager that was going off again he would have missed the book of matches on the floor near a table leg at the top of the stairs. Wes bent low, snatched up the matches and checked the pager display. He then got a good look at the match-book cover.

"Son of a bitch!" He took the stairs three at a time.

"Miss Clara Ann!" he called out.

"In the kitchen, baby."

Wesley burst through the door and confronted the old woman. Her puzzled expression tempered his anger a bit, but not much.

"Where is she?"

Miss Clara Ann wrapped a chicken leg in foil. "Where's who?"

"Your niece," he said, stressing the word niece.

"Margaret? I done told you. She got a call from her fancy job up north. Said they told her she had to cut her vacation short and get back up there."

Vacation my ass, he thought. The matches were from the same motel he'd tucked the witness in. And the witness swore up and down he'd seen a maid he recognized. The hazy description of the woman, prompted more by fear than true recollection, fit Margaret.

Miss Clara Ann handed him a brown paper bag. Wes stared at it like it was a dangerous explosive.

"What's this?"

"That's your lunch, child." She smiled up at him. "You sure been some good company to this old lady."

Wes looked at her. She was either a first-rate actress or completely in the dark. His gut gave him the answer.

"You don't know, do you?"

"Know what, baby?"

Wes smiled and shook his head. "Never mind. May I use your phone?"

He answered the page.

"There's trouble headed your way," Holloway said when he got on the line. "Robbi Langston busted out today while being taken to a medical appointment. He has people in the Charlotte area. The all points bulletin says he's armed, dangerous, and may have a hostage with him."

Wes swore. Then looked at Miss Clara Ann and mouthed "Sorry."

Langston was a bank robber who'd killed three people. He'd been serving life in a federal facility. "That's just what I need. Any reason to believe he's in this area?"

"You're in the path to Charlotte."

Wes rang off with Holloway. He'd wanted to ask about Margaret but couldn't, not with Miss Clara Ann standing there. Bending low, he kissed Miss Clara Ann, wished her well, then hightailed it to the Crown Victoria.

If Margaret was who and what he suspected she was, he might already be too late.

Curious about all the commotion a few blocks away, C.J. headed in the direction of the flashing lights after leaving Amber's apartment.

"This sure is a bustling little place," she said aloud as she drew nearer to what turned out to be a police road block.

Saddling up to an officer, she couldn't resist the who, what, when, where, why, and how that constituted a second nature for her.

"Ma'am, I'm going to have to ask you to step back. Going home and locking your windows and doors would be even better."

Itching for a notebook in her hands, she asked, "Why?"

"Bank robber and killer escaped from prison earlier today. Indication is he might be headed this way."

"What's his name?"

The cop eyed her with a look part irritation, part

male interest. "Why? You know some bank robbers or something?"

C.J. laughed then backed off. News gathering was no longer her job. The curiosity, she figured, would be with her until she drew her last breath.

"Can't say that I do."

"You'd be better off in the security of your own home, ma'am. There's no telling what might happen if he comes this way."

C.J. waved as she left, then did what reporters always do, inched her way around to another vantage point.

About to ask another officer the same questions, her peripheral vision picked up an all-too-familiar sight. A satellite news truck rolled up the street and stopped less than three yards from where she stood.

"Excuse me officer . . ."

Her voice trailed off as she watched the television crew set up. What in the world was going on?

"Ma'am," the officer said. "You shouldn't be here. I'm going to have to ask you to leave."

"What's going on?" she asked.

"Escaped convict. A killer and bank robber is headed this way. We're searching every vehicle."

She was about to ask another question when the Crown Victoria rolled up. When Wes got out of the car and strode to where she stood, C.J. found herself struck by two truths: first, she loved this man beyond reason; second, she had to tell him what she did for a living before coming to Serenity Falls. Opening her mouth to just blurt it out and have done with it, she paused. The wraparound sunglasses obscured his eyes, but every inch of him screamed *cop,* from the snug Levi's right on down to the toe of his cowboy boots. She wondered how she'd missed it before.

An image of Marshals of old came to mind: rugged men, ready to lay down their lives for the law. Wes

Donovan fit that mold. All he was missing was a shiny tin star at his breast pocket, a horse, and a six-shooter at his hip. Six-shooters remained a relic of the past though, she thought. Under that jacket he probably had a semi-automatic in a shoulder holster.

"C.J., what in the world are you doing out here? You need to be at home where I don't have to worry about you, too."

C.J. picked up on the inconsistency. "Too? Who else are you worrying about?"

Wes smiled as he tucked the glasses in his jacket pocket. Lifting his hand, he softly ran his thumb over her cheek and down her chin. With his thumb, he lightly rimmed the contours of her mouth then bent for a quick kiss. "I have some business to attend to but I hope to see you tonight or tomorrow."

C.J. nodded. "Okay. But there's something I need to tell you." She glanced at the uniformed cop then back at Wes. "Do you have a minute?"

"Not really. I'm serious though. I'll be less distracted if I know you're safe at home." He pulled out a badge and addressed the cop. "Who's the on-scene commander?"

"That would be Captain Parker. He's over there."

Wes turned to look in the direction the cop pointed and bumped into a man who'd approached him from behind.

"Sorry about that," he said.

"Not a problem. Hi. I'm Reuben Black with Action News. Are you in charge here?"

Wes stepped aside. "No."

The reporter shrugged at the curt tone and looked around Wes to the cop.

"C.J. Mayview! Is that you? I should have known this was something hot. How long have you been down here reporting this story?"

C.J.'s eyes widened. She shook her head to deny the words.

Wes whirled around. "What did you say?"

Unaware of the sudden tension, the reporter continued addressing C.J. He grabbed her hand and pumped it. "It truly is a pleasure to meet you. I'd recognize you anywhere after all those pictures and the award. I always read your stuff. Well, I used to that is before I took this job in Charlotte a couple of months ago. What's it like winning a Pulitzer? That has got to be one awesome feeling."

C.J., ignoring the TV reporter, only had eyes for Wes. What she saw made her wince. The warmth shining in his eyes just a moment ago was gone, replaced by a dull flat glare, the sensuous mouth that had so recently danced across hers was now a tightly compressed line. "Wesley, I can explain. I've been trying to tell . . ."

"You're a reporter?" he asked.

"It's not what you think, Wesley."

"I have work to do." Glancing at the notebook the TV reporter held he looked at her again, "I suppose you do, too." Disdain dripped from his voice.

With a look that in no uncertain terms was reserved for the scum of the earth, Wesley's gaze flicked over C.J. and the TV reporter. Then he turned his back on her and strode to where the on-scene commander stood talking with some cops.

"What's his problem?"

Tears filled C.J.'s eyes. "Excuse me," she mumbled to the reporter then chased after Wes. "Wesley! Let me explain. It's not at all what you think. I'm no longer . . ."

Wes whirled around. C.J. paused in mid-step, mid-sentence. The fury in him radiated across the few feet separating them. His curt voice lashed at her. "Save it,

Jan, C.J., Ja'Niece, whatever the hell your real name is. Go write your story."

"That's what I'm trying to tell you. I'm not writing a story."

"Ma'am, this is now a restricted area," the original cop said. "I'm going to have to ask you to leave."

Wes turned his back on her and went to the officer identified as Captain Parker.

"Wesley!"

The cop blocked her way then took her arm. "Ma'am, I don't think you want a citation."

C.J. sighed as her shoulders slumped. She watched Wes and the cop get in a car. Pulling her arm free of the restraining officer's light hold, she muttered, "I'm leaving."

With one last lingering look in Wesley's direction, C.J. turned away.

Less than ten minutes later, with everything set up to his satisfaction, Wes looked for C.J. She was nowhere in sight. But that other parasite was. Wes wanted some answers. Quickly.

"Excuse me," he butted into the conversation the TV reporter was having with a cop. "The woman you were talking to. Who did you say she is?"

"Oh, don't you know? That's C.J. Mayview. She won a Pulitzer Prize for investigative reporting a little while ago. It was for a dynamite story package on corruption in the day care system. Then she just sort of dropped out of the scene." The reporter grinned, displaying perfect pearly white teeth. "Boy am I glad I got this assignment. If C.J. Mayview is here, it must be something big. Now what was your name again?"

Wes grunted and walked away. He had all the information he needed. A reporter! She was a reporter. No wonder she'd defended that little weasely punk Kenny

Sheldon. Wes shook his head in disgust. Of all the people for him to get involved with.

But he didn't have time to indulge in justifiable anger right now. The cops would see to it that he got through the roadblocks without any hassles. It was time to whisk his witness to safety.

Margaret Shelley was about to head out of town and toward the interstate when she got a deliciously wicked idea. Glancing at the digital clock in her dash, she figured she'd have enough time for one last dig at Wesley Donovan.

It still grated on her that the job was undone and that she'd let her personal conflict with Wes Donovan get in the way. But it was a reaction she found herself unable to control; the one part of her that refused to be a professional. It was like her brain shut down and her body kicked into overdrive where Donovan was concerned.

Margaret checked her hair in the rearview mirror then laughed. She loved this stalking game even more than the final victory of bringing down her prey.

With a sharp left, she wheeled the mid-size sedan around in a U-turn.

Wes took care of business.

The witness whined and moaned but eventually boarded the small charter flight at the municipal airport.

"You know where to find me if you need me."

The witness grinned. "Unfortunately, the answer to that is yes. Hey, thanks for your help, man. I really hate leaving here. More than you'll ever know."

"You gotta do . . ." Wes said.

"What you gotta do," the witness finished. "But I'm gonna pay you back on account of this outfit. Don't you know this priest get up is a cliche? They do it in all the movies."

Wes took in the cleric's robes and wire-rimmed glasses the witness had donned. It was his turn to grin. "We all must carry our burdens."

"Yeah, right," the witness said. "There's saints turning over in their graves right now. I can't even remember the last time I celebrated Mass or went to confession."

"Then you're way overdue. You can practice what you'll say on the way."

A nun with a 9-mm Sig Sauer poked her head out the single door. "Mr. Yardley, we gotta get a move on before we get made."

Wes and the man known as Yancey Yardley shook hands. "Take care. Hope I don't have to see you again."

"Yeah, me too. And thanks . . . for everything."

The Deputy Marshal in the nun's outfit pulled the stairway up. Wes hopped back and watched the small plane taxi to its takeoff spot.

Wes stared after the plane until all that remained was a speck in the sky.

His job was done in Serenity Falls.

He thought about C.J. Mayview also known as Jan Langley. Lightning quick anger bubbled to the surface. He'd opened his heart and his soul to that woman, told her things a reporter had no business knowing. Wes swore. Striding back to the Crown Victoria, he kicked the rear tire so hard that he found some small satisfaction in the pain shooting up his leg.

His witness was safe and secure now. By the time he finished with C.J. Mayview she was gonna need a safe and secure place to hide.

Twenty-five

Serenity Falls, North Carolina, had lost its appeal. C.J.'s quest for peace of mind had been interrupted by a bronzed dark warrior. She would live through the heartache. She'd survive just like she did at every other turn.

Grateful that she'd packed light when she'd left Baltimore, she stuffed the meager contents of the bottom bureau drawer into an oversized duffel bag she'd picked up at an Army-Navy store. Everything else, and it wasn't much, was already in the Cherokee.

She could sell this little house anytime. Right now, she had one priority: run to a hiding place to lick her wounds. C.J. didn't know where she'd go. She just couldn't stay here. Not in a place that in every corner reminded her of Wesley. Even though what happened achieved the very end she'd wanted, she had hoped they could part amicably, maybe even as friends. She'd wanted the memories to be sweet, not bitter.

"Your good intentions were overcome by events, C.J.," she said, walking into the bathroom to cram toiletries in her bag.

Alcohol, she knew, wasn't the answer. Neither were the small pills that used to help her sleep. She'd go this alone, clean, sober, and ever mindful that each day would present a new mountain, a new struggle. Eventually, with time and with care, the heartache would fade, Wesley's memory would dim and she'd look back on this week and laugh.

There was no laughing now though. She'd finally fallen in love and her own desperate need for self-preservation had ruined that love. Her sin had been one of omission; not so terribly wrong when compared to other sins. But she could think of no penance Wesley might accept, not with what she knew about Marcus Kensington's death.

The newspaper stories David sent had spelled it all out: Marcus had been working undercover on the vice squad. An over zealous young police reporter at a small newspaper who was eager to make a good impression on his new editors had chased down a good lead about a prostitution drug ring. With a camera and notebook in hand, the reporter had slipped unnoticed into a warehouse where undercover cops were doing deals.

According to the clips, including one that had been written up in a media journal, repeated pleas to the newspaper not to run the pictures had been made by police officials all the way up to the chief of police. The reporter and his newspaper editors maintained that while the quality of the photos weren't the best, they captured the mood and essence of street life and that no one in the photos could be clearly identified.

The story and pictures ran on the front page of the reporter's small-circulation newspaper and were picked up by the wire services. Marcus Kensington's bullet-riddled body was dumped outside a police precinct the next day and found by officers changing shifts.

The reporter had had the gall to show up at a memorial service. Wesley would have killed the reporter if deputy marshals and cops hadn't subdued him.

So many things made sense now. The perfect vision of hindsight painted a picture she at any time could have altered, if only she'd known beforehand.

She wiped at tears that obscured her view.

"South Carolina. South Carolina has nice little towns in it." Her mind made up, C.J. dragged the duffel bag to the door.

Heavy pounding on the door rattled the front windows. Startled, she gasped and jumped back. C.J. swallowed. She didn't have to look to know it was Wesley.

With a degree of well-deserved trepidation she opened the door.

For a moment he looked surprised to see her. Then a scowl like thunder crossed his face.

"You must be fast at your muckraking."

His self-righteous, accusing tone ticked her off. "If you didn't go flying off the handle and let me explain—"

"What's there to explain?" he interrupted. "You lied to me. Here I was all this time thinking you were a well-protected witness in my agency's Witness Security Program. But no, you're just another parasite sweating for a byline."

He brushed by her and walked in the house.

"I don't remember inviting you in."

Wes turned and leveled a look at her. "Tough. I'm in."

"Now you wait just one minute, Mr. U.S. Deputy Marshal. You come sweeping in here like some avenging angel. Who the hell are you to pass judgment on me and what I do? You don't know me. You don't really know anything about me."

"You're right. I don't, *Jan.*"

His derisiveness on that point was well-deserved. "I told everyone here that my name is Jan. Not just you.

And besides, I told you I came here to get myself together."

He smirked. "Yeah right. That TV reporter friend of yours told me all about your big Pulitzer Prize. You want me to believe you just walked away from that life and now hang out in small-town North Carolina. Well, pardon me if I just can't swallow that bull."

Wes strode into the room and stopped near the coffee table. Folding his arms he stared her down. "So, tell me, what's your big undercover expose?"

Before she could answer, the telephone rang. C.J. ignored it and advanced toward him.

"Do you know what I made the mistake of doing?"

He lifted one eyebrow and looked at her.

"I made the mistake of falling in love with you." C.J.'s laugh was filled with irony. "I guess it serves me right, though. The first time I fall in love, head over heels, and it's with somebody who doesn't have an ounce of compassion in him."

"Compassion!" he thundered. "You're accusing me of not having compassion. You belong to a profession that not only doesn't know the meaning of the word, but makes sure that any ounce of it that might accidentally slip by and get in a newspaper or television report, gets suitably trounced in short order."

She continued as if he hadn't spoken. "For so many years, people would ask me how could I pour so much emotion and compassion in my stories. The answer was simple. I stole all of it from my own life and breathed it into the words that eventually landed me the top prize."

"C.J., this is Max." They both stopped talking and turned toward the answering machine on C.J.'s kitchen counter. "Listen, I know what you said. I know what we agreed to. But David Woods told me about the story you're working on and gave me this number. C.J., please, don't take it to the *Post*. Give me a call, okay. You know the number."

C.J. winced. Of all the times for her old editor to call. She should have known David would take tall tales back but this wasn't something she'd bargained on. Especially not at this moment.

She turned to look at Wesley. Then she got a good look at what he held in his hand: the newspaper clips about him and Marcus Kensington.

She shook her head to deny the cold accusation in his eyes, to refute the damning evidence right before her eyes.

"It's not what you think, Wesley," she whispered.

"What is it you think I think?"

She had no words for him. She could tell him the truth, that she'd been curious. But he would spin that to his own way of thinking and make her honest curiosity about the Kensington case a bad thing. The circumstantial evidence was stacked against her. She *looked* guilty. The silence between them grew then became unbearable.

"Well, I guess that answers that," he said.

Flinging the papers toward her, he stalked her. His smile was cold. "It was all a game to you wasn't it? Were you betting that I'd invite you home?" Wes swore in such a rage that C.J. did back up two steps.

"I took you to Mama Lo's house. I exposed my family to you. You had a hidden microphone on you the whole time, didn't you? What's the story you're working on? Is your big investigative piece on the grieving family six months after the tragedy? Is that the kind of story that won you the Pulitzer? Do you specialize in human suffering and grief?"

C.J. called on all the reserve she'd built within herself during her time in Serenity Falls. She'd chosen the town because she had been in search of serenity.

There was a time in the not too distant past when she'd have been in his face matching him temper for temper, cuss word for cuss word. But what was the point? He would believe what he wanted to believe. Like so many others before it, this storm would pass if she kept her wits about her, if she looked for the serenity that dwelled within her.

Bracing her back, she stood before him. "Wesley, I know you're angry and I know it feeds your anger to feel like a victim now. I have never done anything to hurt you."

Wesley walked around her as if he were inspecting a prime cut of beef at a butcher auction. "You know, you've got a body and a half on you. I'm glad I got myself a taste." His almost jovial tone belied the cruel words. "It isn't often a man gets to meet a woman who prostitutes herself for a byline. You come awfully cheap. You need to tell those newspaper editors of yours to pay you more money. Or do you do your buddy Max like you did me down by the riverside?"

C.J. clinched her eyes shut. Every word felt like a physical blow on her already emotionally beaten body. She'd hate him if she could, but his vicious words echoed too loudly in her ears the same thoughts she'd had about herself. C.J. wrapped her arms around her body to keep within her the scream that threatened to erupt. She turned away from him.

"And to think, I was ready to turn my life upside down for you. I thought you were a hooker or a gang leader's girlfriend." Then, a question, "You know what?"

C.J. didn't bother to answer.

He grabbed her arm and turned her to face him. His mouth crushed hers, the kiss a cruel punishment. Standing stoically under him, she refused to open her mouth. He sought to dominate her. C.J. couldn't deny his superior physical strength. She'd seen how effortlessly he'd grabbed and twisted Eileen's wrist.

When he finally released her, C.J. knew her mouth was swollen and bruised.

"I wish you had been a whore," he said. "At least then I'd know there was a chance of you having a heart."

Unblinking, she stared at him, the heaviness of her heart reflected in the sadness in her eyes.

She wanted to cry but wouldn't give him the satisfaction of her tears. She knew she'd gotten exactly what she deserved. If not for her perceived sin and infraction in Wesley's eyes, for the countless times when she had been in the wrong and flaunted either herself or the First Amendment to get a story. Chickens come home to roost, her mother always said. C.J. understood the statement—now, when it was too late to repair the damage already done.

Humiliated and defeated, C.J. soundlessly turned away from him. She didn't have the energy or the desire to fight him. All she wanted to do was get away. She left him standing in her living room. From a small bowl on a bookshelf she plucked up the stone she'd taken as a souvenir the night she left Baltimore. Hoisting the duffel bag over her shoulder, she walked out her front door without looking back.

Wes stood in the middle of the floor wondering why the sense of euphoria and self-righteous vindication he should have felt was nowhere to be found. As a matter of fact, he was actually feeling kind of sick to his stomach. He looked down and saw his brother's smiling face look up at him from a police department studio photo. He picked the picture up and stared at it.

"Why Marc? Why?"

But the photocopied picture did not have an answer to the why that held so many questions.

She hadn't railed, she hadn't screamed. She'd simply said it wasn't what he thought . . . and that she loved him.

Wesley's lip turned up. "Yeah, right. She probably doesn't know the meaning of the word. The only thing she loves is her name on top of a story."

Even as he said the words, Wes could hear and feel the hollowness in the charge. He wasn't about to back down, though. She'd lied to him over and over again. Jesus, she'd even slept with him to get a story. How low would these reporters go?

He conveniently ignored the fact that he was the one who initially pursued her. He was the one who had insisted she go to West Virginia. But, he argued to himself, she'd known he was a man and would be incapable of resisting what she willingly threw at him or what she withheld.

Wes frowned, not quite buying his own rationalizing.

When he heard a vehicle gun up and peel away down the street, he went to the door. He'd parked behind a Cherokee with Maryland tags. It was gone. C.J. was gone.

Wes searched himself trying to see if he cared. He didn't.

C.J. Mayview who ran around with the alias Jan Langley didn't deserve his care or his love.

C.J., crying so hard she could barely see, made her way downtown. There were a couple of people she needed to say goodbye to: Mrs. Charleston at the lawn and garden store and Bettina at the bakery. Both had been incredibly kind to her during her brief sojourn in Serenity Falls.

"You never did find out if there's actually a falls that this place is named after." C.J. wiped her eyes when she realized it didn't matter how the town got its name. She was no longer a resident.

She put on a dab of lipstick to cover the bruise at her mouth. Wesley had kissed her so hard and in such anger that he'd drawn blood.

The garden store was her first stop but Mrs. Charleston was in Charlotte for the day a clerk told her. C.J. bought a small peace lily even though she felt more like the unlucky fly caught inside a venus fly trap. The peace lily would give her courage. Just like the plant, she'd grow and maybe flourish in her new home—wherever it might be.

She pulled the Cherokee to a stop in front of the bakery and got out. Contractors, busy clearing the rubble of the façade, said hello. She returned the greeting.

A closed sign hung in the door. C.J. peered through the glass panes. She knocked and a moment later, the chubby baker appeared dabbing her eyes with a paper tissue.

"Bettina, what's wrong?"

"Oh, hi, Miz Langley." She waved the tissue. "Nothing's wrong. Nothing at any rate that can be fixed."

C.J. looked dubious. "Are you sure?"

Bettina nodded. "I'm sure. I just got some sad news on the phone about a friend. I'll be all right. What can I do for you?"

"Well, I was just coming to say farewell. I'm leaving Serenity Falls."

"Leaving? You just moved here."

C.J.'s smile was sad. "I know. But it's time for me to put down somewhere else."

"I'd give you some of those chocolate brownies you like so much but I don't have anything left. I'm officially closed until the repairs are done." Bettina smiled. "Did you enjoy that chocolate swirl cheesecake your fellow brought for you?"

C.J.'s lower lip trembled. Had that just been yesterday? It seemed a lifetime ago. "Yes," she managed to get out. "It was wonderful like everything you make here."

"I wish you happiness wherever you go next. You write or call, okay?"

"Okay." C.J. and the baker hugged. Then C.J. left the store and climbed back into the Cherokee.

When she pulled from the curb, she didn't notice the car following her.

Twenty-six

Margaret Shelley could afford to bide her time. They had to get through the police road blocks. This whole escaped prisoner thing was a drag. But then she smiled, realizing the bright side of it: All the cops would be focused on the escaped killer instead of the one who could do even greater damage.

Following two cars behind the Cherokee, Margaret hummed a little ditty. The prospect of doing someone bodily harm always put her in a good mood.

She glanced at her nails, done in a bright fuchsia polish. "Sure is going to be a shame to mess up this manicure though."

C.J. spread a map out over the steering wheel and dash. She could stay on the main roads, picking up Interstate 40 and then Interstate 77 South. Or she could meander her way through the little back roads and state highways.

Given her shattered emotional state, she figured it might be better to stick to the big roads where she wouldn't have to pay so much attention.

Inching through a roadblock, she thought about the encounter with the cops at the other one, and of

Wesley's reaction when that TV reporter announced her identity. C.J. sighed.

An officer checked her license and registration, peered in the windows then waved her through.

Folding the map with one hand, she tucked it away and reached for her worry stone. A tiny bit of the surface had been worn smooth by her constant rubbing, particularly her first weeks alone in North Carolina. It would take a long, long time for the entire stone to be smooth.

"Just like it's going to take a long, long time for your heart to heal," she said.

Sighing again, she leaned forward and turned the radio on. Tuning beyond the all-talk news station, she settled on a country music station, the closest thing she could find to blues. After a few minutes, the somebody done me wrong songs got to her and she tuned the knob to mindless Top 40 music.

She drove for about twenty miles without thinking or feeling. Then she noticed a car that was following her too closely.

Impatiently, Wes waited while Scotty's computer did its thing. He would have killed for a cigarette.

"Bingo, Donovan," Scotty exclaimed on the other end of the line. "But you're not gonna like this."

"Just give it to me straight."

"I ran lots of combinations on the name. Your Margaret Shelley at one time was Margaret Shelton. She was also Peggy Shellaberg and Meg Shelton. And get this, when she worked for us she was Shelley Ann Grayson."

"What do you mean 'when she worked for us'?"

"Shelley Ann Grayson worked a year as a Deputy

Marshal. Then she got kicked following a substantiated charge of excessive force and abuse of privilege.

"What?"

"I'm just reading you what NCIC spit out. You want it or not?"

"Keep reading," Wes said. The National Crime Information Center's incredible database had helped a lot of cops locate and then put a lot of scum bags behind bars.

"Lost her job, was put on probation for six months, and was never heard from again."

"Shelley Ann Grayson. I could swear that rings a bell. So what's with the aliases?"

"Fingerprints. Some small-time criminal stuff with vague links to organized crime, and a manslaughter conviction. Did her time on that, then poof! disappeared again."

"Grayson. Average height, fat, brown hair?" Jesus, if it was the same woman, he remembered her. They'd worked together once and she'd come on to him. He'd let her know he wasn't interested. Shortly after that, she was transferred. Or fired as it may have been.

He could hear Scotty keypunch.

"Um, not a bad looking woman. The agency pic is just head and shoulders though and it's several years old."

"Anything else from NCIC?"

"Has relatives in North Carolina," Scotty reported.

That was all Wes needed. "Scotty, man, I owe you one."

"Whatever happened with the other name you had me run? That Langley woman."

"It's a short, ugly story. I'll tell you about it over a beer."

Wes rang off with Scotty. Could Shelley Ann Grayson still be holding a grudge because he wouldn't sleep with her? The idea seemed ludicrous. Until he stopped to think about how many times he'd rebuffed Margaret at Miss Clara Ann's house. If Shelley Ann and Margaret were the same person, and deep inside Wes knew that to be the case, she'd have more reason now to want to strike out at him. She'd looked vaguely familiar but he never would have made this connection. The woman had lost a lot of weight, and done something to her hair and face. Margaret was an attractive woman in her own right, but she just didn't inspire the lust Jan Langley could stir up in him with just a look.

Jan. C.J.

Margaret. Shelley. Shelley Ann Grayson.

Wes swore out loud. His witness was safe, well on his way to a new place and a new identity. But Margaret was still on the loose. She'd apparently killed before. Was being spurned by him enough to make her kill again?

He didn't like the answer to his own question: Yes. Particularly if it was personal. He'd snubbed her again. A woman spurned could be a dangerous entity. Someone had already deliberately tried to run C.J. over. Had Margaret been driving that car?

Wes didn't know where to look first. C.J. was in danger and it was all his fault.

Then he remembered the roadblocks police had set up as a precaution in case the escaped con rolled through. Officers were checking every vehicle. C.J. was driving and would have passed through one of them at some point.

In her rearview mirror C.J. could see a woman with a bob haircut following her way too close for comfort. If she had to stop suddenly or even brake the other car would collide with hers.

"These nondrivers really get on my nerves," she said as she accelerated a bit to get some distance between her Cherokee and the woman's car.

But the woman stayed on her tail. C.J. frowned. Then gasped. That nut was going to hit her. The sedan ran so close up on her back bumper that C.J. swore out loud. Then, at the last moment, the car swerved to the left and came up along side her. C.J. powered her window down to yell at the other driver.

The woman smiled, grinned, then pointed her index finger and thumb like a child pretending to shoot a gun.

Too late, C.J. remembered she was supposed to be searching for peace. Letting rude drivers get to her was something she was to have left in Baltimore. She powered the window back up, shook her head and watched as the other driver proceeded ahead of her in the left lane. The North Carolina license tags and a bumper sticker advertising the company proclaimed the car a rental.

Five minutes later though, C.J. swore. That same driver had drifted back and was at her side again. And once again the woman grinned and did the finger pointing thing.

Had C.J. been in her own car, the one she'd sold before moving south, she'd have used her cellular phone to call the cops on this nut case. As it was, all she could do was speed up and hope to lose the woman. It went against her grain though. C.J. had few idiosyncrasies. Driving the speed limit was one of them. While most drivers took posted speed limits as a suggestion instead of a rule, C.J. believed posted speed limits were there for safety reasons. In her early days as a reporter, she'd covered too many accidents involving high speeds to take lightly the damage cars could do to each other on the road.

Accelerating a bit, she eased ahead of the woman. She looked to the left and breathed a sigh of relief. The other car was gone. The relief was short lived though. Right up on her back bumper was the woman in the blue sedan.

Wesley's hunch had played out. An officer remembered seeing both C.J. and Margaret pass through less than twenty minutes before.

With a Serenity Falls cop in a squad car backing him up, Wesley wheeled the Crown Victoria to the interstate. As he slapped a single blue flashing light on his dash, he prayed he wasn't already too late.

The speedometer hit sixty-five then shot past seventy-five and eighty-five as Wes raced to catch C.J.

If his own pigheadedness caused her harm, he'd never forgive himself. When he stopped being angry at her and thought things through he realized she had already been in Serenity Falls when he arrived. Even if she had been a working journalist, no way would she have known he would be headed there. He hadn't even known until the last minute.

Wes swore out loud. With the squad car close behind, the Crown Victoria ate up the miles separating Wes from the woman he loved.

And love her he did. With everything in his being. She personally had not had anything to do with Marc's death. Every journalist wasn't like the one who'd gotten Marc killed. He had no right to judge C.J. the same way he judged that other scum.

"But she lied," argued the still angry part of him.

And you didn't let her explain, he shot back. How many times had she tried to tell you something, something she said was important only to have you cut her off with a kiss? If C.J. was guilty, he shared in that guilt.

The two police cars whizzed by the little traffic there was on a Monday afternoon. Wes glanced at the speedometer in his dash, the red bar beyond ninety now. He was driving way too fast but he could no more slow down than he could stop breathing or stop loving C.J. She was in danger and it was his fault for not recognizing Margaret.

C.J. looked at the plate of glass in front of her. The used Cherokee she'd bought didn't have an air bag. If she crashed or that woman ran her off the road and into something, there was going to be a lot of shattered glass.

She gripped the steering wheel and glanced in the rearview mirror.

A gun! The woman had a gun.

About five or six miles back she could see the flashing lights from police cars.

C.J., who didn't necessarily believe in God, hoped and prayed those cops were coming to rescue her.

She jerked forward at the sedan's first impact on her rear. She swerved to the left but the car stayed with her.

They passed a white Volkswagen. That driver ran off the side of the road when he saw the gun and the two cars practically attached to each other.

C.J. swerved to the right again but was quickly coming up on a tractor-trailer. A school bus chugged along in the left lane.

"Hurry up. Hurry up." She begged the driver as well as the police.

The sedan crashed into her bumper again. Then the woman pulled up alongside the Cherokee and hit the driver's side. The school bus pulled into the median and the trucker blew his horn.

C.J. chanced a quick glance out her side window. The woman aimed the gun at her. C.J. ducked, cussed, and slammed her foot on the accelerator. A bullet shattered the back passenger window.

"Oh, Jesus. Help me, please."

She leaned on the horn in a vain attempt to get the van driver ahead of her out of the way. She could hear the sirens from the cop cars now but a glance out her window told her the help had come too late. The Cherokee wouldn't go any faster and the woman, driving with one hand, had the gun pointed straight at her.

Wes swore and floored the Crown Victoria. The cop behind him must have radioed for backup because two state police cars were crossing the grassy median to join the chase.

He saw the first shot fired and helplessly watched the Cherokee swerve to the left and then the right.

"Hold on, baby. Don't lose your cool. I'm coming."

Seconds later he rammed into the back of the sedan. Margaret's gun went off. He knew the moment she recognized him behind her. She took her eyes off the road to aim at him. Her back window exploded from a hail of gunfire. Wes swerved to the right.

Too late, Margaret turned her attention back to the road. Rubber burned and tires screeched, but her last-second attempt to slow the impact was a failure. Margaret's car crashed into a guardrail and flipped over twice.

Wes looked for the Cherokee in front of him, but saw it in his rearview mirror. The state cops could take care of Margaret. He whipped the car in a U-turn and drove along the shoulder back to C.J.

Margaret's last wild shot had taken out C.J.'s left rear tire. Skids on the road surface were evidence that she tried not to hit the airport limousine van. But the van driver had either moved in the same direction or not been fast enough. The van sat in the middle of the roadway with a smashed in rear. The Cherokee's front end was crushed. The battered and bent Cherokee sat disabled and turned in the wrong direction in the road. Steam poured from under the hood.

Wes barely brought his car to a stop before he dashed out and ran to C.J.

He ripped the door open.

"No, God! Please no!"

The first thing he noticed was the blood. The second was that his heart had stopped beating.

Twenty-seven

C.J. sat in the bed at Serenity Falls General Hospital and picked at the bandage on her forehead. The doctors said she'd have a headache for a while. This pain thing was getting old. Another bandage over her shoulder and left arm concealed the place where she'd been grazed by a bullet and cut by flying glass.

The last thing she'd remembered was pain shooting everywhere and crashing into that van. C.J. closed her eyes and prayed those people were all right.

At the knock on her hospital room door she opened her eyes. "Come in."

Wesley poked his head in. "Hi. Up for company?"

He was the last person she wanted to see. She turned her head away.

Ignoring the rebuff, Wesley came forward.

He thrust a bunch of flowers, red and yellow roses with baby's breath, at her. "I brought these for you."

She turned to face him, looked at the flowers and ignored them. "Why are you here? You made it perfectly clear what you thought of me. Just go away and leave me the hell alone."

"C.J., please. Hear me out. I'm sorry for the things I said. I know I hurt you. I'm sorry."

"And you think some flowers will make it all better?"

The ice and the hurt in her voice cut through Wesley. He deserved it though. She'd almost died because of him. It wasn't until he'd lost her that he realized how terribly wrong and unfair he'd been. Now it was looking like she had no forgiveness in her. Frankly, Wes didn't blame her.

"Please, C.J., take the flowers. I'm sorry."

"Oh, so now it's C.J. I distinctly remember being called let's see, a parasite, a muckraker, and a whore. I think you covered all the bases. Get lost Donovan."

She reached for a pillow to prop behind her back but Wes was there, fretting, assisting. She flinched away from him.

"Are you comfortable now? Do you want a drink of water? Should I call a nurse?"

"I'm going to call security if you don't leave me alone. I don't have anything else to say to you."

"Well, fine," he fired back. "Just shut up and listen to me then."

C.J. glared at him. She looked away for a moment then forced herself to look him in the eye. Why *was* he here? He'd made it painfully clear exactly where they stood and what he thought of her as a person. Somehow, someway, someday she'd get over the pain of loving him and losing him.

Realizing that harsh words and anger weren't going to carry him very far, Wesley changed his approach. He couldn't afford to mess this up.

He handed the flowers to her again. "Would you please accept these as a token of my regret for what I said in anger?"

C.J. accepted the flowers and inhaled their rich scent.

"Thank you," she said.

Taking that as encouragement, he pulled up a chair and sat close. Taking her hand in his large one, he pressed a kiss to the back of her hand. C.J. pulled her hand away and tucked it under the hospital blanket.

Wes winced at the rejection. "C.J., please forgive me. Can you find it in your heart to forgive me? I said some things to you and did some things I regret. I know I no longer deserve your love and I won't blame you one bit if you hate me. But do you think you could, maybe with some time, find it in your heart to forgive me? Please."

C.J. smiled sadly. "You told the truth as you see it. I'm the one who should be asking for forgiveness Wes. I wasn't totally honest with you, or for that matter, with anyone in Serenity Falls. What I told you was true. I quit my job at the newspaper because I no longer wanted to do what I'd been doing."

She picked at a yellow rose petal. "The why and wherefore's of that aren't really important now. Just suffice it to say journalism had stopped being fun for me long before I won the Pulitzer. I sold my condo, my furniture, and my car and gave most of my clothes away and came down here to find myself. I was in search of peace and serenity and was on my way to South Carolina to try to find it when that woman started shooting at me."

"About that woman . . ."

She silenced him with a finger over his lips. "Shhh. Let me finish then you can explain." When Wes nodded and looked down, she continued.

"What I discovered in those last minutes when I knew it was all over for me on that highway, was that you can't run to peace. You have to find it within yourself wherever you happen to be. And you can't control who you fall in love with. You just have to deal with the cards you're dealt."

"And of love?"

"What about it? Love is for fools and people who can afford the luxury of a foolish emotion."

Wes watched her. "I don't believe you. And I don't think you believe that either."

C.J.'s answering smile was tentative. "Well, there's this sexy dark warrior I bumped into on the street the other day. I've been wondering if he's available."

Wes smiled and relaxed. "He is. About that name. How did you know?"

"Know what?" she asked.

"That Dark Warrior is my code name."

"Code name? You people really use those things?" At his hesitant nod she smiled indulgently. "The first time I saw you on that motorcycle, all I could think of was you in a sheik's outfit or in the ceremonial robes of an ancient Saharan warrior king. Dark Warrior."

"That's what made me think you were in the Witness Security Program."

"Who was shooting at me, Wes?"

"Her name's Margaret Shelley. She used to be a Deputy U.S. Marshal but got kicked out. She's in custody now, charged with an arm's length of things including attempted capital murder. The man she hired to run you down sang like a bird to cut a deal."

"I don't even know the woman. Why was she after me?"

Wes smiled to himself. Holloway did his best work as a spin doctor. He'd already put the appropriate and plausible explanations out to the media. Margaret was going to be in prison for a long, long time. Only she, Wesley, and Holloway would ever know that Margaret had been behind the explosion at the recycling plant, and that the car crashing through the bakery window had been to scare the witness. In her few days in the town, Margaret had picked up on Yancey's habits and favorite hangouts. Stalking him had been part of her game plan.

As far as the service and Wesley was concerned, everything else that had happened could be chalked up to a woman spurned . . . or just plain coincidence in small-town North Carolina.

"She had a grudge against me and that's why she went after you. She figured out how much you meant to me."

"What are you saying?"

He took the flowers from her lap, placed them on the bed then took her free hand in his.

"I'm saying I love you no matter what your name is, no matter how you earn a living."

"What about your brother's death? I'm not now and I was never working on any story, Wes. I was simply curious about the little you and your family said about Marcus. I might be retired from daily journalism but I'm still a reporter."

"When I saw you unconscious at that steering wheel with blood all over the place I was able to put things in perspective. Marcus is gone. I can better serve his memory by thinking about the good times we shared growing up rather than how he died. That doesn't mean I'm going to instantly declare a love fest with reporters. I'm just going to judge each person on his or her own merits. Marc left behind two beautiful children. I'm the godfather," he said proudly.

"Those kids need to grow up without the bitterness the rest of the family has. It's going to take some time." He paused, then looked into her eyes. "I have a journalist in mind who might teach me the error of my ways."

"Oh, really? What's his name?"

Wes grinned. "I love you, C.J. . . . Jan . . . Ja'Niece. Now what exactly is your name?"

C.J. hit him with a pillow then sank into the mattress

when his welcoming weight settled over her. Their kiss held promise and hope for tomorrow.

"Hey, C.J.?" Wes murmured as his lips feathered across hers.

"Hmm?"

"Let's go fishing just as soon as they spring you from this joint."

C.J.'s laughter echoed through the room then swiftly changed to a soft moan when Wes buried his head in her neck and demonstrated how he planned to love her forever.

Dear Reader:

C.J. Mayview and Wesley Donovan managed to live happily ever after. But they, like so many real people, have issues to deal with in their lives. While C.J. resisted counseling and Wesley internalized his feelings about his mother, they both needed the help so readily available from programs like Alcoholics Anonymous and Al-Anon.

Like C.J. eventually learned, getting help isn't a pride thing, it's a life thing. If you or someone you love is in a situation like C.J.'s, Wesley's, or Amber Baldwin's, help is available for you. Call a counselor or a domestic violence hotline, find AA in your telephone book. Choose victory over darkness.

Thanks for reading SEDUCTION. I hope you have a true-to-life happily ever after. And if you're wondering what happened to Frankie Baldwin and that fugitive bank robber, that, as they say, is another story for another day.

Keep your eyes peeled for my upcoming book, tentatively entitled RHAPSODY. The characters are all new, but the romance sizzles.

I love to get mail and would be interested in your comments on C.J. and Wesley's story. When you write, I'll send you a newsletter and put you on my mailing list if you'll send a long, self-addressed stamped envelope to Felicia Mason, P.O. Box 1438, Dept. S, Yorktown, VA 23692.

Joy and peace to you.

Felicia Mason

About the Author

Virginian Felicia Mason is a journalist and has worked as a newspaper reporter, columnist, copy editor, editorial writer and as a college journalism professor. She is active in several writers' groups and is a member of Romance Writers of America.

Look for these upcoming Arabesque titles:

September 1996

WHISPERED PROMISES by Brenda Jackson
AGAINST ALL ODDS by Gwynne Forster
ALL FOR LOVE by Raynetta Manees

October 1996

THE GRASS AIN"T GREENER by Monique Gilmore
IF ONLY YOU KNEW by Carla Fredd
SUNDANCE by Leslie Esdaile

November 1996

AFTER ALL by Lynn Emery
ABANDON by Neffetiti Austin
NOW OR NEVER by Carmen Green

DANGEROUS GAMES   (0-7860-0270-0, $4.99)
by Amanda Scott

When Nicholas Barrington, eldest son of the Earl of Ul-
combe, first met Melissa Seacort, the desperation he
sensed beneath her well-bred beauty haunted him. He
didn't realize how desperate Melissa really was . . . until
he found her again at a Newmarket gambling club—being auctioned off by her father to the highest bidder. So,
Nick bought himself a wife. With a villain hot on their
heels, and a fortune and their lives at stake, they would
gamble everything on the most dangerous game of all:
love.

A TOUCH OF PARADISE   (0-7860-0271-9, $4.99)
by Alexa Smart

As a confidence man and scam runner in 1880s America,
Malcolm Northrup has amassed a fortune. Now, posing
as the eminent Sir John Abbot—scholar, and possible
discoverer of the lost continent of Atlantis—he's taking
his act on the road with a lecture tour, seeking funds for
a scientific experiment he has no intention of making.
But scholar Halia Davenport is determined to accompany
Malcolm on his "expedition" . . . even if she must kidnap
him!